A Merry Little Christmas

DONNA ALWARD

Copyright

Cover by Ecila Media

Contents

Deck the Halls

DONNA ALWARD

Chapter 1

GEORGE REILLY TWISTED THE wire on the back of the red velvet bow, anchoring it to the wreath frame. He frowned, looked at the bow, and adjusted it so it was even on the front of the cedar-and-spruce wreath.

This morning he'd arrived at The Ladybug Garden Center before anyone else. The clock on the cash register had said ten past seven. He'd had a whole hour and twenty minutes to work in the quiet before his boss, Laurel, arrived. Pregnant and beaming, Laurel worked nearly every day, waiting on customers, ordering stock, and doing the accounting for the business. George was there to do the heavy lifting, and a college student who'd worked for her over the summer was putting in some hours over the holiday break. Between the three of them they managed just fine.

Now it was after four, and he was finishing his eleventh wreath of the day. This time of year, they opened at nine and closed at five, and traffic was sporadic. In the summer, the greenhouse was filled with flowers and shrubs and vegetable plants, bags of soil and mulch, and fertilizers and pest control products. The interior store held gardening accessories, fresh produce, and small gifts.

Right now the whole inside of the store was decorated for Christmas. There were lights, and three different Christmas trees, and all kinds of decorations made by local artisans. Ornaments, signs, table linens...not to mention the section of holiday baking that was supplied by two local businesses. George hadn't celebrated Christmas in thirteen years. This year he was going to change that...somehow. The wreath making seemed like a good start. The past year had been filled with new starts, it seemed. He was still getting used to it all, but it felt good to look forward to the future.

He sat on a stool next to an apple bin filled with evergreen boughs, the stack of wreaths beside him. Laurel had brought some of the greenery in from suppliers, but most came from the supply of Christmas trees on the lot, standing in tilted rows where the shrubs and fruit trees sat in the spring. The idea had come to him as he'd collected errant branches rather than throwing them away or into the compost. Then he'd looked at a wreath hanging on the door at the Sugarbush Diner and got an idea of how it went together. When he'd mentioned it to Laurel, she'd zipped off, in typical Laurel fashion, and returned with a half-dozen wreath forms, floral wire, and spools of wired ribbon. A few failed tries later, he got the hang of it and started a little side hustle.

He sold them on consignment and added a little extra money to his bank account. More than that, though, he enjoyed doing it. Especially days like this, when it was cloudy and gray. A weekday, too, so the tree lot wasn't running the brisk business it would on the weekend. Laurel was inside marking new stock. George gathered more branches, bundled them together, and pressed them into the frame. The only sound was the cars going by, people on their way home from work, and the snip of his cutters as he trimmed branches and cut wire. He liked working with his hands. He liked the quiet. And though he wouldn't say it out loud, he really liked the idea of adding something of beauty to the world, even if it was just a potted plant or holiday wreath. He'd seen enough ugliness to appreciate beautiful things, no matter how small.

A car pulled into the lot and he looked down at his watch. Twenty after four. Someone looking for a poinsettia, perhaps, or some ivy sprigs. Maybe a gift for an office party or a neighbor. He looked up as a dark-haired woman stepped through the gate, and her heeled boots clicked dully on the stone floor. He frowned. She hadn't noticed him sitting amongst the trees and greenery, but something about her looked familiar. Maybe he'd seen her around town before. Or maybe she was from Montpelier. He'd certainly spent some time there over the years. On the streets, so it was unlikely anyone would recognize him. Even in the rare cases when people had made eye contact, they tended to see what he had been and not who.

He grabbed a handful of white pine and picked up his clippers, snipping the boughs to the right length.

Then the heels clipped on the stone again and he looked up. The woman was staring at him now, and the curious look in her eyes hit him right in the chest. He'd seen those eyes before. A long, long time ago, and the breath froze as he came face to face with Ian Merck's twin sister.

"George?" she asked, her voice soft. "It's me, Amy."

Amy.

His tongue felt swollen; thick and clumsy. It had been close to fifteen years since he'd seen her, and she'd changed a lot. People changed from when they were twenty-five to when they were forty. She wore a tan wool coat that covered her from neck to mid-thigh, and a soft-looking scarf around the collar. Expensive looking trousers, too, and those fancy boots that had tapped on the concrete floor of the greenhouse. It was her face that was the most different, though. There was a maturity to it that he understood. A loss of innocence, or a deeper knowledge of reality, perhaps, that had put the tiny lines at the corners of her eyes. A strain around her mouth that spoke of troubled times. Guilt piled on top of guilt when he considered he might have been able to prevent at least some of that stress.

"Amy Merck," she clarified, taking a single step forward.

"I remember," he finally said, despite the tangled mess that was his tongue.

Silence fell between them and he gripped the boughs tighter. A pucker formed between her brows. "And?" she asked. "Is that all you have to say?"

His fingers tightened so much that the rough ends of the boughs dug into his palm. He welcomed the pain. It was a touchstone in a situation that felt surreal and very unwanted.

"What are you doing here?"

It was hard to keep the grit out of his voice. Amy had her brother's dark hair, which only served to highlight the blue of her eyes. It was like looking at an older, female version of the man he'd failed so horribly. The man he still thought of every day —George's best friend. Ian had been more than that, even. He'd been family.

Her lips dropped open in response to his curt question. "Uh..." Her cheeks flushed, two dots of color on the crests as words deserted her. George's stomach tangled and turned, wondering how five minutes ago he'd been contented making holiday wreaths and now he was face to face with his worst nightmare.

He'd never wanted to see any of Ian's family again. He'd spent years trying to put it all behind him. There was no way it could be a coincidence. Somehow she'd found him. Why? He was just starting to really move on.

"I came to...that is, I found out you were here, and I..." Despite her polished appearance, which he actually found a bit intimidating, she was stammering over her words. It made him more nervous rather than putting his mind at ease.

She took a deep breath. "You look different."

He spared her a glance. "I am different." And he jammed the boughs into the frame, grabbed some more, and ruthlessly started clipping. This wreath wasn't going to be fit to sell, but he had to do something with his hands.

"Have you...have you lived in Darling long?"

"No."

It wasn't exactly the truth. He'd been in Darling off and on for several years, but not at any particular address. Ending up here had been entirely by chance. He'd been drifting around Vermont, hitchhiking from place to place and a truck driver had been making a delivery to one of the local businesses. George spent a few days and found he didn't really want to leave. Darling had been, for the most part, a safe little town, and he'd been tired of running.

He'd spent the coldest and wettest nights at the homeless shelter. It was only because of Laurel and her new husband, Aiden, that he had this job, VA assistance, and a tiny apartment across the bridge, in the older part of town.

"Have you worked here a long time?"

He looked up again, wanting desperately for her to go away. The little tremor of her lips reminded him of the last time he'd been at Ian's house in Brooklyn. Ian had a great family, so different from how George had grown up. A mom and a dad and a sister who'd thought the sun rose and set with him.

"No," he answered. Grabbed another set of boughs. Ruthlessly trimmed them—too short. He fought back a sigh. He was mangling the hell out of the wreath, trying to create some order to the maelstrom of emotions running through him. Most confusing of all was that there as a part of him that was happy to see her. She'd meant the world to Ian, and she'd always been smiling and laughing when he'd visited her family. Like a ray of sunshine.

When he glanced up, she was studying him with a strange look on her face, sunshine under a cloud. "You..." She paused. "You're very different."

Of course he was. The last time he'd seen her, he'd been young and full of piss and vinegar. Full of confidence and bravado and sure he had life right by the balls. Ian had been all of twenty-two, three years younger, and the closest thing to a little brother he'd ever had. Ian had shown up in George's company straight out of basic, still wet behind the ears. George had taken him under his wing and the bond between them had been forged. That had been before deployments, before taking actual gunfire, before—

His brain shut out the memory. "People change," he replied. "Time works that way."

The frown deepened. "Did you forget how to smile, too? Or basic manners?"

He didn't change his expression. Didn't dare, though her words hit their mark. He did smile more lately. He'd started over—with this job, with a home, with friends. Having Amy in front of him seemed to erase all his progress and reduce him back to the man he'd been before. Someone he didn't really want to be again. Plagued with guilt and hopelessness.

He sighed, looked up. Tears shimmered in her eyes. God, not that. They looked all big and bright and hurt. Her lower lip trembled the slightest bit. It cut right to the heart of him. This was why he'd never gone back to the house in Brooklyn. Why he'd never sent a note to Ian's family. He had never wanted to see the pain on the faces of his best friend's family, knowing he was to blame for it all. He'd been a coward, plain and simple.

"What do you want from me?" he whispered, hating that the rasp in his voice mirrored the pain he saw in her eyes.

"I want to know what happened," she said, a tear spilling over her lashes. "What the hell happened to Ian, and to you?"

His fingers tightened on the wreath form, bending the wire frame. "You don't have any idea what you're asking, Amy."

"You don't know what it's cost us!" Her voice was a strident hiss, laced with frustration.

And that was the point at which George lost his cool just a little bit. Didn't know? Like shit he didn't know. He'd been there. He'd come home and watched as his life imploded. He'd spent years on the streets, chasing away demons, trying to forget, sinking into a mental space that said he didn't deserve any better. It had cost him plenty. And there was no way in hell he was going to say that to Amy Merck. Not when he knew he'd let her down, too. He hadn't totally forgotten everything that had happened at that last visit to her home. Or the things he'd promised, when he hadn't been in any position to promise anything at all. Perhaps his biggest lesson had been that there are never any guarantees and that promises can be wiped out in an instant.

"I'm sorry," he said, stronger than he expected, because he was shaking on the inside. "I can't go there, Amy. I just can't. I just got my life back. I'm sorry you came all this way. There's nothing for you here."

Guilt at disappointing her yet again drilled into him, like an auger boring into a maple and the sap trickling out. He could only be tapped so many times before there was nothing left. He'd thought he was done disappointing the people in his life. Apparently not.

He set his jaw and looked down at the mangled wreath. He started removing the boughs to start over. He'd have to re-shape the frame, too.

This time he didn't look up, even when she stood before him for a few minutes that felt more like an hour. Finally, she turned and the click of her boots sounded on the floor again as she left. Ten seconds later the sound of her car starting gave him leave to breathe fully again. He cursed and flung the ruined boughs on the floor, then threw the wreath frame into the pile of odds and ends.

"Wanna talk about it?"

Laurel's soft voice interrupted the cacophony of self-deprecation in his head. He looked up, aware that his body was shaking and that Laurel was watching him with a steady gaze that spoke of understanding and patience. The fact that she didn't come closer also told him she was wary. It hurt a little bit, that she recognized there was a part of him that was unpredictable.

"The last thing I want to do is talk about it," he grumbled. "Leave it alone, Laurel."

"Okay."

His runaway train of hateful thoughts came to a surprising halt. "What?"

She smiled a little. "I said, okay. George, I remember the man you were six months ago. I'm smart enough to realize that that woman is tied to your past somehow. If you don't want to talk about it, I'm not going to force you. You're a man who does things on his own time."

The quiet acceptance went a long way to easing the tension in his muscles. Slowly they started to unwind; all the coiled-up tension from keeping his composure let go and the shaking in his legs and hands stopped.

"Thanks." He couldn't smile yet, but he looked up at her and gave a nod. She rested her hand on her recently blooming baby bump, and something wistful wound its way around his heart. Laurel was his friend. At times he considered her a bit of a guardian angel. A lump formed in his throat when he realized all he might have had if he hadn't driven his life off a cliff. Aiden was a lucky, lucky man.

She came forward and picked up the wire frame. "Wow. You did a number on this, though." She laughed a bit, and put a hand on his shoulder. "Listen, it's nearly five. I'm getting ready to close up. Why don't you come back to the house for dinner with Aiden and me?"

"Thanks, but I'll pass. I'm not very good company."

"I was thinking we might be good company for you."

"Don't worry about me. I'm fine. I'm just going to go home, make something to eat, watch some TV, and go to bed early. Snow's coming tonight, so I'll come in before opening to clear the parking lot."

"You sure?" The hand on his shoulder gave a reassuring squeeze. George wasn't much into physical demonstrations of affection, but Laurel's friendship was different. He'd made other friends in Darling, too, but Laurel had been the first one to take a chance on him, and he wouldn't ever forget it.

"I'm sure." He reached up and patted her hand. "I need to be alone, Laurel. But thank you. For everything."

"Of course."

Her hand slipped off his shoulder and she started to walk away, but then turned back and faced him. "Just remember. You're not the person you were then. You've come a long way since last summer. You're a good man, George Reilly."

His throat tightened at her words, though he didn't quite believe them. Laurel only knew what she'd seen since last June. And the past six months were just a small part of the picture.

Still, there was some truth in what she said. It hadn't been easy to trust someone again, or start working, or ask for help. It hadn't been easy going through the process to get VA assistance, or to start the counseling he was doing now. His psychologist told him he needed to take credit for the positive things in his life. He'd finally started over. He wouldn't let Ian's sister derail him. Her appearance was an ambush. A surprise attack. That was all. He'd had no time to prepare.

"You're a good friend," he answered, blowing out a breath. "And my focus is shot. I'm all thumbs now. Is there anything you want done before we lock up?"

"Naw. You sure you don't want dinner? It's spaghetti night."

"Maybe another time," he said, a little bit sorry to miss it. Spaghetti night was one of his favorites.

She accepted his answer and together they closed up for the night. When it was time to leave, the snow had started and nearly an inch was down. George took Laurel's elbow and walked with her to her car. The last thing she needed was to slip and fall with that precious cargo she was carrying.

"You drive carefully," he cautioned. "And if it's bad in the morning, get Aiden to bring you to work. Or stay home until it's better. I can handle things here."

"Yes, big brother," she joked, and laughed up at him. "Last chance. Spaghetti and garlic bread dripping with cheese."

His stomach nearly growled thinking about it, but he shook his head. He needed to be alone tonight. "I'm good. Drive safe."

He got behind the wheel of his old pickup and started the engine with a throaty rumble. It wasn't much, but considering last winter he'd been huddled wherever he could find a warm spot, the idea of actually owning a vehicle was a big deal. It was responsibility and independence rolled into one.

The road was slick on the drive to the apartment building and took him a few minutes longer than usual. He wondered about Amy; if she'd started the long drive back to New York or if she was staying in town for the night. Regardless of their awkward exchange, he hoped she was safe and off the roads.

He opened a can of soup and made a couple of grilled cheese sandwiches for his supper, imagining how good Laurel's spaghetti was, still thinking of Amy. How had she found him? How long had she been looking? Just recently? A few years? Or since the beginning, when he'd come back home a few months after Ian's body made the journey?

After the dishes were done he went to his living room, sat on his second-hand sofa, and turned on the TV. He looked around the room and realized that by most standards it was plain and unattractive. But it was his, and he was proud of it, regardless of Amy Merck and the memories her sudden appearance brought back.

He couldn't change the past. He could only make sure he didn't make the same mistakes twice.

Chapter 2

AMY DROVE DOWN DARLING, VT's main drag and wondered how George Reilly had ended up here. It was so quaint and. cute. Like a postcard. Not that she didn't like small towns; she did. But Darling, with its colorful buildings and mom-and-pop businesses, reminded her of a set for something like Gilmore Girls. A little too perfect, right down to the charming little bridge right in the town's center. And George...well, the George she remembered was a little rougher around the edges, a bit dangerous and exciting. A bad boy. Ian had told her once that George had grown up in the foster care system and that the army was the first stable place he'd ever felt he'd belonged. Seeing him crafting Christmas wreaths today had been a shock.

And then seeing his face, meeting his gaze with hers...another shock. He'd aged, looking older than forty. There were creases beside his eyes and a dusting of gray hair at his temples. And yet there was still a rough attractiveness about him that echoed back to the soldier she remembered. The strong jaw, she thought, and the determined set to his lips. What she didn't recall was the rudeness. She'd come all this way to talk to him and he'd been, well, "curt" was probably the best word she could think of. And the most favorable. Jerk had come to mind a time or two since she'd got back into her car.

She stopped at one of the few stop signs and waited for her turn to proceed through the intersection. It was six o'clock and snow had begun to fall, just fat, fluffy flakes, but in the darkness of an early December evening, she wanted to find her accommodations and get settled. She touched the gas, felt the tires slide a little, and eased through the intersection, scanning for a sign that said Bridge Street. She had to take that and then turn onto Sycamore Avenue and then she'd be at the cottage she'd rented for the two weeks leading up to Christmas.

Two weeks was all she had to convince George to tell her, once and for all, what had happened to her brother, Ian. Oh, her family knew what the official report said, but there were so many unanswered questions. Had he been happy in those last days? Had he died instantly, or alone? Her heart nearly broke thinking of her twin brother being alone on some battlefield, taking his last breath. What she and her parents were missing was some sort of closure.

George was the only one who could give them that, and ever since he'd returned from deployment, he'd fallen off the radar. Now that she'd tracked him down, she wasn't going to let him slip through her fingers.

She found Bridge Street, appropriately named as the parking lot to the town's icon, the Kissing Bridge, was on the left. She passed it and kept her eye open for Sycamore. Walnut, Beech, Maple... she sighed, squinting through the snow. Was every damn street named after a tree? White Birch Crescent...for Pete's sake.

Then there it was. Sycamore Avenue. The houses were further apart here, and back from the road a little. Tree-lined driveways obscured the view, but the house numbers were visible on reflective signs at the ends of the driveways. She braked, reached over for her directions, and double checked. Number 153.

She kept driving, using her wipers to brush away the increasing snow. How far out of town was this place, anyway? On the vacation rental site, it had said less than five minutes to downtown Darling. Now she knew even the term "downtown" was a stretch. The groceries in the back seat were from the only full-service market in town.

Finally she saw the number and carefully turned in the lane. The cottage was set back from the road about fifty feet, with only a smattering of evergreens in the front yard. A little white-and-black sign swung from a post, announcing *Bedford Cottage*. She skidded past it and stopped in front of a small garage. The opener was inside the house, and tonight she figured she'd just leave the car outside and move it in the morning. Right now she was tired, hungry, and relieved to be done with the nearly seven-hour drive from Brooklyn. Her first meeting with George had been less than satisfactory, but she hadn't come this far to give up after one ten-minute exchange.

The key was in the mailbox by the front door, just as the owners had said it would be. Amy heaved a sigh of relief and put it in the lock, then grabbed the handle of her suitcase and tugged it over the threshold and into the house.

Another trip to the car produced a small tote and three big grocery bags, enough to get her through the first few days in the house until she found the best places to eat. Shouldn't be too hard. There couldn't be more than half a dozen places in Darling.

Then she flicked on the light.

It was a nice cottage, as cottages went, she supposed. Certainly more spacious than her one bedroom apartment in Clinton Hill. And decorated nicely, if a little sparsely and "modern" for her taste. She slid off her boots and put them on a mat, then stepped through the small foyer into the living area. There was a lot of white and tan in the furniture; it looked a little like an ad for Ikea. The coffee table was impressively rectangular, the chairs before the fireplace looked more functional than comfortable. Hopefully she'd be proved wrong in that regard.

She reached into her pocket for the notes about the cottage. Then she went to a switch on the wall, flipped it, and a few seconds later, *poof!* The fireplace flickered to life, casting the room in a warm glow.

She explored the rest of the space, tugging her suitcase down the hall. The master bedroom was decorated in light blue and white, and Amy had the odd feeling it was like a hospital room—just missing the rolling table and mini TV on a retractable arm. The bathroom was done in the same colors, with a splash of beige. "Way to mix it up," she murmured, laughing a little to herself. And the kitchen was like something from the future. All white cupboards and furniture and stainless-steel appliances. Even the countertops were white marble, marred only with veins of light gray.

She put her food in the fridge and leaned against the countertop. None of this really mattered. It was a nice home, and comfortable, and it was in the same town as George, which was the main thing. Her family deserved some closure, especially her mom and dad. If she could provide that for them, she'd be happy. It wasn't like she was distracting them by producing all kinds of grandkids. And they never said a word about it, but she knew it had to cross their minds. She and Liam had divorced. There were no little Merck babies on the way, nor would there be-ever. And Ian had been killed in action.

That was all they really knew. KIA. The only person who knew what really happened, who could give it any context, was George. After today, she knew it wasn't going to be an easy job getting him to open up.

Amy rooted through the cupboards until she found the glasses. She took out a wine glass and was glad she'd bought a bottle with a twist-off top, since she didn't want to go searching for a corkscrew. Then she grabbed a bag of pita chips and a container of hummus and carried it all to the very white, utilitarian dining room table just off the living room. The heat from the fire was starting to kick in and she munched on the chips and sipped away at the cabernet until some of her edginess melted away. Maybe she'd just been hungry.

She filled the glass again, went into the living room, and sank into one of the chairs. It was, thankfully, more comfortable than it looked. She leaned back and sighed again, wishing she were home in her apartment, with the little artificial tree in the corner and Christmas lights in the windows. She'd put them up December 1, as always, even though she'd booked the cottage until Christmas Eve. If she found out what she wanted, she could go home early. Or she could stay for a vacation, since she'd already paid for two full weeks. Still, the owners hadn't done any holiday decorating. The house felt...sterile. And definitely not Christmassy. The holidays were coming and she was fighting the holiday blues, just as she did every year.

In the end she dug out a book, had another glass of wine, drew a bath in the large ensuite tub, and then went to bed as the snow continued to fall outside. As she lay in the darkness, she thought about George, and his big hands twisting the evergreen boughs as he worked at a wreath. Wondered what he'd been doing since leaving the army. Did he have family? A wife? Girlfriend? Was his place decorated for the holidays? Did he buy presents for certain someones?

Or was he as lonely as she was?

She flipped over to her side and sighed. Well, one thing she knew for sure. At least she'd made an attempt to do the "normal" things, like put up decorations, and host Thanksgiving dinners for her parents and grandparents. She helped plan office Christmas parties and remembered cupcakes for co-workers' birthdays.

So what if it was going through the motions? She knew why she did it, and it was wrapped up in her failed marriage. George had been off the grid for years, and she was determined to know why. He owed her that much.

———ee———

George threw his shovel in the back of the truck and made it over to Bedford Cottage before daylight. The snow had continued during the night, easing off just as he was up and making his coffee. He was bundled lightly; the physical exertion would warm him in no time, and so he wore boots, a knitted cap, and work gloves on his hands. The temperatures weren't too bitter, and there was a hush to the early morning that he appreciated. More so now that he wasn't sleeping out in it, or in a doorway somewhere trying to keep from freezing.

A little Toyota sat in the Bedfords' driveway, covered with snow, and announcing the latest renter's arrival. The Bedfords had gone south until the end of February and listed their cottage on one of those vacation rental places. While they were gone, they'd hired George to look after snow removal. There was a blower in the garage, but today, the snow was light and only four or five inches deep. He could shovel it no problem and get some exercise.

The scrape of the metal blade broke the silence as he pushed it across the paved driveway. While most would consider this an early morning inconvenience, he appreciated it. He had work. He had value. Things weren't perfect, but the day Laurel Stone—now Gallagher—had sat beside him on a bench and offered him a job was the day his life had begun anew. He was forty years old, and he lived in subsidized veteran housing and worked at a garden center. It wasn't what he'd planned all those years ago. But right now, it was perfect. Right now, it helped heal his soul.

And there was a lot of healing to do.

He'd awakened just after four, sweat popping out on his skin as he was thrust out of his dream. He hadn't had the dream in months, but mornings like this reminded him of Ian, and his time in the army. Sitting around, chewing the fat about memories back home. George was from South Dakota and Ian had been from Brooklyn. Both had stories of winter storms and power outages and school cancellations as kids, though Ian's had always been about his friends and close family, and George's stories had varied, depending on which foster home he'd been in at the time. Sometimes those memories had kept them going in the brash desert heat. Ian had always talked about going home for Christmas that last year they were deployed. He hadn't made it back. Neither had George. He'd finished out his deployment, then done another. And then he'd been medically discharged after taking a bullet to the knee. The knee had healed. The rest of him had stayed a mess.

The dream always ended the moment before the Humvee exploded. He couldn't help but wonder if Amy's unexpected appearance had been the finger that pulled the trigger on the nightmare.

The shovel blade ground against the asphalt over and over as he tossed the snow onto the lawn, working off the residual adrenaline. When he got to the car, he used his gloved hand to brush off the windows and most of the windshield. He wondered for a moment who rented the house and why. Skiing, maybe? The hills hadn't been open long. A simple getaway? George whistled as he shoveled the front walk and step. His life now seemed more like a vacation than anything. He had a place to put his head at night. People who cared about him—that fact still amazed him. A job. Things he never thought he'd have again.

Things he hadn't thought he deserved.

Amy's surprise appearance was just a bump in the road. He certainly hadn't been forthcoming with any information, though he resented the intrusion of her presence. He was trying to move on from the past, and seeing Ian's sister felt like a giant step backward.

He finished the driveway and tried to push away the little bit of guilt that pricked at him as he walked back to his truck. He wasn't a cruel person, but he'd been rude. Sure, it had been pure self-preservation yesterday. He hadn't had time to prepare. But that didn't erase the fact that Amy had come all this way for answers and he'd given her nothing. There'd been hurt on her pretty face, along with annoyance and frustration.

He'd broken promises to her, too.

He tossed the shovel into the back of the truck again and then climbed behind the wheel. The truth was, he could only deal with so much guilt at a time, and his feelings for Amy didn't need to pile on. Because he'd done her wrong in two ways.

He hadn't brought her brother home safe.

And he'd kissed her and told her they'd pick up where they left off, when he hadn't been free to make that promise at all.

Once he arrived at the garden center, he parked the truck, took out the shovel and cleared the pathways, and then went to the shed where they kept the garden equipment. He started up the small tractor and backed out, then began the job of blowing out the driveway and parking lot. Laurel drove in around seven thirty, gave him a wave, and went inside. When he was done with the yard, he cleaned out the auger of the blower then put the tractor back inside and locked the door. His jeans had a film of fine snow on them, and he brushed them off best he could, then went inside and hung up his outer jacket to dry and pulled on a Ladybug Garden Center fleece.

Laurel came over to him, carrying a huge mug with steam rolling off the top. "Coffee. Thanks for cleaning the lot."

"Of course." He took the cup and inhaled deeply. "It wasn't bad, anyway. We've got months of snow ahead of us. Wait'll a good Nor'easter hits." He shivered just thinking about the unrelenting New England storms. He took a restorative sip of coffee.

"You don't seem so upset this morning. You want to talk about what happened yesterday?"

The coffee turned bitter in his mouth. "Not particularly."

"She have something to do with why you ran away from your life?"

He looked up sharply. Laurel watched him with steady eyes. Lord, but she was a strong woman.

Second friend he'd had in years, with the first being her cop husband. Both had been able to see beneath the damaged exterior to the man inside. He was sure of one thing. Laurel would never judge.

"Something like that," he admitted. "Indirectly. She just wants to dig it all up again, and I'd like to move on."

Laurel nodded sagely. "Of course you do. And you've been working so hard, so I guess seeing someone from your past is a bit of a jolt."

He sighed and grabbed the stool behind the cash register, perching on the seat. "You gave me the nudge I needed, you know? And I love working here. It's just..." He hesitated, unsure of what he wanted to say.

"It's baby steps, and seeing her feels like a giant leap?"

His breath came out in a whoosh. "Yes."

She pulled up another stool. "Were you in love with her?"

His chest tightened. "No. I barely knew her." It was true; they'd only met three times before Ian's final tour. But the last time, there'd been something. It was years ago, but he could still remember how she stole his breath when she came down the front steps of the Merck house in a pair of faded jeans and a Yankees T-shirt. Her hair had been up in a ponytail, long enough that the tips still kissed her shoulders. Twenty-two years old and freshly graduated from NYU, her eyes full of laughter and fun. He and Ian were there for only three days before having to leave again. Ian had begged him to come home with him instead of staying on base. His on-again, off-again girlfriend, Jennie, hadn't been too happy about his decision to head to New York instead of spending his short leave with her. But he'd promised he'd be back in time for a hot date. Truthfully, he'd liked Jennie a lot. Each time he'd been stateside, she'd been around and, well, waiting.

She'd certainly deserved more that the bits and pieces of himself that he'd given her.

"George?"

His gaze snapped back to Laurel. "Sorry. I guess I got caught up in some memories."

"Good ones?"

"Sort of." He smiled a little, gave his head a small shake. "The woman who was here yesterday is the sister of this guy." He lifted up his arm and revealed the black memorial bracelet on his wrist.

"Ohhhh," Laurel said, understanding instantly, her eyes softening. "Oh. No wonder it was tough."

"Yeah. And she wants me to dig up the past. I just...don't. I think she got the picture last night."

Laurel nodded. "She definitely didn't look happy. So what now?"

George took another drink of his coffee. "Now I get back to work. What needs doing today? I know there's a new shipment of trees arriving after lunch. Any other heavy lifting?"

He was thankful she took the subject change with ease. "Nothing I can't handle. It's just us today, so it'll be busy. I've got fresh baked goods coming from the bakery and The Purple Pig, and I'm placing my poinsettia order later today. It'll come in on Friday so we have fresh stock for the weekend." She frowned. "I'm also ordering an extra fifty, for the banquet a week from Saturday. Do you think you could help with delivery to the golf club on Saturday morning? I have Jordan here all day, which should help."

"I don't see why not." Laurel was also helping her sister-in-law, Hannah, with a literacy fundraiser just before Christmas. Whoever said the Christmas season was relaxing was out of their mind, but Laurel seemed to be handling it all with grace. Her glow—which he figured was pregnancy plus happiness—never faltered these days.

"Are you going to the banquet?" Laurel asked, then laughed when he raised a skeptical eyebrow as if to say, are you kidding?

"That kind of event isn't for me. But I don't mind helping behind the scenes."

"Fair enough. But there'll be lots of ladies there in pretty dresses."

Now she was just teasing him. He grinned and got up from the stool. "All right, enough fun and games. This place doesn't run itself. I'll get the lot ready for the new shipment. Yell if you need anything."

"You got it."

George got on with his day's work and decided to forget about Amy. She was probably on her way back home by now, if she hadn't gone last night. And he could go back to keeping the past where it belonged. In the past.

Chapter 3

AMY STEPPED INSIDE THE Purple Pig Café and was immediately assaulted by the scent of cinnamon and fresh bread. The place was delightfully funky, with its purple logo displayed on the counter and then accents of purple, pink, and turquoise brightening the cream walls. Christmas decorations in the same colors—no red and green to be seen—added a festive cheer to the storefront. There was a line to the counter, but she didn't mind. It gave her time to browse the menu and the specials on the chalk board. She adjusted her purse strap and set her lips. George wasn't going to get rid of her that easily.

Since last night, she'd realized that ambushing him might not have been the best strategy. Today she was determined to try again. An hour ago she'd stepped outside, prepared to shovel the drive, and had found it mysteriously done. It seemed like a good omen for the day, so she'd packed up her positive attitude and headed into town to extend an olive branch by taking him lunch. Surely the man got a lunch break.

When it was her turn, a perky young woman with her hair in a messy topknot smiled and asked, "What can I get for you today?"

Amy bit down on her lip, still torn. "How about one of those turkey, cranberry, and provolone paninis, and . . . well, what's the manliest sandwich you have?"

The girl laughed, and Amy immediately felt at ease.

"I can do a roast beef and cheddar with grainy mustard on harvest bread," she suggested. "Pickle on the side. Maybe a brownie or oatmeal cookie to go with it?"

"That sounds perfect." Amy paid and then looked around as another staff member built the sandwiches. It was a neat place, she realized. It emphasized farm-to-table philosophies and organic ingredients. Those came at a significant price, but if the food was as good as it smelled, it would be worth it.

"This is to go?" the woman asked, and Amy nodded.

"Yes, please." She looked at the woman's purple name tag on her apron. "Thanks, Emily."

With the paper bag tucked in her tote, she left the café and made her way down the street to where she was parked. Next to the café was a yoga studio, and then a real estate office. There were all sorts of trendy businesses lining the main street, but no sign of any major retail or fast-food chain. Interesting. She supposed one wouldn't have to drive far to hit a department store or big box grocer—Burlington and Montpelier were less than an hour in either direction. Still, it made Darling feel a little bit personal and special.

Once she started toward the garden center, however, nerves bubbled up in her belly again. George had been very clear yesterday. And sure, she was going to try to butter him up with lunch, but she didn't expect him to just throw up his hands and tell her everything.

In fact, maybe taking a softer approach would work better. Ease into it a bit more. They'd never had trouble talking years ago.

Indeed not. The last time she'd seen him, he'd kissed her until her knees had turned to jelly and her heart had clubbed at her ribs so hard she was certain he could feel it. But that wasn't why she was here. There was enough water to fill an ocean under that bridge. She wanted to know what happened to her only sibling. Her twin. She wanted to be able to tell her mom something good so she'd stop having nightmares about horrific scenarios. She knew very well that the imagination could come up with things that were far worse than the truth.

Amy swallowed against the lump that formed in her throat at the thought. She hadn't known about Liam's affair, either. Hadn't understood why for months and months she hadn't been able to get pregnant. All she'd known was that her marriage was breaking down and that she'd kept hoping finally having a baby would save it.

She'd been wrong on both counts, and once she'd figured it out, she'd been able to let go.

Mostly. If someone pried into the cause of her failed marriage, she expected she'd react much in the same way George had yesterday. A gentler touch was the order of the day.

When she stopped in at noon, the garden center was doing a slightly brisker business than it had the previous day. She gathered the paper bag of food and took a deep breath, hoping this wasn't a mistake. The parking lot was cleared of the night's snow, and her toes were a bit cold in her boots as she made her way to the store again. Once inside she saw him, carrying a large box in his arms. Even with a warm fleece jacket on, she could see the breadth of his shoulder muscles as he adjusted the weight of the box. He smiled at the woman she'd spoken to yesterday, then put the box down and said something that made the woman laugh.

Amy's heart gave a heavy thump against her ribs in response to his smile. When his face relaxed like that, she saw glimpses of the young man he'd once been. That man had been daring, confident, sexy, with an aura of danger—of bad boy— surrounding him. That last summer he'd pushed all of her buttons, even though she'd known there was no substance to their flirting. Still, the easy smile on his face transported her back to a simpler, easier time. Ian had been alive. Her future had been before her, shiny and bright. Everyone had been carefree and happy.

He turned and caught sight of her, the smile slipping off his face.

She stepped forward, determined to get off on the right foot. "Hi," she said firmly, and smiled as one would when entering an office for a job interview—genuinely but with a layer of nerves behind it. "I brought you some lunch. Thought we might talk for a few minutes."

His jaw tightened. "I told you yesterday, Amy, I don't want to talk."

"Then let's just eat lunch. I went to this place called The Purple Pig and got two huge sandwiches. For old times' sake? It's just lunch." She met his gaze. "We got off on the wrong foot yesterday. I heard that the way to a man's heart is through his stomach, so consider this an apology for my lack of tact?"

The woman behind him gave him a nudge. "Go on," she urged. "It's nearly time for your break anyway."

"Just the sandwich," he said, his voice low.

She let out a breath of relief. "Perfect. Anywhere we should go?"

He led her out to where he'd sat yesterday. A heater kept the area comfortable if a bit cool, and she could still see her breath a little bit as he pulled out a folding chair and set it up for her. He swept the little bits of boughs off the small folding table and tucked away the clippers he'd used for cutting. "Will this do?" he asked.

She wasn't about to complain. "It's perfect," she replied, putting down the bag and peeling off her gloves.

He sat while she reached into the bag for the sandwiches. "Roast beef for you. I hope that's okay."

"I'm not fussy." He offered a glimpse of a smile, and it only made her more nervous rather than less. It was so odd; he was a stranger yet not, and she normally had no problem getting a read on people. It was why she worked in human resources. She was trained to assess people and situations, find solutions, bring out the best in staff. She couldn't read George, and it was infuriating.

She handed him the sandwich, then reached inside for her own. "This café is really cool. Has it been here long?"

He began opening the wrapper. "A few years, give or take. The owner is Laurel's best friend."

"Laurel is...?"

He nodded to the storefront. "My boss."

"I see." She took a small bite of her sandwich and found it delicious. "Wow. This is yummy."

"Willow cooks up some weird stuff, but it's always delicious." He took a huge bite of his roast beef, then wiped his lips and fingers on the recycled paper napkin. "She owns the yoga studio, too. She's here a lot."

"You like working for Laurel?"

His brows pulled together a bit, and he hesitated. This, she understood. He was weighing his response. Deciding how much he wanted to tell her. She reminded herself to be patient.

"You want to know where I've been, Amy? I've lived on the street for a lot of years. Last summer, Laurel... Well, she and her husband gave me the nudge I needed. She gave me this job. And Aiden hooked me up with some assistance. So there you go. I've been homeless. I work here now, but for a lot of years, I sat on street corners begging for money. Spent nights at the shelter. Went hungry. All this?" He waved a hand in the air, moving from the top of his head to the floor. "This is all new in the last six months."

"But why?" Her throat tightened. He'd been homeless? Living on the street? For how long, and why? She tried to picture it and couldn't. Not the dynamic, charming guy she'd known as Ian's best friend. Her stomach felt as if it dropped to her toes. No wonder he hadn't wanted to answer questions yesterday.

"My lunch break isn't long enough for that story," he said sharply. "But now you know. I'm a minimum wage laborer in subsidized housing. A real success story."

"You don't believe that," she replied, putting down her sandwich. "God, George. I don't have to know why you were living on the street to know that it's got to be a huge challenge to...to..."

"To what? Be normal? To be a contributing member of society again?"

"I didn't say that."

"I know." This time he sighed. "Listen, Amy, I understand why you're here but I can't go back there, okay? I just can't. So don't ask me to."

"George," she said softly, wondering how to say what she was thinking, wondered if it would be best to just come right out with it. "George, do you have PTSD? Is that what you're dealing with?"

He got up from the table abruptly, the chair scraping loudly against the concrete floor. "I should get back. Thanks for lunch."

Amy pushed away the alarm at his sudden movements. "It's only been five minutes," she said calmly. "And I'm asking because it would explain your reluctance to talk to me, that's all. I'm not judging."

Not in the least. She didn't have any experience with PTSD, but she'd had plenty of "I don't want to get out of bed this morning" moments when her marriage had crumbled. Pain made people do all sorts of things they never imagined.

He stood there looking a little uncertain. "George, please," she said softly. "Please think of me as a friend. I know we weren't really close, but when you were at our house... You were so important to Ian. He was my twin." Her heart swelled as she realized a sudden truth that had nothing to do with what George could do for her, but what she should have done for him all along and hadn't. "He would kick my ass if he knew I hadn't helped you in some way. So please. Finish your sandwich. And let's just talk."

He sat down again, cautiously, his eyes wary.

She reached for her sandwich, even though she'd lost her appetite. "Tell me more about Laurel and Aiden." It was a subject that he seemed to respond to, and she took a bite of turkey and cranberry, hoping to keep him with her. Hoping to build a bridge of some kind.

"Aiden was one of the few people who really saw me," George confessed. "I'd split my time between here and Montpelier. When I was here, in Darling, Aiden would sometimes grab me some food, or take me to the goodwill and get me some clothes. He looked out for me and was probably the only person in this town that I trusted. Until Laurel."

He smiled then, and she couldn't help but smile back. He was gorgeous when he smiled and the stress lines on his face relaxed. Like an older version of the young man she'd known. He should smile more often.

"Laurel offered me part-time work under the table last summer. She did more than give me a broom and a hose to clean up around here. She gave me her trust, and a purpose. Then when I was in the hospital, she and Aiden found out I was a veteran, and they helped me access some assistance and services. Now I work full time and have a little crappy apartment." His eyes warmed.

"It's not much, but it beats sleeping in an ATM vestibule."

She found herself stuck on a previous sentence. "Wait. You were in the hospital?"

He nodded. "A couple of punk ass kids thought it'd be fun to take on the local bum. I got a few shots in, but, well, I wasn't as strong as I used to be. And they were a couple of football players. I ended up with some cracked ribs and stuff."

Amy sat back and stared at him. How could he be so casual about it? Her life had fallen apart but she'd always had a place to sleep and food to eat. She'd never actually had to worry about her personal safety. She tried to imagine anyone thrashing the man who sat across from her now. He was tall and strong, not weak. Most men would think twice before provoking him, but two teenage boys had beaten him up?

It was clear she really knew nothing about him at all.

"I'm so sorry," she said, leaning forward. "That must have been awful."

"It wasn't so bad." He treated her to another small smile. "Landing in the hospital is what started all this. Working full time and having my own place, I mean. It was a new beginning. So you can see, Amy, why you coming into town and asking questions isn't exactly a happy thing for me. I'm trying to move beyond the past, not relive it again." His smile slipped away. "I can't relive it again."

He said the last bit with such conviction that she was surer than ever that something horrible had happened that he didn't want to talk about.

And it wasn't fair of her to come in and start making demands. She could see that now. When she'd left home, she'd been determined to talk to him at any cost. It had made sense when she hadn't had to sit face to face with him. How could she demand he rehash something that clearly caused him so much pain? What could have been so bad that he'd ended up homeless?

As she met his gaze, she realized she wanted to know. And not for her parents' closure, or for Ian's memory, but because of him. George. Something had changed him from a larger-than-life soldier with a constant smile to a man who struggled daily. He deserved to be happy again.

Didn't they all?

"The wreaths," she said, changing the subject. "You make them all yourself? That's what you were working on yesterday, right?"

He nodded. "I mentioned wanting to do it one day, and Laurel ran out and got me the forms and wire and more ribbon than I knew what to do with. I like it, though. I like working with my hands a lot." He finally took another bite of his sandwich, chewed, and swallowed. "And how about you? How long are you in Darling?"

"Until Christmas Eve." She hadn't realized she meant to stay the whole two weeks until she just said it, but the decision felt good. "I rented a house over on the other side of the creek. Like one of those Airbnb things."

He tilted his head. "On Sycamore?"

"That's the one. Why?"

He grinned. "So that's your Toyota. I shoveled your driveway this morning."

"You're the one?"

"The owners hired me to do it while they're south for a few months. I wondered who had rented it when I saw your car in the yard. I'm a few streets over, in a little apartment building. Eight units."

It gave her a funny feeling to think he'd been the one clearing the snow while she'd been tucked in bed, sound asleep. She'd assumed it was some company that the owners had hired. The thought of him cleaning off her car was surprisingly intimate. "Well, thank you. It was nice to not have to worry about it this morning."

She reached into the bag and took out the cookies she'd bought to go with their meal. "Here. I was told these are the best." She reached over and handed him one.

He took it, and their fingers brushed a little. There was no strange hesitation or weird looks between them, and yet Amy got a little ripple of something in the pit of her stomach as his warm fingers touched hers. She tried to imagine what he might have looked like before, when he'd been living on the street. Had his hair been long, had he had a beard? He'd probably been skinnier... She just couldn't reconcile that image with the young man she'd known, and the grown man sitting across from her now.

"Amy?"

"Hmm?"

"How did you find me?"

Her stomach knotted. "I have a friend at the VA. At first, I just kept checking and checking. I know you did another deployment. I know you came home. We kept waiting for you to come see us, and by the time I went looking for you, you'd fallen off the radar."

"And?"

She folded her napkin into little squares. "For the first few years I kept checking. Lately I've only had her check once a year. On...the anniversary."

She didn't have to say what anniversary; the wary look in his eyes told her he understood. The anniversary of Ian's death.

"I see."

"I admit I convinced her to bend a few rules."

He nodded, his eyes warming just a little. "Of course you did. Ian did always say you were determined."

She blinked. He'd mentioned Ian; this progress, even though it was small. "I think he probably said stubborn. Or bullheaded."

"Maybe," George agreed, and the energy between them relaxed.

"Where's a good place to get some dinner around here?" she asked, needing to change the subject while they were in a good place. She didn't want to push too fast. "I didn't get Mom's cooking genes, and I bought a few things last night but I'll probably try the local places while I'm here."

He switched topics with what she could only describe as relief in his eyes. "You looking for some place fancy? There's an inn not far from Darling. And there's a new Italian place—Roberto's, I think—a few blocks north of Main. If you're looking for something more casual, you can't beat the Sugarbush. It's a family restaurant and the food's good and big servings." His eyes twinkled at her a little. "Enough you could probably take leftovers home and have a second meal."

"Maybe I'll go somewhere fancy another time, but the Sugarbush sounds good. If I were home, Mom would have me over for dinner and send me home with leftovers." She laughed. "I guess that's what moms are for."

A shadow passed over his face again and she could have kicked herself. He'd never had a mom like hers.

But the shadow passed and his face softened. "Your mom made a wicked lasagna, if I remember right," he said. "Ian and I went through a whole one on our own, I think."

"He always did have a massive appetite," Amy agreed, sensing that dropping Ian's name into the conversation—twice now—was a big concession on George's part. "George, do you want to join me tonight? Have dinner?"

His gaze held hers for a few moments. "I don't know if I should. There are things..." He lifted his hand, as if to run his fingers through his hair, but he encountered his hat and dropped his hand again. "Amy, I have a lot of baggage. I'm barely back on my feet."

She laughed a little. "It's only dinner. I'm not looking for a big commitment."

His cheeks colored a little as he chuckled back. "True enough. Sorry. After so many years, my social skills are kind of non-existent."

"Well, we can start with the Sugarbush. Do you want to meet me there? Around six?"

"No questions about the past?"

"I'll try really hard." He was thawing bit by bit, but she didn't want to promise when she wasn't sure she could follow through. Ian was the link between them. What else would they have to talk about?

A transport truck pulled into the far side of the lot, creeping forward carefully and giving a raucous honk with his horn. George sighed. "Well, I'd better cram the rest of this in my mouth. The new load of trees is here, and I'll be busier than a one-armed paper hanger for the next few hours."

She laughed unexpectedly, pleased that something of the sense of humor she remembered was still inside him somewhere. He shoved the last bit of his sandwich into his mouth and crushed the wrapper in his hand as he chewed.

"Thanks for lunch."

"You're welcome."

"Tonight is my treat."

She wondered if he made enough money to do that. She didn't want to assume and leave him strapped for the month, but she wouldn't insist on paying, either, since she was sure there was some pride involved. "Why don't we go Dutch? We can each pay for our own. It's not like it's a date or anything."

"All right." He accepted the terms so easily she was a little deflated. She still felt a little of the old attraction. It was surprising, but not unpleasant. George, on the other hand, seemed completely unaffected by her. Maybe he didn't even remember kissing her before he left on that deployment. He'd probably kissed a lot of girls.

He stood and she followed suit, picking up the paper bag and the discarded wrappers. "I guess I'll let you get back to work."

"Thanks. And thanks for not pushing today. There are just some things I can't talk about. I hope you understand."

She did and she didn't, but she knew better than to push. If they could be friends, maybe he'd open up on his own. She had time. And truthfully, George's hesitation aside, she was enjoying being away from the city. She spent so much time commuting and working and commuting again that being at loose ends with no set schedule was remarkably freeing. She was overdue for a vacation, even one as low-key as a trip to Vermont.

"I'll see you at six," she said, and smiled. "Have fun with the trees."

He retrieved his work gloves and headed to the transport. As she got in her car, she saw him swinging one of the back doors open, his strong body pushing it aside as they prepared to unload.

Just dinner. So why was she already nervous?

Chapter 4

HE'D WANTED TO HAVE time to go home and shower, but the unloading process had taken longer than he'd expected, and just when he was getting everything tidied up, the poinsettia delivery had come and he'd helped with that, too. There'd been an afternoon rush on trees—it seemed a few people had taken the day off from work due to the previous night's snow and were taking advantage of the time to decorate. He and Laurel were run off their feet all afternoon, and even after they'd closed at quarter after five, because of a few late stragglers, there'd been cash to ring off and things to stow and tidy before they could leave for the day.

There was no time to go home and change. Not that he couldn't show up at the Sugarbush this way; the place was super-casual and counted on post-work traffic. It was more because of Amy. He didn't want her to see him fresh from an afternoon's labor. His knitted hat had flattened his hair and he knew his jeans were dirty from being around the trees all afternoon. But he had no choice.

He parked a block away—Main was busy tonight —and headed to the diner, breathing in the scent of fresh snow and smiling at the Christmas lights adorning the streetlamps. With only a few weeks to the holiday, every storefront and home was decorated in some way—twinkling lights, lush wreaths, evergreen boughs, and painted windows. In other years, the sight had made him feel incredibly lonely and isolated, but this year he found himself anticipating the holiday. It was dark by the time he reached the diner, but he stepped inside to a brightly lit, colorful display of Christmas cheer, right down to the carols being played over the sound system—barely audible over the cacophony of voices.

Amy was already there. He caught sight of her at a small booth about halfway down the left wall, a glass of soda in front of her as she stared at her phone. Lord, she was pretty. Her hair curled around her shoulders in tumbling waves, and the slender girl he remembered now had the delicious curves of a woman. The sweater she wore had a floppy sort of neck that seemed to cradle her chin without the tight constriction of a turtleneck. And here he was in a flannel shirt and a pair of dirty jeans. Oh well. Nothing to be done about it now, and he sure as hell wasn't going to stand her up over it.

She looked up and caught him staring at her, and he felt the strange zing again, the same one he'd felt at lunch when their fingers had touched. Wasn't that inconvenient?

He made his feet move forward and slid into the booth across from her. "Sorry if I'm a bit late. And a bit scruffy. I didn't have a chance to go home."

"Busy day, huh?" She smiled easily at him, then picked up her glass and took a drink through the white straw.

"Crazy. We seriously just left. I think last night's snow put everyone in a holiday mood."

"I suppose." Her brows wrinkled together, and she laughed a bit. "Hang on." To his surprise, she stood a little, leaned across the table, and rubbed her thumb over his cheek. "It's sticky!"

Heat rushed to his cheeks, flustered by her touch and embarrassed by the fact she'd caught him with dirt on his face. "Damn. It's probably pitch from the trees."

"Let me," she suggested, and she dipped a paper napkin in her water glass and then rubbed it over his skin. "There. That's better." She sat back, then handed him a menu. "So what's good here?"

He didn't even open it, but instead sat there wondering how she could act as if nothing had just happened. Oh, the touch was innocent enough. Platonic, even. But it had been important to George. Occasionally Laurel teased him, but this... this was the first time he'd been touched by a woman in a very long time—even if there was nothing sexual about it. It still felt intimate.

"Everything's good," he got out. "But I don't know what you like, so I can't really make any suggestions."

She looked at his closed menu. "You don't have to look, I suppose."

He didn't want to tell her that over the years, he'd tried a lot of the Sugarbush offerings simply by accepting the charity of others. Sometimes it had been a meal specially purchased, but more often than not it was someone's leftovers boxed up to go home. Either way, he'd had a lot of hot meals courtesy of the Sugarbush's large portions.

It wasn't that he was really embarrassed, exactly, because with the Gallaghers' help he'd pulled himself out of that life. But to say there wasn't a little bit of pride at stake would be a lie. "My go-to items are either the meatloaf and mashed potatoes or a club sandwich and fries. They use real turkey, none of that deli sliced stuff. But since I had a sandwich for lunch, I'll probably go with the meatloaf."

She opened the menu and scanned the items. "There's split pea soup. I haven't had that in years."

He nodded. "They use yellow peas, not green, and big chunks of potato, ham, and carrots. I think it comes with a mini loaf of French bread." He grinned. "I like to think of it as the porridge of the dinner hour."

She frowned and tilted her head.

"You know," he explained, "it sticks to your ribs."

A waitress came around and they placed their orders. Once she was gone again, an awkward silence fell that George didn't know how to fill. He'd asked her not to talk about the past, but that didn't leave them with a lot of options. Ian was the main thing connecting them.

The waitress came back with his drink and he took a moment to sip and scramble for a topic.

"So," he finally said, "what are you doing now? Last time I saw you, you'd just graduated and the world was your oyster."

She fiddled with her straw. "So we're talking about me, now? Does that technically qualify as the past?"

He raised an eyebrow. "Only if it makes you uncomfortable or you don't want to talk about it. It's only fair."

Her gaze softened as she looked at him. "Deal," she said softly. "Well, the short version is I did my masters in HR, started working at a little company in Hoboken, then I got married. Then I got divorced, moved back to Brooklyn, got a new job at a bigger company in Manhattan, and that's where I am."

"That really is the short version."

She shrugged. "It's not very exciting."

He doubted that. A woman as pretty and vibrant as her? And her summary prompted more questions than it provided answers. "Do you like your job? Plan on staying there?" He really wanted to ask about her marriage but figured it might be a bit on the too-personal side.

"It's okay. I'm good at it. The company's decent. For the most part, the people are, too. I don't get out of bed dying to get to work, but I also don't hate my job."

"But you must like being close to your family."

"I do. What's left of it." Her cheeks instantly colored. "Oh dammit, I'm sorry. Forget I said that. I have my own issues where the family is concerned that have little to do with Ian, really."

But the words had hit their mark. The Mercks had had twins and then no more children. George tried not to feel responsible, but he did just the same. He'd promised to look out for Ian, and instead he'd got him killed. Time and the few counseling sessions he'd had helped him to see that he couldn't go back and change the past. He'd accepted that what was done was done. He hadn't yet figured out how to stop the guilt, though. Or the memories from intruding when he least wanted them to.

"George?"

The touch of her fingers on his brought him back to the present. To his surprise, his food was in front of him, steam rolling off it and smelling delicious. But he hadn't even registered that the waitress had returned, he'd been so deep in his thoughts.

"Sorry."

"Don't apologize. I'm sorry I brought it up."

He dipped his fork into his potatoes, tried them, found them unusually tasteless. "You..." He scrambled once again to find a way to put the focus on her. "No kids?"

"No," she said quietly, and she focused all her attention on buttering her bread. "I discovered I can't have children."

That bombshell was sufficient to clear his head. "Shit. I'm sorry, Amy. Is that what happened with your marriage?"

She nodded, then broke off a crust of bread. "Yeah. Well, some of it. We'd been trying a while, and things weren't going well. It was a lot of pressure, and it took a toll on our relationship, not to mention our finances. Right around the time I found out I couldn't have kids, I discovered he'd been seeing someone else."

"Rat bastard," George grumbled, and then felt pleased when she choked out a laugh.

"I might have called him that a time or two," she replied. "But truthfully, his affair was a symptom of a bigger disease, not the disease itself. I'm not blaming myself," she rushed to assure him. "He made his choices. But I'd be lying if I didn't admit that things were already a mess."

"So he moved on, and you moved back to Brooklyn."

She nodded, tasting her soup. "And he and the other woman have a couple of kids now and a dog and...yeah. This soup is fantastic, by the way."

So she'd lost her hopes for a family and a husband all at once, and she was now casually commenting on the soup. He knew the tactic well. Make it sound like no big deal when it was a big deal indeed.

And with her revelation, he also realized that her parents, Ian's wonderfully kind and warm parents, would never have any grandchildren. Amy wouldn't have kids of her own and she wouldn't ever be an aunt.

It was hard not to feel responsible for it all. He'd made the wrong call, broken his promise to bring Ian back in one piece. And when he'd come home, he'd been too much of a coward to go to Ian's family and apologize. To admit out loud what he knew in his heart. It was his fault.

"George?"

He shook his head, realizing he'd blanked for the second time. "This probably wasn't a good idea," he said, his voice rough. "You were right. You haven't asked any questions but the past can't really be avoided, can it?" He fumbled to reach for his wallet, drew out a twenty, and dropped it on the table. "I'm sorry, Amy. You want to know what happened to Ian, and all I can say is I didn't protect him like I promised. You want a place to put the blame, put it on me." All their lives would have been so different if he hadn't told Ian to stay put.

"Don't go. Please, George…"

But he stood and shrugged on his jacket. "I've gotta go. I'm sorry. This is too hard."

He left her sitting there, her lips parted in surprise and her eyes wide with confusion. What would she think if she knew the whole truth? Ugh, he was such a mess. He jogged to the truck and jumped inside, then drove a little too fast down Main before turning onto Bridge. He had to get home. Away from people, away from everything.

He needed to just be for a while. Slow down his breathing, be calm.

Once he got inside, he went to the cupboard and took out a glass, then filled it with water. His throat burned for a whisky right now, but he didn't keep the stuff in the house, and for a very good reason. It hadn't taken much for him to understand that he'd self-medicated when he'd first come home, and it had contributed to his downward spiral. Maybe Amy had set him off tonight; maybe it had been the most difficult day he'd had in a long time. But he wasn't ever going back to being the shell of a man he'd been after he was discharged. Instead he went into the bathroom and took a hot shower, then got into bed and put in a CD Willow had given him to help him relax. He hadn't quite got up the gumption to actually attend one of her yoga classes at her new studio, and he couldn't afford the extravagance, anyway. But he'd accepted the CD and found that it helped when he was having a hard time settling.

And he thought of Amy, what she'd lost, how pretty she was, how he'd been a dumbass fool to kiss her all those years ago and a bigger fool tonight for running out.

She deserved better. And she'd already been disappointed once in her life. He wasn't about to make things worse.

When he woke, hours later, it was still pitch-black outside. He looked at the clock—4:00 a.m.

He'd gone to sleep so early that he was up and fully rested.

Last night's dinner played through his mind and he sighed, rubbing a hand over his face. He'd run out on her, leaving her with food, the bill... Sure he'd thrown money on the table, but he was ashamed of his actions. There were days he felt as if he'd come so far and had a good handle on life, and then other days where it seemed to kick him in the teeth again and all he could do was react rather than be in control. Maybe Laurel was right. Maybe he did need more counseling. But accessing it was proving harder than he had anticipated, and the VA doctor's solution had been to put him on meds to help with his symptoms.

Truth was, despite jumping up yesterday when Amy had asked, he was pretty sure he did have PTSD, though no one had come right out and diagnosed it. When he'd got his shit together and got this job and an apartment, he figured he was on his way to handling it on his own. When days like yesterday happened, he wasn't sure "on his own" was a good enough strategy.

He got up and dressed, then poured a bowl of cereal and ate it standing over the sink. He took his daily pill and knew that the one thing he had to do today was find a way to apologize to Amy.

It wouldn't be light for hours yet, but he knew exactly what he could give her as a peace offering.

Amy woke and stared at the ceiling as sunlight filtered through the blinds. Last night had been unexpected. For one, she should have never rubbed that pitch off George's face. He'd frozen beneath her touch and for a few moments he'd stopped breathing. She'd struggled to remain casual, as if there weren't these strange undercurrents running between them, but it hadn't been wariness that had made him freeze. She was sure of it. The vibe between them wasn't awkward—it was aware.

Then she'd made that dumb comment about her family and he'd instantly backed away. There'd been moments, too, that he'd gone somewhere else in his mind. Did the memories still haunt him? The last thing she wanted was to make it worse. Could she let her questions go? For his sake?

She flopped over in the bed and pulled the covers to her chin. Each time she asked herself that question, she came up with the same answer. Avoiding the issue wouldn't actually help him at all. He had to deal with his feelings. It had taken her two years of therapy to be able to put her own insecurities and issues to rest, and even now she had moments it was difficult. She just knew how to handle it better. George, she reminded herself, had spent years living on the street. She could only assume that self-blame and unworthiness were two emotions he'd dealt with daily. A person didn't get over that overnight.

She finally crawled out of bed and headed for the shower, still filled with more questions than answers. While the cottage was nice, and certainly well-kept, she didn't find it particularly homey and certainly not very festive. Today she'd give George a break. Instead, she might wander down Main Street and do some shopping. While most of her gifts were bought already, there was nothing like a little retail therapy to give a girl a boost.

Cheered by her plans, she dressed in her favorite skinny jeans, boots, and a tunic-style sweater that gently cradled her curves and, in her opinion, made her look a little taller than she was. She did her hair and makeup and made sure her phone and wallet were in her bag. With a satisfied sigh, she opened her front door and—

Smelled the pungent, sweet scent of spruce and pine, all in the form of a lush, green wreath hanging on her front door.

She didn't need to see the tell-tale red ribbon to know it was from George. And it didn't take a genius to figure out this was his way of making an apology. She closed the door gently behind her and then stood staring at the gorgeous creation. He somehow knew how to blend the different kinds of evergreen into a perfect combination of color and fullness. It was hung on the door with some sort of a brass magnet in the shape of a knob.

The wreath also took the front step of the little cottage and suddenly transformed it into something Christmassy.

She blinked away the sudden tears in her eyes. Such a small gesture; it shouldn't affect her this way. The truth of the matter was she was always the person doing little things for others rather than being the recipient. Quite often Amy felt invisible, or at least taken for granted. She baked cookies for staff members. She picked up flowers for her mom, or candles in a friend's favorite scent. She liked doing those things, but the same consideration and thought wasn't often reciprocated. George's small gift was actually a very big deal in the overall scheme of things.

She didn't want to pressure him, though, so she locked the door behind her and headed downtown. She'd find a way to thank him later.

The sun was out and once she parked she gained a better appreciation for the town. Darling was quaint, with an old-fashioned vibe blended with a younger, funky feel. The vibrant colors of The Purple Pig and the Fisher Creek Yoga studio next door brightened the street, and while other buildings were more traditional in their main colors, the same didn't necessarily hold true with their doors and shutters. She spotted greens, deep reds, bright blues. The flower shop sported a unique door, painted in a distressed red and with a heart-shaped window in the top third. She passed Pen 2 Paper, a book and stationery store, a lawyer's office, and a large brick building that she realized was the bank.

Across the street was a walkway that traversed a long stretch of park. A sign quietly announced it as the Darling Green, and she could see a little bridge beyond, crossing the creek. Snow clung to the branches on the trees, and with the rampant Christmas decorating that had been going on, the entire effect was festive.

She stopped at The Purple Pig and got a green tea, then went for a walk along the Green, enjoying the fresh air and the scenery. She understood why George liked it here. It didn't matter that it was small, with only a few important intersections. It wasn't far to either Montpelier or Burlington, when it came right down to it. She was sure a good part of the population commuted to either city, but preferred small-town living. It was the same in city neighborhoods, like where she lived. Families knew each other. There was a sense of community and connection.

Once she'd ambled along to her heart's content, she popped into a few shops to browse. The F Bomb was advertising a Christmas Explosion of Savings—everything 25-50% off. She frowned, staring at the pastel and lace curtains in the window, wondering at the disparity between the name and the appearance of the store. She couldn't resist a step inside and was immediately immersed in a bouquet of scents as bowls and boxes of fizzy bath bombs filled every surface— fizzy being the "F" word, she assumed. She grinned and bought herself two, both in the shape of cupcakes. Then she bought a little assorted box that she'd tuck into her "emergency" cupboard. There was always a last-minute invite to a birthday or shower, or even just a dinner that required a hostess gift.

Back outside, she took a deep breath of fresh air, leaving the heavy perfumes of the soap shop behind.

At the bookstore she bought a hand-painted thank you card for George. She couldn't keep showing up at the garden center every day; it was his place of work and she didn't want to be a pest. She also grabbed a little booklet at the cash register that contained a history of the area, including the legends of the town's Kissing Bridge. A little boutique was set on a corner, tucked away and private, but inside she splurged on a butter-soft pashmina that rivaled anything on Fifth Avenue and for a fraction of the price.

But it was the General Store that stole her heart. It sported a deli counter, grocery basics like milk, bread, and some canned goods, touristy souvenirs, seasonal decorations, and what her parents would call a "dry goods" section, with clothing essentials like underwear, socks, and baby onesies.

It was charm and practicality all rolled into one, and it was easy to tell the locals from the visitors just by listening to the cadence of the speech. There was a familiarity and warmth to the way neighbors spoke to each other that made her smile.

While she'd enjoyed The Purple Pig's delightful offerings, today she stepped up to the deli counter and ordered a thick pastrami sandwich with a side of kettle-cooked potato chips. A can of soda rounded out her order, and when she left the store she crossed the street to the Green and found a vacant picnic table. It was cold with her gloves off, but she didn't care. It felt positively indulgent to browse and then sit in the park—snow and all—to eat one of the most delicious sandwiches she'd had in her life.

"Room for one more?"

She swiveled around at the voice behind her. George stood there, dressed in a puffy jacket and the knitted hat that he always seemed to have on, a whisper of a smile on his lips. Heat crept up her neck; her mouth was jammed full of pastrami in a most unladylike manner, and instead of trying to speak around it, she raised one hand in supplication.

He laughed. He'd smiled occasionally since they'd met again, and even had a low-grade chuckle, but his laugh did something to her insides that she wasn't comfortable with. She couldn't be attracted to him. It would be such a huge mistake. But the twinkle in his eyes as he sat across from her didn't lie. In another life she would smile back, flirt a little. But this was George, who admittedly had a ton of baggage weighing him down, and a history with her family that was fifteen years late in being resolved. And he was laughing at her.

She chewed and swallowed and used a paper napkin to wipe her lips. "Sorry. You caught me with my mouth full."

"So I see. Am I intruding?"

"Of course not." She still wanted answers. And now she could say thank you in person. "I saw the wreath this morning. It's beautiful, George."

His gaze sobered. "I was rude last night. And you said the cottage didn't have any decorations, so..."

"Apology accepted," she offered softly, meeting his gaze. "I know this is hard for you."

"I wish it weren't," he confessed, and her heart softened even further.

"Would it...would it be easier for you if I left?"

"Yes."

The immediate answer hurt. And she didn't want to go yet, really. She was enjoying her time away from home. She felt lighter somehow. Despite their rocky beginning, she wasn't ready to say goodbye and leave George behind forever. He was the last person to see her brother. He was the key to the closure she so desperately needed. Just being near George was like being close to Ian again in a strange way.

"But I don't want you to go."

Her fingers tightened around her soda can. "Really?"

He nodded. "I was thinking about it this morning. I was up early, making your wreath, thinking about last night at the diner. I know I'm not being fair to you, Amy. I should have talked to you years ago. You deserved to know. Your family deserved answers. I just didn't want to see the look in your eyes when I told you what happened. I didn't want you to think badly of me somehow."

She took a deep breath and told him the truth. "Ignoring us for fifteen years didn't exactly endear you to us."

He nodded slowly. "I know. I was a mess, Amy. A real mess, and it just kept getting worse and worse until I couldn't have made it to New York if I'd tried."

"I figured as much. It has to be bad when the end result is homelessness, you know? And I'm not judging, I promise. Truth is, it's a shit situation all around. Us with questions, you dealing with... everything." She reached over and put her hand on his arm, feeling the strength there even beneath the thick jacket. "I just can't help feeling like maybe we can help each other. Finally lay some of those ghosts to rest."

He let out a big breath. "I'm not sure that'll happen, but I'll talk. Hard as it is, I tried running away long enough and it didn't work. Starting over means facing all of it. And if you hate me forever, I'll live with that somehow."

"I could never hate you, George."

Their gazes caught. Her hand was still on his arm, and he slid his elbow back until his gloved fingers covered hers. "I hope not," he said quietly. "But I'll understand if you do."

They sat in silence for a few moments, until George slid his fingers away. "You should finish that sandwich before it freezes," he noted, nodding at her waxed paper. "I didn't mean to disturb your lunch."

"It's too much for me. Do you want some?"

But he shook his head. "Can't get in the habit of you bringing me lunch every day, can I? I already ate, anyway. Packed myself a lunch from home. I'm just running an errand for Laurel. I should be getting back."

"Oh." She couldn't help the disappointment she felt at his words. They'd really connected just now, and not in the flutters-in-the-stomach way from before. This was different. The park didn't seem the right place for a confessional, though, so she wrapped up the end of her sandwich and tucked it into a little bag to take home.

"I'm free tonight if you want to, I don't know, talk," he said, sliding his legs out from beneath the table. "My apartment isn't much, but you're welcome to come over."

Amy tried to keep her mouth from dropping open. She hadn't expected him to invite her into his space, and she wasn't about to turn it down. "Sure," she replied. "Give me the address and a time and I'll be there."

He grabbed one of her spare napkins and she handed him a pen from her purse. He scribbled on his address and handed it back. "Put that in your phone, though all you have to do is turn right at the end of your street, go past the stop sign, and turn left at the next intersection. There's only one apartment building there, and I'm unit seven."

"Should I text you first?"

He chuckled again, the lines in his face smoothing. "Well, you could if I had a cell phone." He took the pen back from her fingers, and the napkin, too. "I do have a landline. Here." He jotted down the number.

No cell phone? Who did that in this day and age? And then she was reminded again that George was a man living with the bare necessities, and what most people defined as necessities were really conveniences with a disproportionate amount of importance.

"Seven sound okay?" she asked, tucking everything into her bag.

He nodded. "Just...well, it's a bachelor pad. I don't have much for furniture or anything."

But he was willing to let her in, and she knew that had to be a big step, a show of faith on his part. "Hey, it's warm and dry, right? Decorating is overrated anyway."

"Sure. If you say so." He smiled again. "Okay, I really have to get back now or Laurel's going to be wondering where I am." He winked. "Not like she can text me, huh?"

"I think that's just you playing mysterious," she said, surprised at the flirty tone in her voice.

Where had that come from?

He angled his head and stared at her. "Mysterious is not a word I'd use to describe me. There are lots of others, but I'm trying to move past them."

"I didn't mean to tease."

"It's okay," he nodded. "In fact, it's good. Not many people are comfortable enough with me to crack a joke." His gaze held hers and warmed. "Actually, it makes me feel kind of normal."

Oh, there were things about George that were normal right enough. And in the last few days, the tough barrier he'd put around himself was weakening. It made him more approachable, and more than a little alluring.

"I'll see you later, then. Should I bring food? I'm not a great cook like my mom, but I can manage to put something together."

He smiled. "You don't need to keep feeding me, but I'll confess, I'm a horrible cook. If you happened to bring food, I'd be happy to eat it."

"It's a deal."

George turned to walk away and took half a dozen steps before she called him back. "George?"

He turned.

"Thank you," she said quietly, serious again. "I know my showing up here hasn't been how you planned to spend the days leading up to the holiday. I appreciate your effort."

He nodded again and strode off through the snow.

Chapter 5

AMY DETOURED TO THE market and bought the ingredients for Shepherd's Pie, something she could make in a casserole and transport to his place easily, but a sturdy enough dish to give him a hearty meal and perhaps leftovers for the next day. She added a French bread to her basket, as well as a little tub of whipped butter and a pre-made garden salad. She bought dessert, too, a lemon meringue pie from the market bakery that had golden-brown meringue that was two inches high and was beaded with the slightest bit of moisture beneath the plastic domed lid.

Back at the cottage, she spent the remainder of the afternoon cooking ground beef, adding vegetables and making the gravy, then boiling potatoes, whipping them until they were perfectly smooth, and adding her mom's special ingredient: sharp cheddar.

At five thirty she put the casserole dish in the oven to bake, sliced the bread, put the salad in a large, covered bowl she found in the cupboards, and wondered how she was going to get it all to her car and then up to his apartment. It took her a couple of trips to her car, and she put the casserole on the passenger side floor so it wouldn't tip. She found his apartment building with no trouble. She took the salad and bread first, and went inside the main door to find his unit number. There it was, Reilly, next to number seven. She hit the buzzer and waited.

"That you, Amy? Come on up."

The door buzzed, long and loud, and she opened the door, balancing the bread on top of the salad as she pulled on the handle.

The carpet covering the stairs was worn and the wood railings scarred, but the building seemed clean. She only had to go up a small flight, turn a landing, and go up another small flight to the second floor. He was the last unit down the hall on the left; he'd opened the door and stood in the doorway waiting for her. "There's more in the car," she said. "If you have a spare set of hands..."

"Let me grab my keys." He took the dishes from her and put them inside, and she heard the jingle of keys as he came outside and the door shut automatically behind him.

"You found it okay?"

"No trouble at all. Darling's not that big."

They started down the stairs. "If you keep going to the edge of town, there's an industrial area. There's a food bank and shelter over there. I used to sleep there a lot. Since I started work and got the apartment, I haven't had to use the food bank. I'm pretty proud of that, actually."

She wasn't sure how to answer. The fact that he'd been in a position to sleep in a shelter and rely on donations to eat—something she took for granted

—well, she would never know what his life had been like. Not if he told her a million times. She figured it was one of those things that you couldn't understand until you'd lived it. But she could imagine, and it gave her a whole new respect for the man who'd somehow fallen from grace and had picked himself back up again. As well as a genuine affection for the friends who had stood by his side.

They'd been better friends than she. Though, to be fair, she'd been looking for him for a long time, and it had been as if he'd dropped off the face of the earth.

He helped her carry up the casserole and she took the pie, and he exclaimed about the good smells as he led the way back to his apartment.

He'd been right; it wasn't much. A scarred table with two chairs sat in the small dining area, and the living room held a battered sofa, a chair, and a small wood stand with a television. There were no pictures on the walls, though there was a coffee table with a remote on it and a newspaper of some kind. And in one corner sat a Christmas tree. Just the tree, in a homemade stand, without any lights or decorations. It was the loneliest Christmas tree she'd ever seen.

Still, his apartment was tidy and it was warm and dry and her heart wept a little bit at the defiance she saw in his face when she turned back to face him.

"It's a good size, isn't it?" she asked, putting the pie down on the counter in the little galley-style kitchen. "But seriously, you need a woman's touch. Something on your walls, a print or something. Some little things."

His jaw was tight, and she knew the barriers were back up again, protecting him against hurt or criticism. "Well, we didn't have a lot of that stuff in barracks, so I'm right at home."

"I suppose you're right." She made the comment with a deliberate sort of ease. "And the important thing is it's yours, right? After my divorce, I stayed with my mom and dad for a while until I found the new job and my apartment. Once I moved in, I didn't have a lot of money to decorate the way I wanted. But it was mine, all mine, and I didn't care."

The lines around his forehead smoothed. "Nice try."

She shrugged. "Hey, it's true." The tree was now kind of like the elephant in the room, so she figured she might as well mention it. "Do you have special plans for decorating your tree?"

He shrugged, looking over at the naked, green branches. "Not yet. I need to get some decorations, I guess. This is the first Christmas I've celebrated in years. To be honest, I'm finding it a bit overwhelming."

"Well, it can be as elaborate or as plain as you want. You're the boss." She wondered, too, if there would be any presents under his tree. She decided then and there that she'd get him something and wrap it up beautifully so he could put it beneath the branches.

"Do you want to eat now?" she asked. "The shepherd's pie is still hot."

"Yes, let's."

"Do you have any wine? I never thought." She faltered. She should have picked up a bottle at the market.

He met her gaze. "I don't drink anymore. I drank too much when I came home. And once I lost everything... I know some people have this idea that homeless people are all drunks and addicts, but I wasn't. At least, I wasn't for long. I wasn't just homeless, I was hopeless. But I gave up booze. I stayed sober."

She melted at his honest response. Her respect for him kept growing exponentially, as well as her empathy for what he'd gone through. She went up to him and on impulse, gave him a hug.

He hesitated a second, then his arms came to rest around her. She was still wearing her jacket, so the contact wasn't all that close, but even so, it was an intimate gesture.

"What's the hug for?" he whispered, his breath warm against her hair.

"For being strong."

"Oh Amy, I'm not. If I were strong, I would have held my shit together."

She lifted her head and looked into his face. "You're holding it together now. That says all I need to know. I'm proud of you, George."

Emotion flickered over his face before he shuttered it away. "Well, let's eat. I'm starving."

Too much, too soon, she thought, but let him take the lead. If he wanted to talk to her tonight, she knew it had to be on his own terms.

George couldn't remember the last time he'd eaten so well, unless it was at Laurel and Aiden's and their weekly spaghetti night. The shepherd's pie was delicious, the potato topping melt-in-your-mouth smooth and flavorful. The salad was fresh and the bread crusty on the outside and soft on the inside, just the way he liked it. When she said there was lemon pie for dessert, he wondered if he'd died and gone to heaven.

It was the first time he'd invited anyone to his apartment. Aiden and his brothers, Ethan and Rory, had helped George move in the meager furnishings when he'd first got the place, but he'd never entertained. Hah. The very word made him want to laugh. He didn't have many friends, but years of being alone had taught him that a few good ones were worth far more than tons of acquaintances.

But he'd invited Amy here. Because he liked her. Because she reminded him of Ian, and the affection they'd shared, and because he knew that he owed her, even if it was hell to think about, let alone talk about. He'd run from this moment for fifteen years; it was time he faced it.

And deep down, while he expected her to hate him, he wondered if she might just offer him a glimpse of forgiveness for what he'd done—or rather, what he hadn't done. He hadn't protected Ian as he promised. She'd lost a brother and he'd lost his best friend in the world. Ian had been his brother, too, in all the ways that counted.

The meringue on the pie suddenly lost its flavor. He pushed the plate aside as dread slid down his chest to settle in the pit of his stomach.

"What's the matter? You don't like the pie?"

"I'm just full." He forced a smile. "I haven't eaten like that in ages. That was delicious."

She smiled at him, and he wished she wasn't so pretty or so accepting. She made him want things he had no right to want or expect.

"I bought most of it. To be honest, by the time I'm done my daily commute, I don't go to a lot of bother to cook for just me. There's a shocking amount of convenience food in my freezer."

He toyed with his water glass. "Are you lonely, Amy? You must have friends." He hesitated a bit. "A boyfriend."

"Friends, yes. Boyfriend, no." He watched as she pushed a fluff of meringue around on her plate, mushing it a bit with each touch of her fork. "I haven't really dated since the divorce. If I'm being honest, too, I'm sitting right on the edge of forty. Most guys are looking for someone younger."

George frowned. Thirty-seven wasn't exactly "on the edge" of forty. Who cared about age, anyway? Amy was beautiful and kind. "Well, that's just dumb," he replied, and was gratified when she laughed a bit.

"Oh, George." She met his gaze. "I can't have kids. That stops a lot of people in their tracks."

"And it stops you in your tracks, too, doesn't it?" He stopped moving his glass around and stared at her. "Maybe more than the men in your life." He frowned. "Did you want children badly?"

The meringue was obliterated now. "Yes, I suppose I did. The stress of trying to conceive took a toll on my marriage. The divorce...well, it felt as if it was my fault. I mean, I know I didn't do this on purpose, but I was bitter and hard on myself just the same."

"I'm sorry."

She smiled a little. "Don't be. Besides, in another few years, I'm not sure I'd want to start with the mom thing, you know?" She shrugged. "I considered adoption, and I considered IVF a few years ago, but both are really expensive. I make a good living, but it would be a strain. Maybe I just have to realize that some things aren't meant to be."

She'd make a good mother, he thought, and felt badly that she probably wouldn't ever experience it. She'd lost enough over the years. She'd come to Darling for answers, and he was going to give them to her. It was the least he could do.

If she left after tonight, it would serve him right. The dinner had been great. He'd loved hearing her laugh, or just the sound of her voice as they talked about Darling and little things about the town. He'd just have to carry the memory of that with him. He was pretty sure her friendship was temporary. Once she knew the truth, she'd head home and celebrate the holidays where she belonged—with her family.

"Let me help you clear the table," she said, rising and gathering their dessert plates.

"I'll get it later, don't worry. You cooked; the least I can do is the dishes. Why don't we have a seat in the living room?"

The meal had been comfortable and easy, but now an awkwardness surrounded them as they made their way to the sofa. They sat down together, but with a few feet separating them. This wasn't about relaxing and making small talk, this was about getting down to the real reason she'd come. He was going to have to tell her the truth and see her face and maybe wipe her tears. He'd rather do anything than see her cry.

He was afraid, too. Afraid of what might happen when he went back to that day in his mind. Sometimes he panicked if he thought about it or the dreams were too vivid. And then he only remembered bits and pieces from those hours of stress, not quite losing time but not having clear recollection, either. When he'd mentioned it to the doctor, he'd been told simply that he was dissociating, that the medication would help, and that after a panic attack his recall was off because of hyperventilating and heightened adrenaline and the brain trying to protect itself or something.

He took a few calming breaths. Remembered what Willow Gallagher had told him about dealing with the bad times.

"George, are you okay?"

He opened his eyes and met Amy's concerned gaze. "Kind of." He smiled weakly. "This is just hard."

She reached over and took his hand, her warm fingers circling his. "As much as I want to know about Ian, I don't want to put you through something that's going to traumatize you."

"It's just hard to go back."

She simply waited, her thumb rubbing across his fingers, creating an anchor that he so desperately needed. She couldn't know what a help that simple touch was, or the sound of her voice.

He stared straight ahead and began.

"It really wasn't anything different from any other day. We'd been up the night before, playing poker, having a few drinks, talking. That morning we were part of a supply convoy, and we were all joking around and feeling good, you know? There hadn't been a lot of action lately, and things had been quiet for a couple of weeks. We made jokes about getting out for a Sunday drive. Talked about what we were going to do if we made it home for Christmas." He frowned. "Ian was saying he was going to look up some girl. Melanie? Melody? I can't remember." He smiled a little. "He kept saying they'd gone to school together and she had big jugs." He cupped his hands in front of his chest and laughed a little. "I can't believe I remember something stupid like that."

He found her hand again and held it. Still liked having that anchor.

"Melody was a girl in our neighborhood," Amy supplied. "She was maybe three, four years younger than us, so he'd never asked her out in high school." Amy laughed a little. "And she did end up with some substantial assets. Consensus is she had a boob job."

George nodded. He could still see the joy on Ian's face that morning as he swung up into the passenger seat, and it stabbed at his heart. He swallowed thickly. "So we started out, Ian and me in a Humvee, singing stupid songs. He started on Christmas carols and said I had to go home with him for the holidays because I didn't have anywhere else to go. I told him I was going to look up Jennie—I'd been seeing her off and on—and he said no, I needed to be with family."

He looked over at Amy then. "I know I promised to come back to see you, too, Amy. I shouldn't have done that. I wasn't free to."

She smiled a little. "I knew that. I didn't wait around."

He chuckled a little. God, he loved her honesty.

"What happened then, George?"

He shrugged, let himself be pulled back into the memory. "I don't know. One minute we were driving, and the next minute the vehicle ahead of us hit an IED. Shooting started; we were ambushed. I told Ian to stay in the Humvee while I got out and returned fire. He yelled at me that he was going to help and I told him to stay put and that was an order. It was the only time I ever pulled rank on him."

George could hear the sounds, taste the dust. The rapid smack of gunfire, shouts from the men, the grittiness of the sand in his teeth. The smell of gunpowder and blood.

"He stayed where he was. A minute, maybe a few seconds later, the Humvee was hit with an RPG. That's a—"

"I know what it is," Amy interrupted, her voice tight.

He looked over at her, but it took a moment or two for his focus to settle, to pull himself out of the memory and register the look on her face. She was pale, her eyes wide. With horror? Revulsion? He didn't know, couldn't move past his own emotions to analyze hers.

"He was in the Humvee . . ." she began, prompting him to continue.

"He was halfway out the door when the grenade hit. Never stood a chance. One moment he was there and the next..."

George stopped talking. He couldn't tell her any more of the details. She knew what had happened next; she didn't need the visuals of the aftermath. It was enough that one of them would remember, and he'd live with those images for the rest of his life.

She was crying, he realized. Silent, salty tears that streaked down her cheeks in a straight line and dripped off her chin. Oddly enough, George felt...nothing. He felt empty, numb. Like he should console her but didn't know how, nor did he deserve that honor. "I failed him, Amy. I promised to protect him, and I got him killed instead. He never knew what hit him."

"You didn't kill him, George. The enemy did."

He frowned. "I told him to stay in the Humvee. You don't think they knew he was in there? Of course they did! If he'd got out with me, we—"

"He could have got shot just as easily. You both could have."

But he shook his head. He was the one who'd been there. He'd been the one to shout for his best friend, his brother, to stay inside. He should have anticipated the enemy's firepower.

"You don't know," he said harshly, shaking his head. He couldn't stop seeing the image of Ian on the ground, blood and pieces everywhere. "I failed him, I failed you, I failed my unit. I should have been more vigilant instead of treating that day like a goddamned Sunday picnic."

She slid over on the sofa and leaned up against his arm. "It's not your fault."

"It is my fault," he insisted harshly. "He's gone and it's my fault. I took him away from his parents, and you, and even what's-her-name with the big boobs. I took away his chance to get married, have children, be a dad. I took away the only family I'd known since I was twenty-one." George shivered all over, wanting to stop talking, wanting to hide and shut down, but somehow he couldn't. "You wonder why I dropped off the radar for so many years? Because he died and I didn't and every damned day I knew it should have been me. No one would have missed me. I didn't deserve the chance to have the things that he'd never have."

To his surprise, Amy reached up and cupped his face, forcing him to look at her. "So you trashed your life, thinking it was your penance? That you deserved to feel unhappy and worthless?"

"Yes!" He twisted out of her arms and jumped up from the sofa. "God, yes."

She met his gaze evenly. She'd stopped crying, but he could still see the streaks from the tears that had run down her face. "George Reilly," she said sternly, "that is the biggest load of bullshit that I've ever heard."

His mouth dropped open.

"Don't stare at me like you're an idiot. You're not, not really. Your thinking's pretty warped, but you're a smart guy." She pointed at the sofa. "Sit down. Because now I have a few things to say."

He obeyed because she had issued an order like a CO might, or his third-grade teacher, Mrs.

Olson, who had terrified every single kid in her class but had commanded a crazy amount of respect at the same time.

"You listen to me, George. If Ian was getting out of that truck, he was either disobeying your order or he knew what was coming and was trying to get out. Either way, he left himself exposed and you're not to blame for that."

"But—"

"Shh. It's my turn, remember?"

He stayed silent, waiting for whatever decree was coming next.

"As far as you trashing your life after you got home...what a fucking waste."

His brows lifted. He hadn't expected that particular word to come out of her sweet little mouth, but there it was. Her eyes were bright and her lips set, the color back in her cheeks.

"You were spared, and you threw it down the toilet. You want to know something? I'm not mad at you about Ian. What we were told was simply that there'd been an IED incident and the location and nothing more. We wanted to know what he was like, if he was happy, what exactly happened, if he suffered long. Now I know those things and I'm not angry at you for that stupid order or whether or not Ian disobeyed. That changes nothing. What I'm pissed off about is that you were spared, and you came home, and instead of honoring his memory by doing all the things he couldn't, you checked out."

"Jesus, you don't know—"

"I know I don't. I don't know what it's like to go through what you went through. To try to get past the guilt, even if it's misplaced. But to disappear... what, so Ian wouldn't ever have a home, so you decided you didn't deserve one either? No wife, no kids, so no personal relationships for you? You just decided to punish yourself forever? Do you think that is what he would have wanted for you?"

George's throat tightened. He struggled for a few moments, trying to slow his breathing, get a hold of his emotions. When he finally had some semblance of control, he spoke again.

"The topic of mortality only came up once, and I told Ian to shut up about it. But Ian was so down, almost depressed, so I made him promise that if anything happened to me, he'd go out and do all the things we said we'd do after our tour was over. Find a pretty girl and have lots of sex. God, he laughed at that one, and said it was a no brainer." George smiled a little, remembering. It was bittersweet. "Drink beer and watch sunsets. Take a motorcycle trip from Carolina to Maine in the fall, when all the leaves were changing."

"But you didn't do those things."

"Oh, I did. But it didn't go the way it was supposed to." He sighed and leaned back against the cushions of the sofa. "I tried, Amy. God, I tried. I came home and looked up Jennie. We did have all kinds of sex, until she clued in that it wasn't love I was looking for but escape. Step one

—I blew up that relationship. Oh, and I drank a lot of beer and watched sunsets. And sunrises, and the sun at any time of day, unless it was cloudy, and I drank then, too. And I did take the bike trip, but only got as far as Concord. It seemed pretty pointless so I ditched the bike. Ditched everything. Lived in a shitty old dive until my money ran out and I was kicked out. I tried a few jobs but nothing stuck. I kept missing days and I'd get fired, over and over again. A year after I got home and I was on the street, drifting from town to town."

Amy was quiet for a long time. George waited for her to say something and yet she didn't. He looked over at her and tried to figure out the look on her face, but he couldn't read that, either. "What is it? Just say whatever you're thinking. It can't possibly be worse than anything I've said to myself over the years."

Her brows pulled together. "I just don't know how to ask this."

"Ask what?"

Her gaze touched his and her lips worked a bit before she finally said, "If it was so hopeless, why did you stay? Why didn't you…did you…I mean, something kept you going from day to day."

"You're asking if I thought about suicide, and why didn't I do it?"

She nodded, but he could tell by the worry in her eyes that she was afraid of his answer.

"I thought about it at first. And then I thought that would be taking the easy way out. For a long time I thought I was meant to suffer. After a while I stopped feeling that so sharply, you know? But then, homelessness is just a hard cycle to get out of, even when you start wanting to. Getting your life back seems like such an uphill climb it feels like it's impossible to take the first step. Laurel treated me like a human being instead of a thing that needed to be dealt with or given charity. I started to stand taller and feel like a man again. And for the most part I do. But days like today, when I relive what I've done, it's hard, Amy. It's fucking hard not to go back to feeling like that failure who let everyone down."

She lifted her hand and placed it on his cheek. He leaned into the touch, even though he knew he shouldn't. He'd been without real human contact for so long that he couldn't resist. "You're not a failure," she whispered, sliding closer. "You're not. You're the walking wounded, George, and you were the one who was let down when you came home. You should have had supports in place. You should have had family to turn to...God, I wish you'd come to us. I wish it hadn't taken fifteen years for me to tell you that it's okay and that I don't forgive you because there's nothing to forgive."

He didn't realize he'd started to cry until she pulled him close and put his head on her shoulder. His lip wobbled and his chest cramped so hard it hurt to breathe, and the sobs came out harsh and ugly and painfully. He cried for the friend he'd lost and the years he'd lost and the benediction he'd just received, and when it was over, he realized her arms were wrapped around him and her fingers were stroking his hair as a mother would a small child. He'd never had that in his life, not really. He didn't remember his parents, or even when he'd been put into "the system." As a foster kid he'd had more mothers than he'd had grade school teachers. He'd just get used to a place and then he'd have to leave, all his belongings in a single bag, on to another family. He'd had his heart broken so many times that as a teenager he'd made sure he didn't stay in one situation too long so he couldn't get attached. He'd run away or been too much trouble. He'd certainly never felt the unconditional acceptance he did in this moment.

He still didn't feel as if he deserved it.

"You've been waiting a long time for that, haven't you?" she asked softly.

He pushed out of her arms, even though they felt so good. "Yeah." His voice was rough and unsteady.

"George, I don't know what kind of support you have in place now, but you've got to talk to someone and get the right treatment."

He snorted a little, then briskly wiped his eyes and rolled his shoulders. "Yeah, right. Going through all that red tape? It's ridiculous."

"Then let me help you navigate it." She smiled at him. "I'm in HR. Policies, forms, and red tape are my specialty."

"I can't do that. Don't worry about me. I'm getting by. And I'm getting things together..."

She rubbed his knee. "You deserve more than to just 'get by.' A few years ago, a woman in our office was raped. She was a mess for a long time, but then she did some therapy to help her get through the PTSD. It was so helpful, you know? We can find a qualified therapist for you."

He let out a breath, feeling more than a little raw. "Can we talk about it another time? It's been an intense night already."

"Of course." Her fingers squeezed his knee. "I just want you to know that Ian would want this for you. He'd want you to be whole, and happy. So do I. You're not alone anymore, George. You have friends here, and a job you like, and you have family, too."

He wasn't sure her magnanimity would extend to her parents; they'd lost their son, too. But at the same time, he wanted to accept what she was offering so much. Learning to reach out for help, for friendship, had been so hard. He was still learning how to be that person again. To be able to not only accept friendship, but to give it in return.

And then he looked at her, her eyes red and slightly swollen from crying, her lips full and red, and knew that he'd never wanted just friendship from Amy. Not since the first time he'd clapped eyes on her back in Brooklyn. She'd been his best friend's sister and off limits then. She should still be now. Instead she'd snuck right past all his barriers. He wouldn't kiss her; Lord, he wasn't in any position to do such a thing, but he wanted to. Despite how weak he'd felt tonight, confessing what had happened, crying on her shoulder, for God's sake...despite that weakness, right now he felt more of a man than he had in over a decade.

Chapter 6

AMY SHRUGGED ON HER coat and wrapped her scarf around her neck. "Have you got everything?" George asked, and she nodded. Her lids were heavy, both from the crying and the fact that it was 1:00 a.m. and they'd spent the whole evening talking. First about Ian; once George had let out the truth, it seemed as if a dam had opened up and the good memories of their times together on deployment came rushing out. She'd laughed at some of the stories, tucking them away in her heart, the little pieces of her brother that she had missed over the years. They'd done the dishes together, him washing, her drying, and then shared a hug when George got a little misty again over a particular memory of Thanksgiving in the desert.

But now it was late, and she wasn't sure where to go from here. There'd been a moment, when George had looked into her eyes, that something had happened, a tenuous, invisible connection between them that frightened her. He'd always been attractive, but now he was a bit weathered from time and experience and damned if she didn't find it sexy. At the same time, he was so damaged. Even considering anything happening between them would be a mistake.

She knew better than most that going into a relationship trying to fix someone was a recipe for disaster.

She should leave. Go back to Brooklyn, spend the holiday in her brownstone and with her parents, and...

And do the same damned thing she did every year. It sounded disgustingly dull and a bit sad.

She looked up at George, who was holding out the salad bowl. "Thank you for dinner."

"Thank you, for everything," she said softly. Her gaze lit on the plain Christmas tree in the corner. Thought about George trying to celebrate the holiday alone and knew exactly how he felt. It wasn't that she was a Grinch or a Scrooge and hated the holiday; she didn't. But sometimes decorating for one, showing up at all the gatherings alone, and having only her own presents under the tree was depressing.

He had his hand on the doorknob when she looked up into his face. "Do you want to go for a walk tomorrow night?"

He hesitated. "A walk?"

She nodded. They had to do something other than eat if they were going to spend some time together, but she didn't want to suggest anything elaborate that could be misconstrued as a date. "I was just thinking that we could walk around Darling and see all the different Christmas lights. And if you wanted, we could put some decorations on your tree."

He looked over his shoulder at the tree. "Oh. Yeah, I was going to get around to that."

She smiled a little. "I put my artificial one up on December first, but I can't really enjoy it while I'm in Darling, can I? And I can't really put one up in the rental. I was kind of hoping there'd be one already." Even though the holiday often felt lonely, it felt worse to ignore it altogether. "If I'm going to visit, I might as well make the most of it. I heard there's a big tree at the town hall."

"There is. And there are lights through the Green as well, and around the bridge. If the weather agrees, that might be nice."

"Do you want to meet somewhere?"

"I'll pick you up. We can park at the lot off Bridge Street, walk over to town hall, and then back along Main to the Green." He grinned, and she loved seeing his eyes light up. "If we take my truck, we can maybe pick up a few decorations. If you still feel up to decorating."

He looked so pleased she knew she'd make sure they dressed up his tree in style.

She tucked the casserole dish and bowl under her arm and put her hand on his wrist. "George, thank you for telling me what happened. And for more than that, for sharing all those memories. There were so many parts of his life that we didn't get to see or share. Tonight I felt close to him again."

"Me, too."

She nodded, her throat tight. "You know, the grief isn't the same after so many years, but the questions...they were a real loose end." She smiled a little. "You gave me a wonderful Christmas gift tonight. Now I'd better go so you can get some sleep. Work comes early for you, I'm guessing."

She was surprised when he grabbed his apartment keys and walked her to her car. A dusk-to-dawn streetlamp created a disc of light toward the end of the small parking lot, but the night was silent and still. Their feet made crunching noises in the snow as they crossed to her car, and her breath puffed out in a white cloud in front of them. He took her keys and unlocked her door, the hinges squeaking in the quiet. He handed her the keys.

"Good night, Amy," he murmured, his hands resting on the top of her car door.

"Good night."

He shut the door behind her, and she put the key in the ignition and started the engine. She let it warm for about thirty seconds, until she got self-conscious of the fact that he was standing at the front door to his building, without a jacket, making sure she got out of the parking lot okay.

When she drove away she looked in her rear-view mirror and saw he'd gone inside. Then she let out a breath and tried not to overthink what was happening—to her, to George, and to the two of them together. They were just friends. That's all they could be. The closeness she'd felt tonight had simply been a reaction to their emotional discussion, nothing more.

It couldn't be more.

—ele—

George rushed home and showered after work, washing away the dirt and pitch from working with the branches and trees all day. He dressed in clean jeans and a button-down shirt, ran his hand through his hair and wondered if it was time for a cut again, and let out a big breath.

This was not a date. Hell, the idea of dating was crazy, wasn't it? He and Amy were connected by Ian, and George was just going to show her around town. It wasn't like he had such a surplus of friends that he could justify turning a friendly face away. But it was more than that, too. It was how she'd smiled at him, held his hand, let him cry. They weren't just connected through Ian's memory— they were connected through shared grief.

Damn. Crying. At one time he would have been embarrassed as hell to let anyone see his tears, but last night had been different. He'd felt safe. And today he felt different. Lighter. More at peace with himself and the world around him.

Maybe confession was good for the soul. Maybe forgiveness lifted the burden on his heart. Whatever it was, he stared in the mirror in the bathroom and realized that tonight was yet another step on the journey toward normalcy: a walk in the snow with a pretty woman. He was going to celebrate that.

It was dark when he pulled into her driveway and got out of the truck. Nerves bounced around in his stomach as he made his way up the cobbled walk to the front door. He knocked and stood back, feeling sick to his stomach.

All those feelings fled when she opened the door. He couldn't think much of anything except how beautiful she was. She wore a cream-colored jacket and a fluffy pink scarf that highlighted the roses in her cheeks. Her hair was tucked beneath a matching hat, the dark waves of it just visible around her collar. But what really struck him was that she seemed genuinely happy to see him, and excited for their outing. He found himself smiling back at her.

"You ready?" he asked, though he didn't expect an answer.

"Let me grab my purse," she replied, and disappeared for a moment. She came back with a cream-and-pink shoulder bag. "Now I'm ready. I even charged up my phone so I can take some pictures."

She locked the door behind her, and by the time she reached the truck he had the door open for her. Was he imagining things, or did the pink in her cheeks deepen as he shut the door? He pushed away the feeling that this was somehow all too surreal and hopped into the driver's seat. "Brace yourself. It's a whole minute and a half to the parking lot."

She laughed a bit and still buckled her seatbelt. The truck was a little too loud; he hadn't paid enough attention to the exhaust when he bought it. And it was an older model, with a few rips and tears in the interior. Her little sedan was much newer and in perfect shape, but tonight he didn't care. He had his own wheels and he could drive a pretty woman to town for a date.

Whoa. He pulled into the parking lot and reminded himself this was definitely not a date.

And reminded himself again when he jogged around the front of the truck to open her door, only to find she'd already got out and was putting her bag over her shoulder.

"Let's go to the town hall first," he suggested. They used the sidewalk on the regular traffic bridge to cross Fisher Creek, then turned left toward town hall. The evening was cool and cloudy, with no stars, but the odd errant snowflake drifted down, adding to the festive feel without being a nuisance for pictures or walking. When they got to the town hall, Amy pulled out her phone and took a picture of the towering tree, lit with hundreds of colorful bulbs.

George stared at it too, and felt a contentedness spread through him. "You know, it's not Rockefeller Center, but it's pretty, don't you think?"

"I do. The whole town is really great, George. Friendly and warm. I can see why you like living here."

They moved past town hall and the adjacent emergency services building, then ambled toward Main Street and the businesses there. "You know, I wondered if I should stay here, or go somewhere that people didn't know my...well, background is probably the best way to put it. But with my job, and the few friends I've made, I really didn't want to go anywhere else. One new start seemed like enough to tackle."

They passed the church and stopped for a moment to admire the Nativity scene, lit by spotlights. "Oh, this is lovely." She sighed. "You know, we used to go to midnight mass every Christmas Eve. Mom used to dress us up, too, in special clothes for all the Sundays in advent. God, how Ian hated putting on a tie, even the little clip-on ones when he was a boy. There was always a crèche inside, but never room for a really pretty scene like this. The church was right on the street and parking all around it. This is restful, don't you think?"

Her remembrance reached in and wrapped around his heart a bit. It wasn't hard to imagine Ian as a boy, all dark hair and sparkly eyes full of mischief. More than that, she'd unwittingly drawn a picture of a family and a childhood that he'd always longed for and never had. "It's beautiful," he replied, and looked over at her. "I'd like to come here for a service sometime." He didn't mention that twice a month the church women provided a hot meal for those in need. He'd eaten his share of homemade soups, stews, and baked beans in the small hall at the back of the building.

They walked further on Main, remarking at the decorations on display at businesses and residences alike. She tugged him into the General Store and pulled him to the holiday corner where a small selection of decorations were kept. She picked up a flat box containing thirty little wooden ornaments. "This is cute, don't you think?"

"They're not bad."

"You don't strike me as the shiny glass ball type."

She looked so excited he didn't have the heart to tell her that he was actually exactly that type. He couldn't explain why, except that he'd had one Christmas as a boy that had been wonderful. He'd been six, maybe seven, and there'd been three other foster kids in the family. But the tree had been beautiful, and he'd got a toboggan from Santa. He hadn't minded that he'd had to share, and hadn't minded that the rest of his presents had been underwear and socks and jeans and T-shirts instead of all the latest toys on TV. He'd spent two whole months tugging that sled back up the hill before zooming down again. Before he'd had another switch to a new foster home.

He honestly didn't give a damn what the decorations on his tree looked like. The fact that he even had one was enough.

"They're nice," he answered, but she'd already tucked them under her arm and was looking at tree toppers, namely stars covered in some sparkly something-or-other. "What are you doing?"

"Getting you decorations for your tree."

He frowned. "Then here. I'll get them."

"Nope. My gift to you."

He stopped her with a hand on her arm. "Amy, I can get a few decorations."

She tilted her chin in the air. "Let's look at it from my point of view, shall we? I don't have a tree at the cottage, and every year I decorate mine alone. You already have the tree and stand. And helping you..." Her big eyes shimmered at him. "It'd be nice to decorate with someone for a change."

Amy? Lonely? He hadn't considered it before, but maybe she was.

"Is this a pride thing?" she asked. "Because if it is, I'll let you buy me a hot chocolate at The Purple Pig."

She was so impossible to resist. He should have known that first day she'd driven into town and faced off with him at The Ladybug that he didn't stand a chance. Less than a week later he'd spilled his guts and was out being social of all things.

"I suppose I'll have to say yes," he replied, and dropped his hand. She smiled triumphantly and took the decorations to the cash register. Then she tucked them into the pink-and-cream tote.

"Now you know why I brought the big bag," she teased, stepping through the door as the bell dinged above them.

Snow was falling a little harder now, but still only what he'd call a "gentle flurry." Their steps slowed as they walked along, stopping to admire a few different wreaths. George even stepped closer to a business door to examine the wreath's construction, which led to more teasing from Amy. At The Purple Pig he bought two dark hot chocolates, made with organic cocoa and milk, as well as two holiday shortbread cookies in the shape of snowmen. Further down the block they crossed to the Green at a crosswalk, found a vacant bench, and sat to sip and nibble.

"This is nice," Amy said quietly, tilting her face to the sky. She stuck out her tongue to catch a snowflake, and then giggled. George watched, fascinated, entranced. She seemed so young. And most of the time he felt so old, but tonight that all disappeared. Tonight he felt the weight of his past fade away, and when she looked over at him and lifted an eyebrow, he tilted his head back, stuck out his tongue, and waited for a little cold flake to land on it.

"You look silly," she remarked, and bit the rest of the head off her snowman.

"Who cares?" he asked, grinning. "Want to know something? I went through years of people either not actually seeing me or seeing me and pretending I didn't exist. It taught me not to care so much about things like how I look. What I really have to worry about?" He held his cookie in his hand but pressed his hand over his heart. "How I feel in here. Being square with myself. I spent so much time thinking I wasn't worth it, determined not to accept help. I started over, and if I want to catch snowflakes on my tongue I'm damned well going to do it."

"Good. You should." She gave an emphatic nod.

They were still chatting when a voice interrupted them. "George?"

He looked up and saw half the Gallagher clan walking through the snow. Laurel was there, holding Aiden's hand, her baby bump just visible beneath her jacket. With them was Aiden's brother, Ethan, his partner, Willow, and his two little boys. Willow was glowing; her pregnancy wasn't quite as far along as Laurel's but wasn't far behind.

"Hey, boss." He smiled up at Laurel but felt heat rush into his face. Particularly when everyone seemed to be staring at Amy like she was some kind of curiosity.

"Looks like lots of people are enjoying the lights tonight," Aiden remarked, giving Laurel a gentle nudge with his elbow. She stopped staring and smiled.

"Everyone, this is Amy Merck. I knew her brother a long time ago." There wasn't as much pain at the words as he expected. "Amy, you've met Laurel. This is her husband, Aiden, and his brother Ethan; Willow, who owns The Purple Pig, and Ethan's sons, Connor and Ronan."

Amy smiled widely. "I've heard a lot about you, Aiden, and Willow, I just love the food at the café." She looked down at the boys. "And I suppose you guys are getting excited for Christmas."

Ronan held onto Willow's hand and stared. Connor started jumping around and talking about wanting hockey skates for Christmas, so he could be just like Cam Collier. Amy nodded. "Sure," she said brightly. "But I'm a Rangers fan, so I'm not so much into Collier."

"What?" Connor's mouth dropped open in dismay, and George laughed. "I think you just insulted his superhero," he muttered. He looked at Connor and shook his head. "I know, Connor. I mean, the Rangers? Really?"

With the ruffled feathers smoothed, everyone enjoyed a laugh.

"We'd better keep going. We parked at the garden center. Willow and Ethan are going to take their tree home tonight."

Ronan still hadn't said a word, but George noticed his eyes brightened with excitement.

For a moment a bit of wistfulness hit him. He'd never have a family like this, not now. But maybe what he had was enough. He'd been alone for so long. Having a real family invite him in...it was more than he'd ever expected again.

"You two enjoy your evening," Ethan said. Willow approached George and knelt down in front of him.

"How's the CD working out?"

She was so kind, so generous. "Like a charm."

"You know where I am if you need anything, right?"

He nodded. Willow had surprised him a few months ago by sharing a small bit of her own story. She'd dealt with her own mental health issues and never hesitated to offer a helping hand or a non-judgmental ear. Not that he'd really taken her up on it; he was too private. But she was able to read between the lines without pressing, and he appreciated it.

Willow looked over at Amy. "It's really lovely to meet you. Come on into the café at any time. We should have tea."

"Oh." Amy looked flustered but pleased. "Thanks. I'd like that."

Willow reached over and patted Amy's hand, then stood and reached for Ronan again. "Okay, kiddo. Let's go pick out a tree."

When they were gone Amy looked over at him with big eyes. "Wow. They're really nice people. And Willow is so pretty!"

"That family has been...well, not my surrogate family, but my friends. They're good people. The best."

"The boys are sweet."

"Ethan's first wife died a few years back. But this past year, he and Willow started dating. They're expecting a baby in the spring."

"That's so sad."

"With a happy ending." He shrugged. "She loves his boys and they love her. There are three other kids in the family, too. When they all get together, it's a bit overpowering."

"I bet."

His cookie was long gone. "Do you want to keep walking? There are lights all along here. And you must be getting cold."

She nodded and he took their empty garbage to a nearby receptacle. When he came back, she reached out and took his hand in hers.

His stomach flipped over, and he left his hand in hers while wondering what the hell he was doing. He was in no position to offer her anything. Not materially, not emotionally. But how could he deny himself the simple sweetness of her gesture? There was innocence in it, and trust. Trust most of all.

They passed several little illuminated scenes as they walked along the path, but George barely noticed them. He was too busy thinking about the woman beside him. Ian had spoken of his twin sister often, worrying about her, telling George stories of their childhood, both good and bad. Girls, he'd explained, could be really horrible to each other. Particularly when someone wasn't in the popular crowd. When it had been time for their senior prom, he'd gone with his girlfriend, but his best friend had taken Amy when her date had cancelled on her two weeks before the dance.

George looked at her now, her face lit by the myriad of holiday lights, and wondered if her marriage, and her past experiences, had left her feeling like she was always second best.

She wasn't. No way.

He kept his hand in hers as they approached the Kissing Bridge.

"So this is the famed bridge?" she asked. "It's beautiful."

The town council had strung lights from one side of the stone bridge to the other, making it worthy of a fairy-tale. Other people were strolling, across it, in front of it, taking pictures, even the odd kiss. Quite often kissing and taking pictures.

But George didn't even really see the bridge. He was too busy looking at her, marveling that she was there with him, and smiling, and that for the first time in a very long time, he wasn't just optimistic, he was happy.

"So are you," he said, before he could change his mind.

She turned to face him. "I'm what?" she asked, having lost the thread of their conversation.

He swallowed, even more aware that he held her hand in his. "Beautiful," he said, gazing into her eyes. "I'm sorry if I shouldn't say it, but it's true. You always were, and you still are."

"George," she whispered, and her eyes softened.

"Just in case you forgot," he added. "In case your ex made you feel as if you weren't. Or whatever."

"Sometimes," she admitted softly. "Oh, George. How did we get to be so broken?"

They stood at the edge of the bridge for a long time, staring at the lights, the way they sparkled off the snow, listening to the chatter of people around them. Amy took out her phone and snapped a couple of pictures. After a while they started walking across the stones, over the frozen creek to the other side. George held his breath. He knew the legend of the bridge, didn't really put any credence in it, but didn't want to tempt fate, either. Other couples laughed and kissed; they ambled. When they got to the other side, and the path that led away from the bridge and to the half-full parking lot, they hesitated. George wasn't ready to leave. There'd been something magical about their walk through the snow tonight. Something tenuous and beautiful that reached in and made him feel so alive.

Amy looked up at him, her eyes wide and serious. Then her gaze dropped to his lips and he felt the jolt in his solar plexus. When was the last time a woman had looked at him this way? He still didn't feel he deserved it. As she leaned closer, he realized that his time on the street had left him feeling dirty and unworthy of what most people took for granted as normal.

She stood up on tiptoe and touched her lips to his. She teetered on her heels a little, and reached out to the stone rail of the bridge to keep her balance. Only for a moment, though. He put his hands on her shoulders and held her firmly as they kissed. It only lasted a few seconds, but it was enough to rock his world.

Shorter and sweeter than he remembered, but no less potent.

He pulled away first, ran his tongue over his lower lip. He tasted the soft sweetness of her lipstick. Oh boy. This was not supposed to happen. He was just supposed to be showing her around town.

"Is it okay that I did that?" she asked, her voice quiet and uncertain.

"I don't know," he answered honestly. "It surprised me. I haven't...I mean..." He smiled a little. "Shit, Amy, I'm out of practice."

She smiled a little in return. "I didn't notice."

Damn. Just damn.

"Let's just put a pin in it," she suggested. "Call it a nice moment, maybe? And not read too much into it?"

It sounded like the perfect way to handle it, but it was more than a nice moment. Did she realize the gift she'd given him? He'd done a lot of things in the last few months that had helped give him back his dignity and his sense of self and pride. But this... One sweet, simple kiss had given him back a bit of his manhood. Of his sexuality. He felt desirable.

And if he ever admitted such a thing out loud, he'd be laughed out of Darling. But it didn't change the expansive feeling in his chest, or the fact that he wanted to kiss her again, but this time properly.

"George?"

He shook his head and dropped his hands from her shoulders. "Sorry. Do you want to decorate the tree now? Or would you like to do something else?"

Her eyes twinkled at him. "Your tree. I have some surprises in my bag."

"You do?"

She nodded. "Let's go."

The truck wasn't far away, and within a few minutes they were pulling into the parking lot at his building.

Something new sat between them, a delicious kind of tension that was a hangover from the kiss and had bloomed into what George thought might be attraction. It certainly was on his part. He might be out of practice, but he'd given her the opportunity to call it a night, and instead she'd seemed excited to go back to his apartment and decorate his tree.

A nice moment indeed.

But she wanted to keep it light, and he'd oblige. So they hopped out of the truck, she grabbed her bag, and they headed upstairs to the naked tree that waited for them.

Chapter 7

AMY DIDN'T KNOW WHAT had come over her back at the bridge, but she could still taste him on her lips and was still tingling all over from the possessive way he'd gripped her shoulders, keeping her from tipping over.

She'd kissed him. Kissed him! She couldn't even really explain why, except that something had happened between one side of the bridge and the other. Nothing tangible, nothing specific she could put her finger on, nothing but a connection that ran between them, both poignant and sweet at what they'd lost and what they'd gained over the years since they'd last met.

And when she'd looked into his eyes she'd seen a flash of hunger there, a glimpse of the man he'd once been, who'd looked at her as if there was no one else in the world he'd rather be with at that moment. The same breathless feeling had overcome her.

Back then the kiss had been wild and reckless; this time it had been soft and sweet. But no less devastating.

Now, though, as they entered his apartment, she was reminded of the differences in their lives. Differences that would be impossible to overcome. The very thought was precipitous, wasn't it? He certainly wasn't in the market for romance, and neither was she.

"Home sweet home," he said quietly, shutting the door.

"Indeed." She tried a smile. "Before I dig out the ornaments, do you have a big pot we can use on the stove?"

He frowned, clearly puzzled. "A pot? What for?"

She had to restore some normalcy to their interaction or she was going to kiss him again. Once really didn't seem like enough, and her voice of logic wasn't speaking loudly enough tonight. Distraction was the only way she was going to keep from compounding her mistake of earlier...if it could be called a mistake. It didn't really feel like it.

She reached into her tote and pulled out a bag of popcorn kernels. "We're going to string popcorn for your tree."

He stared at her with such a blank look that she burst out laughing. It helped to dispel a little of the tension still simmering between them. "What, you've never done it before?"

He shook his head. "Never."

For the second time in as many days, she was incredibly thankful for her upbringing. She certainly didn't pry further; she suspected his response would be that none of his homes had really done any of these activities. One day she'd like to talk to him more about his childhood. She knew foster parents, had grown up with foster kids in her neighborhood. Some had flourished, others not so much. It was sad to think that George was one who'd somehow fallen between the cracks. All Ian had ever said was that George had been bounced from home to home, and then when he'd turned eighteen he'd signed up and the army had become his home.

Which meant he'd been homeless in more than one way since he'd been discharged. She hadn't considered that before.

"Well," she said, shaking off the sad thoughts, "there's a first time for everything. Our mom never let us put these on our main tree, but we had this little artificial bottle brush thing that we kept in the downstairs den, and she let Ian and I decorate it however we wanted. We went crazy every year with the tackiest decorations we could find, usually at a local dollar store. I've got everything here we need. Popcorn, needles, string, cranberries . . ."

"Cranberries?"

"And if there's any popcorn left over, we can eat it." She didn't tell him that there was hardly ever any left and that they'd have to pop more than one batch. Baby steps.

But George seemed game for it all, found a big pot, and they began popping. He swatted her hand when she reached for a few kernels, and then laughed when she stuck out her lower lip in mock outrage. They sat at his little table, a huge bowl of popcorn between them, and a large bag of ruby-red cranberries, and started stringing.

Amy didn't see a stereo or anything around, and a cursory glimpse at the TV revealed no cable box...did it even work or was it simply a piece of his furniture? Instead of asking, she took out her phone and splurged, just this once, by turning on her data. A few clicks later and Christmas music filled the silence, a bit thin and tinny in the phone's speakers, but festive just the same.

"You have Christmas music on your phone?" he asked, then put his tongue between his teeth as he poked the needle through a cranberry.

"It's a streaming service. I have a subscription."

"It's nice." He smiled at her and she picked up a piece of popcorn.

"George, about what happened in the park..."

His gaze touched hers. The sparks she'd felt when they'd kissed came back full force, making her breath catch.

Then he looked down again and started to string a piece of popcorn. Her eyes followed the movement, and she saw his fingers were shaking.

"George." She whispered now, though she couldn't explain why. "I'm sorry if I overstepped. That was all I was going to say."

He didn't look at her. "You regret it."

"No! I mean..." Oh Lord. Why had she even mentioned it? "You're still a very good kisser."

Now he looked at her. "Be careful, Amy. This would be a big mistake, don't you think?"

If he'd just said it would be a mistake rather than asking her opinion, she might have left it alone. She put down her needle and thread. "Maybe. I don't know. I just know that I still find you very attractive."

A blush colored the crest of his cheeks, and it delighted her.

"And you're a pretty woman. Not just pretty..." He stumbled over his words a bit, a crease forming between his eyebrows. "Listen, you got what you wanted from me. Maybe it would be best if you went home. This is just going to complicate things."

He was right, but it had been so long since she'd felt anything like this that she didn't want to let it go without at least exploring it a bit. "If we...I mean, I'm going home at Christmas. I'm only here another week. Can't we agree to enjoy the time a bit...together?"

He kept stringing popcorn, faster and faster, forgetting to put a cranberry in at regular intervals. "I don't know how to do anything casual anymore. I know I used to be that way, but things change. I've changed."

She got up from her chair and went to him, squatted down beside him, and stilled his busy hands with her own. "The thing is, George, you see your changes as being a problem. And I see them as a sign of growth and strength and courage. I couldn't give a rat's ass about your apartment, or your rusty truck, or your job. Don't shake your head at me, either. I've seen the look on your face when you think I'm not looking. You judge yourself far harder than anyone else does. Things mean nothing to me. Character does. And you've got that in spades, George. You always did." She and Liam had had a decent life, but in the end their house and favorite restaurants and good jobs and circle of friends hadn't been able to save their marriage.

He laughed, but it was a bitter sound. "Oh, don't be fooled, Amy. I wasn't honest with you back then, and I wasn't honest with Jennie or even myself."

"So you made mistakes. Haven't we all? It doesn't mean you weren't—that you aren't—a good man, in here." She reached up and placed her hand on his chest.

He put his hand over hers.

"Amy..."

She stood up and told herself to not overthink anything, but to do what felt right. She slid onto his lap, heard the sharp intake of breath that relayed his surprise, felt his warm, strong hands settle on her hips.

"What are you doing?"

"Shh," she whispered, closing her eyes. "Just shh."

She sank her fingers into his short, dark hair, then let them slide over his scalp, tracing the hairline of his forehead, down along his cheek where his hair turned from brown to gray. It was soft, silky, and smelled of his shampoo. Her fingertips grazed his cheekbones, slid over his eyelids, down the bridge of his nose where the end turned up just a little. And still she kept her eyes closed, seeing him by touch alone, imagining each feature as she read them with her fingers. She rubbed her thumb over his full lower lip, and a flash of desire darted straight to her core when he grabbed for her thumb with his teeth.

Whatever had happened to him in the intervening years didn't matter. The man before her right now was strong, sexy, and if she were any judge, as turned on as she was right now.

She was debating whether she should kiss him again when he took matters into his own hands. He slid one hand around her neck, pulling her closer, and kissed her.

Kissed her the way he'd kissed her all those years ago, on her parents' back step with the outside light turned off for privacy. And now, like then, her knees went weak, saved only by the fact that she was sitting on his lap and not required to be upright.

She clung to him tightly as the kiss built into something wild and sensual, like she was that last bit of water in the desert, and he'd die if he didn't drink. Her body responded with a rush—God, it was good to feel wanted again—and she curled herself around him, a small sound issuing from her throat.

His body tightened beneath hers and their breath came faster, harder. But still he stayed in the chair and didn't make any attempt to move them in any way. She bit down on his lip, just a light nibble, and he ran his hand up her ribs to cup her breast in his palm. She pressed into it, imagining what it would be like for him to peel off her sweater and bra...

He broke off the kiss and pressed his forehead to hers. "Jesus," he murmured, breathing heavily. "We've got to stop, Amy."

"I don't want to stop," she answered honestly.

"Don't say that."

She heard the longing in his voice. He wanted her, too. What a revelation. And it would be good, wouldn't it? She'd always thought so. Wondered a time or two this week if he'd changed too much, if they'd both changed to a point where the chemistry would be gone. But it was very alive and well, wasn't it?

"It's the truth," she whispered, shifting her head to drop little kisses on his cheeks. "You feel so good."

He didn't say anything, and she drew back to find him with his eyes closed, his jaw tight. Unease settled in her chest. "Did I say something wrong?"

George shook his head. "No. And it's not that I don't want to." He made a strangled sound, halfway between a sigh and a laugh. "Believe me. But it would be a mistake, Amy, and you were right earlier this week. Ian would be ashamed of how

I've acted. I won't compound that with disrespecting his memory further by sleeping with his sister."

He picked a hell of a time to be honorable.

He was also right. Sex right now would be a one-night proposition, and they both deserved better. Her brain and heart knew it. She just had to convey the message to her body, which still hummed from his touch.

"But kissing," he continued, "kissing might be okay. Because I could kiss you all night."

She sat back a bit and cupped his face. He looked into her eyes. There was a vulnerability she hadn't anticipated, and she realized with a start that this was a bigger moment for him than it was for her. She was the one who needed to be patient. Who needed to think of his needs before her own, or at the very least give them equal weight. What George needed right now was affection, acceptance. A slow burn rather than a raging fire. She probably needed that, too, if she were totally honest with herself.

"I like kissing," she admitted, curling into his embrace. "I happen to like kissing a lot."

And so they kissed—what Amy would have called "making out"—in his kitchen chair until they both decided they'd drunk their fill.

And then they strung more popcorn and cranberries, looped the strands around the tree, and hung the ornaments. When they were done,

George stood back and stared at the spruce. "I like it," he decreed.

"Me, too," she answered, standing beside him, leaning against his arm. "It's not a showstopper, but it's yours. And that's exactly how it should be."

Her phone battery had died a while back, so she looked on the little microwave in the kitchen and saw that it was after midnight. "I should probably get back home."

"I'll drive you. Don't forget your bag."

"Do you want to walk? It's not that far, and it's a beautiful night."

"If you want to."

They bundled up and were careful to be quiet on the stairs, then stepped out into the wintery night. The flurries had stopped and the moon was out, its bright light reflecting off the snow as they made their way toward Bedford Cottage. He held her hand, and she wondered at all that had happened tonight. The date, meeting his friends, the surprising physical developments in their relationship. But what would happen in a week when she went back to Brooklyn and he stayed here? What prospect did they have other than a holiday fling or, if they wanted to put a more serious tag on it, a way to find closure from the past? Could she walk away and not see him again?

After tonight, was it possible for them to be just friends?

He'd been right. Sleeping together would have been a mistake.

"You're very quiet." His voice was deep in the snowy silence.

"Just thinking."

"Me, too. Wondering what we're doing. What it means in the big scheme of things."

"Me, too."

"You figured it out yet?" He looked over at her briefly.

"Not even close."

"Me, either." He squeezed her hand. "But if I wanted to keep it simple, I'd say I want to enjoy the next week with you. And that I am fully aware that you're going back to your life on Christmas Eve. That's what I know for sure."

"And you think we can manage that?"

He nudged her with his elbow. "Honey, after the last decade? I can handle a week with you, no problem."

But that wasn't what she'd meant. She wondered if it would be so easy to walk away. She could go right now and put an end to anything between them. Or she could stay and give herself the gift of this one week. If he swore he could do it, she could too, right?

Chapter 8

GEORGE PUT THE LAST of the poinsettias in the bed of his truck and then carefully unrolled the tarp he'd tied to the box to keep them covered for the drive to the golf course clubhouse. Tonight was the Lights for Literacy fundraiser, and as he'd promised, he was taking fifty special potted arrangements to serve as centerpieces.

There were activities planned for all over town. All children's books and resource books were on sale at Pen 2 Paper, and a children's author from Boston was doing a reading sometime in the afternoon. The library was hosting Stories with Santa later this morning, and there was an adult literacy organization's display as well. Businesses all over town had donation boxes and incentives as either free gifts or coupons. George would hold down the fort at the garden center while Laurel and Aiden got ready to attend the banquet and silent auction. The whole thing was the brainchild of Aiden's oldest sister, Hannah. Between her and the town's social media manager, Oaklee Collier, it had become the season's big event.

As he drove out to the golf course, he thought about Amy. They'd spent more time together in the evenings ever since they'd decorated his tree. Once they'd gone to Roberto's and shared a huge sausage and mushroom pizza. Another time they'd stopped at the Suds and Spuds pub, ordered iced teas, and listened to live music.

It had all been so very normal, but today his muscles were tense with nerves. He was dressed in jeans and work boots and delivering plants. She'd bought a ticket for the benefit and was going with Willow and Ethan. Apparently in the past five days, she and Willow had struck up a friendship. She'd even talked about attending one of Willow's morning yoga classes.

They were from different worlds. No matter what she said or how much he enjoyed her company, that simple fact couldn't be denied. She was on holiday. Her real life was back in New York, working at a big company and taking the train to work each morning. Shopping on Fifth Avenue and dinner with her parents.

He didn't mean to get hung up on financial differences, but he did have a bit of pride, and it took a hit when he looked at his own life and hers.

The clubhouse was already a beehive of activity. When George pulled up to the staff entrance, he saw delivery vans outside the kitchen and a flurry of workers bustling around, adding signage and even more Christmas lights to the already impressive array. He slammed the truck door and went inside to check in and ask where to put the flowers. When he poked his nose into the ballroom, he caught sight of Hannah Gallagher, gesturing wildly to someone who was setting up the sound system at the front of the room.

He waited a moment until Hannah shook the man's hand and backed away. "Hey, Hannah? I've got the centerpieces."

"George! Perfect. The tables already have their linens on. We can put them right in the middle. You don't mind helping, do you?"

"Makes sense to only handle them once." He was happy to have something to do. Hannah Gallagher intimidated the hell out of him. She was nice enough, and generous to a fault, but she was incredibly beautiful as well as being one of those women who just got things done. She was also rumored to be the best realtor in the area, and he figured it was her blend of savvy and charm that made her so good at her job.

She followed him out to the truck. "So," she said, taking the first box of six pots in her arms. "I hear your friend is coming with Ethan and Willow tonight."

"Amy? Yeah, she bought a ticket."

"You're not coming with her?"

He hefted his own box. "Not really my scene." Not to mention, a little hoity-toity for his liking. Him, in some fancy clubhouse eating a hundred dollar a plate dinner? Not likely.

"It's a good cause."

He knew it was. "I'm closing up the shop tonight so Laurel can get ready."

"It doesn't start until six. And that's just the cocktail hour."

He was prevented from answering, thankfully, as they entered the ballroom and went in different directions to place the foil-wrapped pots on the tables. Hannah must have gathered that he wasn't going to change his mind, because she didn't bring it up again. Instead they worked along, emptying the truck. When all the tables had a centerpiece, she stood back and looked at the room.

"It's just missing the candles. Once those are lit, it'll be beautiful in here, don't you think?"

Beautiful. He got a surprising lump in his throat. Normally he didn't think about his lost years with a sense of grief, but he did now. He thought of all the Christmases he'd missed, all the good times he might have had if he'd figured things out, kept his life together, made friends. He could never have those years back. And he thought of decorating his Christmas tree and kissing Amy and knew that night was a memory he'd always cherish.

"I should get back," he said quietly, shoving his hands into his pockets. "Laurel's by herself until I get there, and she wants to leave by three. This'll be our biggest Christmas tree day, too."

"Thanks for your help, George."

"You're welcome. I hope your fundraiser's a big success."

He went back to The Ladybug and threw himself into the rest of the day's work. Laurel didn't escape until three thirty, and only because he finally told her if she didn't leave he'd quit and there'd be no one to man the store.

Tree sales were crazy. All of his wreaths sold and the nails on the wood stood empty. There were precisely four poinsettias left in the whole store, and their baked goods were sold out except for one lonely tray of sliced banana bread.

That Laurel trusted him with all this—with her business—still amazed him. That she was going to let him manage it when she had her baby boggled his mind. At five o'clock he shut the gate and locked it, then went inside to ring off the cash, do up the deposit, and make sure everything was set before locking up for the night. Then he'd have to stop at the bank and do a nighttime deposit, because ever since Laurel had been robbed last spring, she didn't like leaving more than the float on the premises.

He'd just tucked everything into the deposit bag when the office phone rang. He looked over at the display and saw that it was Laurel's cell number, so he picked it up. "What's up? Are you okay?"

"Oh good, you're still there."

"Just finishing up the deposit."

"Did I leave the auction item somewhere? It's a Ladybug travel mug with some gardening gloves, a spade, and a gift certificate."

He looked around. "I don't see it."

She sighed loudly. "Argh! I swear I have pregnant brain. Who knows where I put it!"

"Let me have a look around." He pressed the phone to his ear and looked through the office, then started through the store. "Are you sure you didn't take it with you?"

"It's not in my bag. It could be anywhere. I'm such a dunce."

He laughed. "No, you're not." He went behind the cash and looked beneath the counter, where they put their returned items. "Hey, I think I found it. Does it have clear plastic and ribbon on it?"

"Yes! Oh, thank goodness. Could you do me a huge favor? I have to be there in thirty minutes, and I don't even have makeup on yet. Could you drop it at the golf club? I know it's out of your way..."

"Of course I can." He didn't want to; the place would be crawling with fancy-dressed people and he'd be in the way. But he'd do just about anything for Laurel. And he'd try not to think about Amy being there, all dressed up, where she belonged. If anything, it made it easier to think of her leaving next week, when her lease on the cottage was up. He liked being with her, but it was temporary.

And if the thought of her going home burned a hole in his gut, well, he'd handle it. He'd been through worse, right?

By the time he dropped the deposit at the bank and got to the golf club it was almost ten to six. The parking lot was starting to fill, but he didn't see Aiden or Laurel's car anywhere. It didn't matter; all he needed to do was find a staff member to put Laurel's contribution to the silent auction in the right spot and all would be well.

And he'd done just that when a familiar voice called his name. "George?"

He turned and there she was.

It had been a critical mistake to think that he could be somehow indifferent. To think that he could turn off the feelings that had been growing for the past week, born out of their shared history but nurtured by their time together.

Ethan and Willow were chatting with people a few feet behind Amy, but she stood still, looked at George with her luminous eyes, and he knew that indifference was impossible. She was stunning in her black cocktail dress, but it was more than that. It was simply everything. He'd been taken with her at twenty-five and he was equally smitten now. To discover she was also kind, compassionate, and understanding…she was everything he could ever want in a woman. And she was so out of his league it was laughable.

"I was just dropping something off for Laurel," he said, acutely aware that he was still in his work clothes.

"Oh. Of course." Disappointment wreathed her face, and he suddenly wondered if she thought he'd come to see her.

"You look beautiful, Amy."

"A girl should have one good little black dress," she said, taking a step forward in her heels. The added height put her just a tiny bit shorter than him. His hands itched to touch her, he wanted to kiss her as he'd been doing all week, but they'd been in private each time—at her door or as she got into her car or at his apartment.

But now it was all different. He looked around them. Everyone here was dressed to the nines, cocktails in their hands, and waiters were beginning to circulate with little appetizers. Her world, not his.

He stepped back. "I should go. Enjoy your evening."

He slid away, feeling worse by the second. What should he have done or said? Why did she even have to come back and give him a taste of what he couldn't have?

"George, wait."

He went outside into the cold air, took a big lungful, and felt it burn.

"George!" Her heels clicked on the paved parking lot. "This is ridiculous! Why don't you go change and come back? We'll have dinner. It's for a good cause."

"I can't." His voice sounded constricted, and he clamped his lips shut. She hugged her arms around herself to keep warm and frowned at him.

"If it's the ticket, I'll get it. Don't worry about it."

"You don't have to buy me a goddamn ticket!"

A few people looked their way, and George felt about two inches high. Amy, to her credit, simply looked at him as if trying to puzzle him out. "You got something you need to get off your chest?" she asked.

"Forget it." He started to walk away but she hurried after him.

"Oh no you don't. This is how you acted the very first day I came to Darling and I thought we were past all that." She followed him to his truck despite how cold she had to be in her dress with no coat.

He turned to face her. "If I wanted a ticket I'd buy a ticket. I'd buy some decent clothes to wear, too. But I don't want a ticket and I don't want some stupid suit. Because these aren't my people and this isn't my world. So go ahead. Go rub elbows or whatever. And next week you'll go back to your job and city apartment and forget all about the charity case back in Darling."

"That's incredibly unfair, not to mention entirely inaccurate."

"I'm allowed to feel the way I feel."

She nodded. "Yep. You sure are. Except you weren't expressing your feelings, you were passing judgment. Know what, George? You've still got a chip on your shoulder."

"You bet I do. Ninety percent of the people in there used to walk right by me. I mean, they actually took care to make sure they never touched me or made eye contact. Now, I face them every day. In my job, and around town, but on my terms. Not here. Not like this. Not like I'm some...example of...of..."

"You think I've spent the last week with you out of pity?"

A fire sparked in her eyes as she said it, her breath forming an icy cloud. He went to take off his jacket since she looked frozen, but she held up a hand.

"I don't want your jacket. Not when you're pissing me off like you are right now. Know what? Me paying for your ticket is simply a recognition that money's tight for you right now as you get back on your feet. It doesn't have to be a power struggle or a point of pride unless you make it one. But these people? They're not perfect. But they're good people, deep down. At least the ones I've met. The Gallaghers are your friends and Hannah has spent months putting this event together. I'm third wheeling with Ethan and Willow and I thought it might be nice to have a date. But you didn't want to come and I didn't push it. But for you to make this into a battle of the sexes isn't just silly, it's hurtful." Her eyes filled with tears. "I've tried to show you every way I know how that I care about you, the person, and don't give a damn about how much money you make or where you live. You think people have hang-ups about you, George? Take a look in the mirror. The person with the biggest hang-up is you. And until you can make peace with yourself, a relationship between us doesn't stand a chance." She let out a big breath. "I can't do the work for you. And I have to look out for me. I have feelings too, you know. You don't have the corner on baggage and insecurities."

His chest cramped as he looked at her, so angry, so passionate. "You'll go back home and forget all about this week."

She scoffed. "Sure, you keep telling yourself that if it makes you feel better. Then you can pretend that nothing we shared was real."

He didn't know what to say. His feelings were all over the map, and the familiar tensing in his muscles told him he had to get out of there. Why was he driving her away? She was the first really good thing to happen to him in so long. He could hear his heart beat in his ears as she faced him down, and then he realized her face had softened into one of concern.

He held up his hand. "Don't. I don't want your pity."

"I don't pity you. I care about you. I worry about you. And you won't let me in, not really. Please, George." Her eyes shimmered. "Just let me in."

He wanted to so badly it frightened him to death. In her eyes he saw Ian's. He'd let down his best friend so completely, he was sure he'd let Amy down, too. How could he knowingly do that?

How had he ever thought kissing her was a smart move, and that they could come through unscathed?

"I can't. It's for the best," he said roughly, and spun away, jogging to his truck. There were still cars coming into the lot, arriving during the pre-dinner cocktails, and he couldn't spin out the way he wanted. But he didn't look back. He drove out the lane and onto the main road back toward Darling center. Got home and threw the truck into park and slammed the door. Went upstairs to his apartment and went inside, stared at the Christmas tree, and fought with everything he had to not rip the popcorn strands off the branches.

He had to get a grip. He couldn't solve problems by losing his cool, by being impulsive. Adrenaline rushed through him, seeking an outlet. He dropped to his hands and pushed out twenty, thirty, forty pushups, kept counting until his shoulders ached and his arms felt like jelly.

Then he lay on his back on the living room floor and stared at the ceiling, wondering if he'd ever have a normal life again, or if he was just fooling himself.

Chapter 9

AMY WENT BACK INSIDE the clubhouse, darted into the ladies' room to fix her makeup, and then went to the banquet room to find Willow and Ethan. They were mingling near the auction tables, and Amy took a moment to watch them. Ethan put his hand lightly on the small of Willow's back, looking down into her face as if there was no one else in the world. Willow looked up at him and Amy saw the younger woman rest her hand on her belly. Willow's dress was of the flowy sort, so her pregnancy wasn't immediately obvious. But when her hand rested against the fabric, it was easy to see that she had a little bubble at her waistline.

Willow and Ethan had all that Amy had ever wanted. The love of another and a family to call her own. Was that so much to ask? She'd made such a mistake putting her faith in George. Not that he'd disappointed her, no, never. And she'd spoken the truth that she'd thought he needed to hear. But she regretted how she'd said it, and she was sad to realize that neither of them was to blame. George simply wasn't ready. He might never be ready, and she'd allowed herself to hope.

Willow looked over and saw Amy standing there, and with a look of concern excused herself from Ethan's company and made her way over to Amy's side. "Oh dear. What happened?"

"It's okay. We just... Oh, we were fooling ourselves. Said we'd have a nice week of spending time together and then part ways at Christmas. And it worked, until today."

Willow touched her arm. "Any time someone says the words 'no strings' or 'no feelings involved', it's a guarantee that it's going to get messy. It's like we already know we're in over our heads and if we say the words it's not true."

"I think I need a glass of wine."

"Ask and ye shall receive." Willow snagged a glass from a passing waiter and handed it to her. "I didn't ask if you liked red or white. Desperate times."

Amy managed a small laugh. Willow was one of the most likable women she'd ever met. If Amy lived in Darling, she bet they'd end up friends.

For some reason, that also made her sad.

"Come on," Willow said. "I know a quieter place we can chat before dinner starts."

"I don't want to ruin your night."

"You're not." Willow tugged at her hand and led her past the coat check to a second, quieter room. "Okay. Tell Auntie Willow everything."

Amy didn't know where to start. She sat down on a hard plastic chair and cradled her wine glass instead.

Willow pulled up a chair next to her. "Hey," she said softly. "You care about each other. It's not easy, particularly when there are so many mountains to climb. I know. I've been there." She held out her arm and showed Amy the little tattoo at her wrist. "I went through a really shit time. It took a lot of therapy and time to sort myself out. Even then, it wasn't until Ethan came along that I made it the rest of the way. And Ethan had lost his wife. Healing is hard business, Amy. It doesn't happen overnight."

"I know. I was so hard on him just now."

"I've known George a while. For him to be where he is now... He's shown so much courage and strength. You could have blown us all over when we saw you guys on the Green the other night. If you'd asked us two weeks ago if George would be drinking hot cocoa with a date at the Kissing Bridge, we would have laughed in your face. You did that. He has his job and his apartment and the necessities of life, but you reached in and found the real George lurking behind all the practicalities of merely existing."

Amy's eyes began to sting.

"He said that a lot of the people here used to make sure they didn't touch him," Amy said, her heart hurting as she heard the words echoing in her head. "I forget sometimes that there's a different history that I don't know. I have no context."

"It's also true that a lot of people have stepped up and helped him," Willow said. "But the other was an easier way to keep you at arm's length.

Caring for someone is what really scares him, you see? And it's not just that you can hurt him, it's that he could hurt you. Or that down deep, he worries he's not enough. That he doesn't deserve you. And that kind of thinking can be hard to change."

Amy wondered if some of George's insecurities stemmed from his transient upbringing, too. He'd never known unconditional love, never known the security of a family. Even the army had cut him loose without the supports he needed. "I suggested counseling," Amy admitted. "Real therapy, not the 'Band-Aid, come in and talk about it' kind."

"I've mentioned it, too," Willow said. "But access is harder than it should be, and without good private insurance..."

They sat quietly for a few moments.

"Do you love him, Amy?"

The question surprised her, but the answer surprised her more. "Yeah," she answered softly. "I think I do. I know it's been a short time, but—"

"But sometimes it just happens, when we least expect it." Willow laughed a little. "And with the last person we expect. Ethan and I totally did not get along at first."

"George and I always got along," Amy answered. "Even fifteen years ago."

Willow patted her hand. "Then don't give up. Show him he's worth fighting for, if that's what you want."

"I'll think about it."

"Do you want to stay? Ethan can take you home if the evening's ruined for you now."

Amy shook her head, feeling so much better now that she'd talked to Willow. "No, I'll stay. You've all been so kind, and the meal smells amazing, and I want a chance to bid on some of those items. Besides, I need to do some thinking. If I go home I'll wallow."

Willow grinned. "I like you. I'm kind of hoping you're around a little more."

Would she be? Was that even possible? Or would she and George just be able to patch things up as friends?

She enjoyed the evening, even dancing a few times with Aiden and Ethan and their younger brother Rory, who had come with his girlfriend, Oaklee, who turned out to be Cam Collier's baby sister. Since Oaklee and Hannah were rushing around making sure everything was running smoothly, Rory took his turn on the dance floor with some young ladies who looked at him as if he hung the moon. Then Amy had a slower dance with John Gallagher, and one of Ethan's buddies from the fire department, and someone named Brian who owned the pharmacy in town. By midnight she was tired and ready for bed, but when Willow turned into her yard—as the pregnant one in the party, she'd become the default designated driver—the sight of her evergreen in full lights stole her breath.

"Oh, that's gorgeous. When did you do that?"

Amy's throat clogged. "I didn't. Oh, dammit." She sniffed. "I yelled at him and he gave me a Christmas tree."

"George did this?"

"It had to be him." She knew in her heart it was. The tree stood at least twelve feet high, a perfect pyramid of pungent branches. Looped around it, from top to bottom, were large multi-colored lights, shining off the snow.

She got out of the car and went over to the single Adirondack chair placed by the tree. He'd written on the backside of the cardboard from one of the packages of lights and placed it on the seat. *I'm sorry*, it read. And that was all.

Ethan got out of the car and took her her purse. "That's a pretty big gesture," he said quietly. "A man has to feel pretty shitty to do something this nice."

"I know. And he already feels shitty enough. I wish he could see himself the way I do. The way other people do. Not everyone sees him as that homeless guy anymore, you know?"

"Is that what he thinks? Everyone I know of thinks it's amazing what he's accomplished the last few months. Sure, they were wary before, but once you get to know George..."

"I know," she said softly. "I know."

"Call if you need anything," he offered.

"You go get Willow home. She and that baby need some rest."

"I will. And Amy?"

"Hmm?" She kept staring at the tree. Couldn't look away. He'd done this, for her. Not just because he was sorry but because he knew she didn't have a tree of her own at the cottage. How could she see his thoughtfulness and generosity and he couldn't?

"Don't give up," he advised, then went back to the car.

She didn't want to, but she wasn't sure how to proceed, either. She went inside and got ready for bed, and then turned facing the window, so she could see the rainbow glow of the lights in the front yard.

If George couldn't see how much people cared, maybe she would just have to show him.

—ele—

When George didn't hear from Amy after the literacy banquet, he figured it was pretty much over.

He'd waited most of Sunday to hear from her. And again Monday. Then Tuesday...and nothing. No impromptu lunches at The Ladybug, no walks through the park or sharing fries at the Sugarbush. Now it was Christmas Eve, they'd be closing up shop by three, and the words she'd said to him kept running through his head like a constant loop. The one with the hang-ups was him. She wasn't wrong. But she wasn't 100% right, either. There was nothing wrong with wanting to be worthy of someone's trust and affection. Why was it wrong for him to need to be self-sufficient? Why shouldn't he want to have some pride?

God, he was still such a mess. There were only two things he knew for sure. He was determined to move forward with a better life. And he knew that it was possible to love again. Not just Amy, though he suspected that was true, too. But he loved other people, too, like Laurel. Like Jordan, their student employee, who came into work with her crazy college stories and homemade cookies that she baked all the time because she had a sweet tooth and her mom never kept sweets in the house. And right now he was half in love with a tabby cat that he'd found huddled under a stack of Douglas firs a few days ago. He hadn't taken it home, but he'd put out a little food for it in the morning and before he left at night. The damned thing probably had fleas, but George felt sorry for it all the same. The cat watched him with wary eyes, but when George found a couple of burlap sacks left over from evergreen boughs and tucked them into the sheltered corner of the fence, he was gratified to find the cat curled up fast asleep a few hours later.

Letting go of some of the past had made room for the future. He'd apologized, but it was obviously too late. With a sinking heart, he figured Amy wasn't even in Darling anymore. Tomorrow was Christmas. Today was the last day in her rental term.

He was sweeping up the greenhouse floor when Hannah Gallagher came in and brought him a little wrapped present.

"What's this?" he asked, turning it over in his hand.

"Just a little something to say thank you for helping with the benefit. The centerpieces were lovely, George. I appreciate you delivering them and helping put them around."

He frowned. "Oh. Do you want me to open it now?"

She shook her head. "Not if you don't want to. You can put it under your tree. Merry Christmas."

A while later there was a tap on his shoulder. It was one of his neighbors, an elderly man he thought was named Hugh. Hugh also held out a present, wrapped rather raggedly in green paper with a red bow. "Came in to get some Christmas Eve cider," he said in his shaky voice. "But I wanted to thank you for cleaning off my car after last week's storm. I have a hard time reaching these days and I appreciate it."

"Shoot, it was no problem. You didn't have to get me anything."

"Heh," the old man answered. "Don't have many people to buy for anyway. Merry Christmas, George."

The afternoon went much the same. Business owners, neighbors, friends...several popped by with thanks for something he'd done, the littlest thing, really, and brought cards and gifts and one little girl gave him a toilet paper roll ornament she'd made as a way to say thank you for putting her chain back on her bike last summer. He didn't understand why it was all happening, didn't know what to say through his surprise, but at the same time, a warmth expanded in his chest each time someone made a point to say Merry Christmas.

It was nearly quitting time when Laurel came out to see him. The customers were all gone, presumably to their own homes to get ready for the holiday and family festivities. "Big plans tonight?" he asked, pulling the door shut.

"Just dinner at John and Moira's," she said. "Christmas Eve at the in-laws, and then in the morning we'll have Christmas breakfast at Ethan and Willow's. Because of the boys."

Those little boys unwrapping presents, a huge extended family laughing and talking over bacon and scrambled eggs and probably pancakes. It sounded so damned perfect.

"George, I wanted to give you this. I know we didn't say anything about exchanging gifts, but you need to know how much you've meant to me —to us—these last months. Without you, I'm not sure Aiden and I would have worked out our differences. And the garden center... You started by sweeping up and watering and now I know I can have this baby and The Ladybug will be in great hands. It's a load off my mind, and I'm thankful and so stinkin' proud of you it's ridiculous. So Merry Christmas."

She handed him a gift bag. It was fairly big and not heavy but definitely full. "Should I open it?"

"If you want to."

He grinned. He had a whole stack of little gifts to take home—holy doodle, he was going to have presents beneath his tree after all. But this one... It was Laurel after all. He reached inside, pulled away the clump of fluffy tissue paper, and removed a black fleece jacket and two work shirts.

Each one was embroidered with The Ladybug Garden Center logo and had the word Manager written below it.

He met her eyes and raised his eyebrows. "Manager?"

"I know I'm not due for a while, but now is as good a time as any. I can focus my hours more in the office and you can see to the day-to-day running of the place. It comes with a raise, George. Not a huge one, but a little something. And benefits."

He didn't know what to say. Thought he should sit down but there was nowhere to sit. "God, Laurel, you're sure?"

She smiled tenderly. "Amy was right. We have more faith in you than you have in yourself. You've earned this, George."

Amy. The day had been nearly perfect except the one person he really wanted here, he'd driven away.

"I don't have anything for you," he said quietly. He seriously hadn't considered exchanging gifts with anyone this year. He hadn't expected to receive any gifts at all.

"I have all I need, honey. Now you go home and let me clean up here. Aiden'll be by after his shift so I'm just putting in time anyway."

"You're sure?"

She laughed. "Go."

He put all his presents in a shopping bag, put his jacket and shirts back in the pretty gift bag, and carried them all to his truck. The market was still open for another few hours, closing at five, so he ran in quickly and bought himself a single serving turkey dinner at the deli, thought twice, and bought a second one for Christmas dinner tomorrow. Though he'd never been a fan of fruitcake, there was a solid brick of one marked down in the bakery section and he put it in his basket. His last stop was for eggs and bacon. He wasn't much of a cook, but he could make bacon and eggs and celebrate the good things in his life. Even Amy. Even if she'd gone back to Brooklyn, her coming here had started a chain reaction of good things that he could build on.

When he arrived at his apartment, her car was parked in one of the visitor spots.

He took three deep breaths, warned himself not to get his hopes up, and stepped out of his truck.

She got out of her car at the same time, and their eyes met. She smiled—oh, that wonderful, sweet smile—and the bonds around his heart eased.

"You're late," she said, her smile widening.

"I stopped at the market. If I'd known..."

"You would have rushed right home?"

"Damned right."

It must have been the right answer because the spark went sizzling between them again.

"I heard you had quite a day at work."

"I get the feeling you had something to do with that."

She walked up to him. "Do you want to talk about this inside?"

"If that's what you want."

"Let me take one of your bags." She took the bag containing the eggs, bacon, and juice, and followed him into the building and up the stairs. Once inside she pushed off her shoes with her toes and left them by the mat. Then she took her groceries and put them on the kitchen counter, turned around, and walked into his arms.

He wanted to hug her back, but his hands were full of plastic bags. Instead he closed his eyes and reveled in the feeling of her arms around him, her body close to his.

She backed away, let him put down the bags, then took his hands. "I'm sorry," she whispered, rubbing her fingers over the tops of his hands. "I'm sorry I yelled at you and said those things. And I'm sorry that even for such a short time, I gave up on you. That was wrong. You're not in this alone. I asked for you to just get over years of issues and baggage, when we both know that's not how it works. I'm sorry, George. I hope you forgive me."

He pulled her into his arms, close to his chest. "Of course I do. You weren't wrong, you know. I'm just a work in progress." He frowned a little. "I have to admit. After I put the lights on the tree in your yard, and you didn't say anything, I thought you couldn't forgive the things I said, too. I thought you'd left."

She shook her head. "I had to look after a few details. Come, sit down for a minute. By the tree."

He followed her to the sofa and sat down beside her.

She reached into her purse and took out a long, slim box, about the size of a business envelope but maybe an inch deep. It was wrapped in red foil with gold ribbon and bow. "My present to you. Open it."

"You don't want me to wait until tomorrow?"

"No. Not for this one." Her smile was wide and bright with excitement. "This is part of what took up my time the last few days."

He tore off the ribbon and slid his finger beneath the tape on the paper. Inside the box was a sheaf of papers. "What the heck?" He took them out, scanned them quickly, met her gaze. "I don't understand."

"There's a group of veterans that do a bike tour every year. I know you don't have a motorbike anymore, so this gives you a one-month rental and insurance, plus the tour package the group uses. The road trip is for two weeks, the first two weeks of April. I know it's not New England in the fall, but . . ."

He didn't care. It could have been to Timbuktu. He could already imagine the feel of the wind on his face and the road slipping away behind him. "Amy, it's too much."

"It's not. It's just right." She smiled at him. "Say you'll go."

"But Laurel's baby is due—"

"I ran this past Laurel first. She said you're not to worry and to go and have a good time."

He stared at the papers once more. God, what a rush it would be! It was the perfect gift. How could she know him so well after such a short time?

"I don't have anything for you," he said, feeling like a heel for the second time that afternoon. "I feel awful."

She shook her head. "Don't be silly. You put the lights on that tree, and I went to sleep at night seeing them out the bedroom window. And you've given me so much the last few weeks. Stories about Ian...those are better than anything. You can't buy that kind of stuff."

He put down his gift and took her hand in his. "And what about us, then? I can't move quickly on this, Amy. I don't want to hurt you, or get hurt myself. Not that there are ever guarantees, but I don't want to be careless. You're too important for me to mess this up."

"I've been thinking about that," she replied, leaning against his shoulder. "It's a long drive, but we could do it now and again. Or take the train. Spend some weekends getting to know each other better." She put her hand on his knee. "Take it one day at a time, with no pressure about the future."

"You mean try to make this work?"

She nodded. "I'm willing if you are, George. But I have issues too, and I understand if what—" She halted. "The baby thing. I can't ever give you that. I don't want to deprive you of fatherhood if it's something you really want."

He pulled her close. "That isn't even on my radar, and it's you I want. All of you, not just the easy bits. I've a long way to go before I could be anyone's father. So no, sweetheart, that's not a deal breaker for me."

She let out such a deep breath that he knew it had been troubling her a great deal. He wondered how many men had missed out on her love because of her fertility. Their foolishness was his gain. "So we're going to move forward, one day at a time, working with each other's flaws? Hardly sounds exciting," he teased.

But her eyes were soft and serious as she answered. "I don't need exciting. I just need honesty and love. And if we work with that, I think it'll all come right in the end."

"Me, too." And when he couldn't wait any longer, he kissed her, long and deep. And after a very long while they got up and heated up turkey dinners in the microwave, and cuddled on the sofa.

And when Christmas Eve turned into Christmas morning, it was with Amy held close in his arms as they lay spoon fashion on the sofa in front of the tree, sleeping.

Chapter 10

AMY WOKE EARLY, HER arm stiff from being beneath her all night, but loving the feel of George being the "big spoon" behind her. She stretched, then snuck out of his arms and to the kitchen, where she started making coffee and quietly put bacon in a pan on the burner. It didn't take long and George came up behind her. "Merry Christmas," he murmured in her ear, sending shivers down her spine.

"You need a big breakfast. We have a long drive ahead of us."

"We do?"

"Yep. Today's the second half of your present. Christmas dinner with my parents."

"Oh."

She reached for his arm, understanding the wariness in his voice. "It's okay. I went down there this week, and had a long talk with them, and they really want to see you, George. You were his best friend. Now you're my best friend. It's time you came home for Christmas."

Amy was pleased when he didn't argue. Instead they ate bacon and eggs and toast while the sun was just coming up, and then she waited for him to throw a few things in an overnight bag. If they left now they'd be home by mid-afternoon. Just in time for her mom's turkey and mashed potatoes and special sausage stuffing. When they got outside, she handed him the keys to her car. "You can drive if you want."

"You're sure?"

She laughed. "I've driven there and back already this week. I don't mind being the passenger. Or we can swap at lunchtime. Whatever."

The drive provided more opportunities for them to talk, and Amy loved the pride in his voice when he told her about his promotion and all the people who had brought presents. "I didn't even open them yet," he said, shaking his head. "I got distracted."

"They'll be waiting when you get back."

"I didn't know people felt that way. That they even noticed me."

She reached over and took his hand. "People see you. I see you, George."

He pulled the car over and kissed her for about five minutes, and then they hit the road again.

He got quieter, though, as she directed him to her neighborhood, and they dealt with heavier city traffic. "You can see why I use the train to commute," she said quietly, looking over at his tense face. "I love my neighbors and my job, but I have to tell you. I understand why you like Darling. There's room to breathe there."

When he pulled up in front of her parents' house, he killed the engine and they sat there for a few moments. Her heart ached for him. This was a big deal, but she also knew what waited for him inside. He just had to be ready to take the step.

"You thinking about the last time you were here?"

He nodded, and she saw his throat bob as he swallowed.

"Ian was full of it. And the last time you were here you kissed me on the back step." She grinned at him. "If you'd made your move, I'm not sure I would have been able to resist."

His gaze locked with hers. "I wish I had. Maybe it all would have turned out differently."

"Maybe. But we're here now, right? And I'm happy, George. So let's just be thankful for second chances."

"I am," he said, reaching for her hand. He lifted it and kissed her knuckles. "More than you'll ever know."

"Okay. Then let's go inside."

George tried to keep his hands from shaking as he walked to the front door of the Merck house. It was just as he remembered; an older bungalow with a little front porch, but the paint wasn't peeling at all, there was a wreath on the door, and Ian wouldn't be waiting inside.

He looked over at Amy and gathered strength.

And when they reached the front door, it opened before he could knock. Mrs. Merck stood there, an older version of the woman he remembered, lines at the corners of her eyes and mouth, but the same warm, welcoming eyes.

"Welcome home," she said, and held out her arms.

He stepped into them and felt something beautiful slip into place. All the years of running, of wandering, of feeling in the way...it all evaporated with a hug from his best friend's mother. This was what had been missing. Family. That they still invited him into theirs after all that had happened was the most humbling moment of his life—and he'd been humbled a lot.

When he finally let go, Amy and her mom both had tears in their eyes. Ian's father stood behind, unsmiling, his expression filled with emotion. George held out his hand. "Sir," he said quietly. "Merry Christmas."

Owen Merck took his hand and gripped firmly. "We're glad you're here," he said gruffly.

Amy cleared her throat. "Okay, then. Now that we got all that over with, let's lighten things up. I'd say this constitutes an eggnog toast."

Amy showed him to a spare room—not Ian's old room, thankfully—and he stowed his overnight bag. When he got back to the living room, she handed him a glass of eggnog and invited him to sit down and relax. Their tree was a stunner, full of those glass balls he loved so much. Picture perfect, with white twinkling lights and a beautiful white angel on the top. Beneath it were presents, all opened, tidily arranged. There was one left, though, a little cloth gift bag with a wide ribbon and a tag on it. He leaned closer to try to read it. His name was on it.

Mrs. Merck saw the direction of his attention and got up from the sofa. "We have something for you, too, George." She picked up the bag and took it to him where he sat on the sofa beside Amy.

"You really shouldn't have done this."

"We wanted to," Owen said. "We're just so glad to see you, son."

Son. George's heart constricted and he looked over at Amy, who was smiling wistfully. "Open it, honey," she said, putting her hand on his knee.

She'd called him honey. This whole day, the last two days, were like something out of a dream. If it was, he wanted to open this last present before he woke up to reality.

He untied the bow and reached inside the silk bag. There was another box inside, smaller than the one Amy had given him, a little tin one like he'd seen in stores to put gift cards in. He carefully took off the lid and looked inside.

It was a card, the size of a business card, with a doctor's name and appointment time written on it.

"I don't understand." He looked up.

"I told you I was good at red tape. This is an appointment with a counselor in Montpelier. He comes highly recommended, particularly with EMDR therapy." Amy squeezed his hand. "That's for PTSD. I thought you might prefer a male doctor to a female for this, but if you want to change we can find someone else."

"But..." George looked down at the card. Yes, he was going to have benefits now, but would they even cover something like this or a portion of it? "I don't know how to say this. I appreciate the gesture, but I'm not sure I—"

He couldn't bring himself to say the words. That his salary plus assistance allowed him to pay the bills but not have a lot leftover.

Owen spoke into the silence. "It's paid for, George. For as long as you need."

George put down the card. "I can't accept that. I'm sorry, and it's a wonderful thought, but I can't." They couldn't know about what really happened that day if they were being so kind and generous. The eggnog churned in his stomach.

"We never did anything with Ian's life insurance," Owen explained. "Never felt right. But this...he'd approve of this. He'd want it for you. He'd want you to stop blaming yourself and for you to have a happy life." Owen's gaze slipped to Amy. "And if you're going to date my daughter, I have a vested interest in your health. So let us help you, George. It's what we want more than anything."

George's lip quivered but he regained control of it. "It's so much more than I deserve."

"Maybe someday you'll see that's not true," Amy's mom said softly.

"Thank you," he said. "I don't know what else to say but thank you."

"You're welcome."

Amy nudged his arm. "Why don't we go set the table for dinner?"

"Sure." He got the feeling she wanted to talk to him, in private, and the chore was just an excuse.

Once they were in the kitchen, she hugged him. "You're not upset with me? I kind of took over and strong-armed you into everything."

He shook his head, put his hands on either side of her face, and kissed her square on the mouth. "I'm not mad. I'm humbled, but not mad. No one has ever fought for me like you have."

"Fought with you, you mean."

Her saucy smile made him grin. "Tomato, to-mah-to." He got serious again, though, because this mattered too much. "Growing up, I was scared to let anyone help me. Afraid that I'd get too attached to a place, or the people, and then have to give it up again. I'd act out so that I'd get moved— it was somehow easier if I rejected them before they could reject me. But Ian was different. I didn't feel that way with him, and then I lost him. Letting you in should have been difficult, but it wasn't. It was easy. And even when you were angry with me, it was because you were fighting for me. I just couldn't see it. So thank you, Amy. I'm sure I'm not worth it but you sure as hell seem to think I am, and that changes everything. I won't let you down." He swallowed tightly. "I'm so done with running. I'm ready to have a home."

She reached up and touched his face. "People occasionally let each other down," she whispered.

"But then they take each other's hands and get back up again. I'm good at loving people, George. Let me love you."

His breath came out in a rush as he hugged her close. "God, Amy. You're so easy to love. It's way harder to let someone love me. But I'll try."

"Then kiss me and seal the deal," she said.

He touched his lips to hers, his heart hammering against his ribs. How had this happened? Three weeks ago he'd been rebuilding his life, step by slow step. And Amy had blown in with a snowstorm and changed everything.

"Hey, George?" She kissed his cheek, and he felt her lips curve against his skin. "You know that night we first kissed? At the bridge?"

"Yeah." Like he could forget.

"I know what the legend says."

He did, too. That whoever kissed on the bridge would have their love last forever. He gave her waist a squeeze. "Aw, that's just fairy tales. Besides, we weren't even on the bridge. We were across it, remember?"

She leaned back a few inches and grinned at him, her eyes dancing. "Well, I might have stumbled a bit, and put my hand on the railing..."

He laughed, and kissed her again, lifting her off the floor and spinning her around a bit.

The sound of the television came from the living room; some holiday special that had 'Deck the Halls' playing. "That's Mom's cue that we're going to have company soon," she whispered, giggling. "We'd better start rattling some dishes so she knows we're not making out in here."

And as George set plates around the dining table, he realized that living was better than existing, and loving was the greatest blessing of all.

THE END

Turn the page to read Hannah's story in MERRY CHRISTMAS, DARLING!

Merry Christmas, Darling

DONNA ALWARD

Chapter 1

IF THERE WAS ONE thing the town of Darling, Vermont, knew how to do, it was Christmas. Wreaths and bows hung from the streetlamps. Storefronts were decorated with sparkly lights and holiday-themed wares, beckoning passersby to come inside. A Christmas tree sat on the Green beside Fisher Creek and next to the Kissing Bridge, waiting for the tree-lighting ceremony that would happen on the weekend. The air smelled like evergreen and cinnamon and butter cookies. There'd even been flurries overnight, covering the ground with a dusting of pristine snow. Everything looked like a greeting card, and normally, Hannah Gallagher loved every moment of it.

Instead, she let out a frustrated breath, hung up the phone, and slumped against the desk in her office.

The second annual literacy benefit was only three weeks away, and her celebrity author and speaker had just cancelled their appearance. The whole event had been planned around Jillian Jordan's attendance. And now...nothing.

Sure, having surgery was a legitimate excuse. She guessed. But it put her in a horrible pickle. Tickets for the event had already gone on sale. Donations for the silent auction were coming in, with others promised. Local businesses were in on the action. The literacy benefit was her brainchild, her baby, and last year had been a roaring success, raising thousands for local literacy organizations. There was no way she wanted the event to suffer a sophomore slump.

She had to find another celebrity. Someone who didn't mind traveling to a small town in Vermont in three weeks, and a week before Christmas to boot. Someone willing to donate their time, who wasn't already booked up. And someone who would be the *right* person, not just anyone who could fill a chair or stand up to the mic. She'd originally begun this process in March. Now she had to do it all again in a matter of days.

"I hate my life, I hate my life, I hate my life," she muttered, resting her forehead on the heel of her hand.

"Aw, it can't be all bad."

Hannah lifted her head and found Oaklee Collier standing in her doorway, her blond hair pulled into a perfect topknot, one hip resting on the doorframe, and a lopsided smile on her otherwise symmetrical face.

If Hannah had anything to say about it, Oaklee would be her sister-in-law one of these days. She heartily approved of her brother Rory's choice in partners.

"Jillian Jordan just cancelled. She's having surgery in ten days and doesn't think she'll be recovered enough to attend the benefit."

Oaklee's smile disappeared from her face. "Oh, shit."

"Shit is right. Can you think of a replacement? And I don't want it to be us scraping the bottom of the barrel for anyone with a pulse, you know?"

"Of course." Oaklee came farther into the office and sat in the chair opposite Hannah's desk. "I mean, do we have to have a celebrity?"

"Yes?" Hannah pursed her lips. "I'm just...not angry. I can't be angry with a woman who has to have medical treatment, can I? But *why*?" She drew out the last word and punctuated it with a sigh.

Oaklee leaned forward. "You'll figure it out, Han. You always do. No one gets stuff done like you do. You're General Gallagher. You just need to round up your troops."

Hannah stared at Oaklee. General Gallagher? She'd been called a lot of things over the years, and for some reason, this one bothered her a lot. Yes, she was definitely type A. She didn't feel she should apologize for it. She had skills. But the two monikers she'd earned that she disliked the most was this one and Dozer. As in bulldozer. Which was just slightly worse, in her view, than Ballbuster.

She was a doer. She got things done. And that way, she didn't have to focus too much on her non-existent love life. Because in that one area, she was an absolute failure. She had the battle scars to prove it. Hell, an ex was where the Dozer name came from.

"If you start calling me General, I'll fire you."

"You can't fire me. I'm a volunteer."

Hannah angled an eyebrow in Oaklee's direction. "You know what I mean."

Oaklee sat back and studied Hannah, intensely enough that Hannah started to be a bit uncomfortable. "What?"

"It really bothered you, didn't it? I'm sorry. I was just teasing."

Hannah let out a breath. "I know. Don't worry about it. I'm just touchy. I really didn't need this today."

Oaklee leaned forward and reached out to touch Hannah's arm. "I know, sweetie. Listen, I popped in to ask you if you wanted to grab a drink at Suds and Spuds later. Do you want to? Maybe we can brainstorm then."

Hannah nodded. Oaklee was an invaluable volunteer. She managed the town's social media and worked with their marketing and promotions department. She also knew how to get results and be part of a team. She'd designed the event website and Facebook page, and then all the promotional materials...

Ugh. Another thought darted into Hannah's brain. All the signage would have to be redone. Considering the print costs had been donated, it put another layer of wrinkles into the situation. Maybe she could find another sponsor.

"A beer sounds perfect." She wouldn't worry about the calories until tomorrow. "I have a showing at six thirty. Say seven thirty-ish?"

Oaklee got up from her chair and smoothed her hand down her sweater. "That sounds perfect. Rory works late tonight anyway. I just have to run home and feed the dog after work."

Oaklee and Rory had been living together for close to six months. Hannah's younger brother was a veterinarian. He'd given up his bachelor digs above the clinic and bought a house two blocks away from their brother, Ethan, and his family. Oaklee had moved in with him over the summer when the lease on her townhouse was up. They had a dog and a variety of cats or other animals that Rory usually ended up bringing home from the clinic from time to time.

Everyone was settling down. Or at least all the boys in the family were. Hannah was the oldest female and completely single. Her twin sisters, in their early twenties, weren't interested in settling down yet. Heck, Cait hadn't ever had a boyfriend. She was more interested in hanging out with friends than relationships.

But at thirty-three, Hannah was starting to hear a ticking clock and resigning herself to being Fun Aunt Hannah for her nieces and nephews. Certainly no one in Darling was willing to take her on. And there was no one she was interested in, either.

"Perfect. I'll see you then. I'm glad you stopped by, Oaklee. I'm not quite as panicked as I was when I hung up that phone."

"You'll figure it out. You always do. I'll catch you later."

She left with a waggle of her fingers, leaving Hannah in her quiet office. It was too quiet. The real estate market was a bit slow right now, and her office assistant had gone home at noon since her daughter got sick at school. A few doors down, The Purple Pig Café did a bustling business of coffee, hot chocolate, and gingerbread lattes for the Christmas season, replacing the pumpkin spice flavor from Thanksgiving. She considered going for a tea and a scone and then decided against. She could make tea right here and work until she had to leave for her showing. Besides, she was feeling rather cranky and was inclined to stay in her office rather than have to be out in public with her outward facing, energetic, and positive persona.

Sometimes it got tiring being Hannah Gallagher.

She put on the kettle and plopped a peppermint tea bag in a mug, then grabbed a handful of grapes from the fridge and sat back in her chair, the casters making a slight squeak as she pulled it closer to the desk.

With a click of her mouse, she opened up her browser and started a search. Finding a replacement wouldn't happen all on its own. If she was going to be lonely, at least she could be productive doing it.

Cam Collier had been home exactly twice in the last five years. And each time, he was surprised to find that nothing had really changed in Darling. Cute town, friendly people, same stores and shops. Slow, too. He was used to being in Denver, a bigger city with a lot more going on. Heck, Darling didn't even have a movie theater.

He turned off Main Street with its decorated streetlamps and storefronts and went across a bridge, then over to the other end of the park. One thing Darling did have, however, was an ice rink. It had been as much a home to him as anywhere in town, and that included his own house and that of the Gallaghers. As a kid, if anyone wanted to find Cam, it was in one of those three places.

Rory Gallagher had been his best friend for years, until Cam had moved away in high school to play major junior hockey. After that, he'd been drafted to St. Louis as a second-round pick. Traded to Boston. And for the last few years, he'd been in Denver, wearing the big C on his chest. He'd had a fairy-tale career, really. Some playoff runs and a Stanley Cup. One of his two trips home had been after that win, when he got to bring the cup for a visit. It had been surreal for a guy of twenty-six. There'd been a parade.

He'd also taken a few rough hits. He'd been sidelined for knee and shoulder injuries, though they'd been minor, and he'd been back on the ice quickly. This time was different. This was concussion number two, thanks to a cross-check that had nailed him into the boards. They were only eight weeks into the regular season, and he was now benched until cleared by the doctors.

At twenty-nine, he still had a lot of career left. Another head injury after this one, and he could be sidelined permanently.

The rink was quiet now, the parking lot empty with the exception of Cam's rented SUV. Weekdays weren't busy. All the kids were in school. Oh, there was ice time in the morning, and after school, and in the evenings there'd be practice, since the high school team used the rink as their home ice as well. And on the weekends, the lot would be crammed. But right now, it was quiet. Cam shut the car door and walked to the entrance, his feet crunching on the light dusting of snow that had come this week, just a few days after Thanksgiving.

The door was open, and Cam figured there was a custodian on duty or something. He made his way to the middle of the seats—all benches—and stopped where he could look over center ice.

It had all started here. Skating lessons at age three. A hockey stick in his hand at age four. Hockey had been in his blood from the beginning. In some ways, it was all he'd ever known. The one thing he could count on.

And now he was home, feeling uncertain and already missing his team. Missing the ice under his blades and the feel of the stick in his gloved hands. The sound of skates cutting up the ice; the smooth sheen of it after the Zamboni did its work.

He was home because the doctors had told him that he absolutely needed to take time to recuperate or else there would be no more hockey. And a world without hockey was... inconceivable.

His sister, Oaklee, had convinced him to come home for Christmas. She and Rory were hosting a New Year's Eve party, and there wasn't a hope that he'd be cleared for play that soon. He'd been put on four weeks of medical leave. After that, he'd only be cleared for practice if he stayed symptom free. Once everyone was confident in his ability to return, he'd be put back in the lineup.

Four weeks in Darling.

He wasn't sure he was going to make it. But his folks were thrilled he was going to be home for the holidays. He was at least glad he could make them happy about that. And he'd be eating his mom's cooking, too. Her spaghetti and meatballs and the Christmas shortbread she made each year.

But not playing hockey.

Some people got holiday depression. Cam didn't. But this year, he had anxiety, and it had little to do with Christmas. He was worried his fear of another injury would cause him to lose his edge. He had two more years left on his contract. If it wasn't renewed, he'd be a free agent. Or he'd have to consider...retirement. But the check still loomed in his mind. The sight of the other player in the corner of his eye. The force of the impact, and then...nothing. He didn't remember blacking out, or regaining consciousness, or leaving the ice on a stretcher because of the possibility of a neck injury. Instead, he'd seen the news replays. Every time, he got a horrible sick feeling in the pit of his stomach.

But if he wanted to play, he couldn't play afraid.

He took a big breath and let it out slowly, trying to push the thoughts away. Right now, he was at the rink, breathing in the cool air, remembering sweet memories from his childhood. He was here, and he might as well make the best of it. If recovering was what he had to do, he'd do the best job of it ever.

Because failure was absolutely not on the agenda.

When he had restored himself with the cool sounds and scents of the rink, he returned to his SUV and made the five-minute drive to his parents' place. The house was small by most standards, barely over a thousand square feet of bungalow, with three bedrooms, a single bathroom, and an oversized deck overlooking the back yard. He kept offering to buy or build them a new house, something that wasn't built in the eighties and with more amenities. But they insisted they liked it just fine, so here they stayed.

He got out of the SUV and stood for a moment, breathing in the crisp, cool air. Thank God, he'd been cleared to drive. It was bad enough he couldn't play. That his life was on hold. At least he had some freedom.

But for now, he was home for the holidays, and moping about it wasn't doing his mood any favors. Maybe he needed to start counting his blessings instead. Including time spent with his parents and sister.

"Cam? Is that you?"

A smile broke out on his face at the excited sound of his mother's voice, and his heart lightened. "Yeah, Mom, it's me." He rounded the hood and went up the short drive, his shoes leaving footprints in the dusting of snow on the paved surface. His mom wore a huge grin and opened her arms to him.

"About time you came home for Christmas."

"I know, I know." He enfolded her smaller body in a big hug and then set her back, holding her by the arms. "You look good, lady." She was graying a little bit, and her laugh lines were getting a little deeper, but she looked happy and healthy.

She laughed. "Go on." Then her laugh softened, and she peered up at him. "Be honest. How're you feeling?"

He shrugged, deciding he might as well tell her everything. She'd get it out of him anyway. "Tired. Frustrated I can't play or even practice." He sighed. "Afraid of what lies ahead."

"You're not done playing yet. You just can't rush things. And you always like to rush things."

"I know." He smiled. "Let me get my stuff and come in. We can order something for dinner and hang out."

"Order?" She shook her head. "Don't even think about it. I made a roast for tonight. And cake."

He went back down the drive to the SUV and opened the tailgate. "What? You cooked?"

"Brat. I do know how, you know. I did it lots when I wasn't running to the rink all the time."

He knew it, but he loved bugging her about it anyway. "You mean I won't be eating frozen lasagna and Shepherd's Pie from a box?"

"If you didn't have a concussion, I'd box your ears."

He laughed again, and it felt good. Okay, so maybe this wasn't the best situation. But he did love his family, and it had been too long since he had a good visit.

His dad had retired, and Cam found him inside, watching the news channel. "Hey, Dad," he said, putting down his duffel and toeing off his shoes.

"Hey, yourself!" His dad rose and came to the entry. "Gosh, it's good to see you. How're you feeling?"

Cam figured he was going to get that question a lot, so he might as well practice patience. "I'm okay. Feel fine, mostly. But restless."

"You're not used to sitting still. Even in the off-season, you're training. Gotta be tough."

Cam wasn't sure what he was going to do with himself for four weeks. Christmas shopping would take up an afternoon. There were doctor appointments already set up. But how would he fill his days?

His mom popped back in the foyer. "Your old room is ready for you, Cam."

Lord. He hadn't actually lived in this house for over a decade. He hefted his duffel and started down the hall, stopping in front of Oaklee's old room. He was looking forward to spending more time with her, actually. And Rory. They'd been together just over a year now, and once he'd got over the surprise of them hooking up, he could see how perfect they were for each other.

He wasn't jealous. Nope. Besides, he was traveling a lot, and trades meant moving cities. Lots of his teammates were married with families, but he'd always thought a stable upbringing was better for kids.

Like he'd had.

His mom opened his bedroom door and he went inside, then turned around and hugged her again. "Thanks, Mom," he said.

She laughed. "For what?"

"For everything."

She stood back, and he thought he saw a glimmer of moisture in her eyes, but then she grinned. "That must have been some knock to the head," she quipped, winking at him. "You're all sentimental."

He smiled back but shook his head. "Naw, just realizing how much you guys sacrificed for me."

"Well, you're home for Christmas. Even if the reason isn't the best one, I'm glad to have you around for a while. Now you chill out, and I'll see you at dinner. You don't need me all up in your business."

He chuckled and nodded. She left and shut the door behind her, while he stood and surveyed his room—the double bed, plain chest of drawers, and a bookcase that held trophies rather than books.

Suddenly weary, he lay down on the bed and stared at the ceiling.

He was going to be bored out of his mind.

Chapter 2

HANNAH WAITED AT THE bar for a good fifteen minutes past their agreed time before Oaklee showed up. She'd sipped on water, but she was starving since she hadn't yet had dinner. She was dying for a plate of chili cheese fries. And then tomorrow she would do a longer run to work them off. Ninety-five percent of the time, she ate clean and said no to sugar and fried food. Tonight, though, she had zero willpower. The showing hadn't gone as well as she'd hoped, either. It had been a shit day all around.

Oaklee blew in on a cold breeze and peeled off her coat on the way to the table. "I'm sorry I'm late! I totally forgot I had a family dinner, and I thought I'd be finished on time. But Cam got telling stories, and I lost track of time."

"Cam's home?" Hannah lifted an eyebrow. Cam had always been Darling's golden boy. While he and Rory were best friends, Hannah could remember Cam being a bit big for his britches in school. She wondered if his ego was still as huge, considering what a superstar he was now.

"Yeah. He's off for a while. Another concussion." Oaklee's happy expression faded as she hung her coat over her chair. "He put on a good show, but I can tell he's worried."

"For how long?"

Oaklee sat and let out a breath. "Oh, well, he's home for the holidays. Going back to Denver after our New Year's party. You are coming to that, right?"

Hannah smiled. "Of course." She loved that Oaklee was already planning something a month away. She did the same thing. They really did get along well.

They each ordered a beer and Hannah ordered her fries, then the door opened again, and her sisters-in-law, Willow and Laurel, blew in. Hannah waved them over. "What are you guys doing here?"

Laurel shook a bit of snow off her hair. "We called Rory, and he said you guys were meeting here. The guys are watching the babies."

Willow had married Hannah's oldest brother, Ethan, and Laurel and Aiden had hooked up just before that and had a surprise wedding at the town's fabled Kissing Bridge. Hannah had always felt rather lucky that her best friends were now her sisters.

Food arrived, and another round of drinks, and before long, Hannah found herself relating her bad news about the benefit. "So we're without any sort of celebrity headliner, and only a few weeks to find a replacement."

Laurel tapped her fingernails on the table. "Hey, you said Cam is home, right, Oaklee? Why not him? The kids around here would adore having him take part. He's like a local hero."

Hannah had been scouring her brain for a guest author, but the idea of having a famous athlete held appeal. Kids looked up to athletes as superstars. Having someone like Cam endorse reading? It would be a great thing.

"What do you think, Oaklee? Would he do it?"

"We can always ask. It wouldn't hurt. And it would solve your problem."

A weight seemed to lift off Hannah's shoulders. "I'll think about it. We could maybe have him do the reading at the library, you know? And then speak at the dinner. Maybe even donate a jersey or something to the auction."

Her day was starting to turn around. And all because Cam Collier had graced Darling with his presence for a few weeks. She'd never once considered Cam the kind of guy who would come to her rescue. But then she'd never in her life actually needed rescuing.

Right now, Cam could be the solution to all her problems.

—ele—

Hannah hadn't quite decided how to broach the topic with Cam, though she'd thought about it all through her morning run. She ran the same route every morning. She left her renovated colonial and headed toward downtown, then to the golf course, back up through the park, over the Kissing

Bridge, down the Green to the Ladybug Garden Center, and then back along the main route into town. It was about four miles altogether, and Hannah considered the rhythmic sound of her breathing and the slap of her steps conducive to deep thinking. She solved a lot of problems during her run, but today, she'd conjured and dismissed a half dozen scenarios. She knew Cam, but they weren't exactly friends. She thought about getting Oaklee to facilitate some sort of meeting, where she could accidentally show up, but he'd see that ambush for what it was the moment she asked for the favor. Ditto with getting Rory involved as a middleman. She thought about showing up on the Colliers' doorstep and simply asking him, but she figured he got requests all the time and didn't want him to think she was cashing in on his celebrity— which of course, she was. Or wanted to, anyway.

No idea felt right, so she went home, showered, and left for work bundled in her warm coat, scarf, and her favorite knee-high boots. The cold weather was sticking around, and she didn't want to be frozen after her walk to the office.

Within minutes, she was inside the homey warmth of The Purple Pig Café for her daily coffee, with the scent of cinnamon and coffee around her. The display case showed a variety of muffins for the morning crowd, and she looked longingly at the blueberry-oat ones before ordering her coffee and, as her stomach growled, an egg-white breakfast sandwich and bowl of fruit salad.

Willow came out of the kitchen and lit up when she saw Hannah there.

"Morning, sunshine," her sister-in-law called, and moved to pour Hannah's coffee herself. "Long time no see."

Willow had opened The Purple Pig a few years ago, serving light, healthy fare that was organic and locally sourced. The menu was simple but satisfying, and the business had taken off. Then, when Willow and Ethan had their baby, she'd leased the space next door and opened a yoga studio. Nowadays, the running of the café largely fell to the manager, Emily. Seeing Willow behind the counter was a treat.

"Not teaching classes today, Wil?" Hannah took the coffee cup and sipped while she waited for her sandwich.

"I have a chair yoga class at the senior center at ten thirty," Willow said with a smile. "I stopped in to give Em a hand with the morning rush."

"And where's Brenna?" Willow and Ethan's daughter was just six months old and as cute as a bug's ear with Ethan's rusty hair and Willow's calm temperament.

"In her playpen in the back. I'll pop her to the sitter before my class." Willow tucked Hannah's sandwich in a paper bag, as well as the fruit salad and a spoon. "Here you go."

"Thanks," she said, just as a strange quiet settled over the busy café.

She turned around and immediately saw the reason why. Cam had walked in the door, leaving the patrons gaping with expressions of what Hannah could say for certain was hero worship. And no wonder. She'd seen him on TV, of course, most often dressed in his hockey uniform and sweaty from playing. Not today. Today he was dressed in jeans and a bomber jacket that made his shoulders look impossibly wide. Hannah was tall at five-nine; Cam was well over six feet and made her feel small in comparison. It wasn't just his height or the way his ass looked in his jeans, though. He had ridiculously thick hair that curled just that little bit over the collar, and full lips that often smiled when he spoke on camera. Right now, they were smiling at the girl behind the counter, who was blushing to the roots of her hair as she took his order.

"That's him, isn't it?" Willow whispered close to Hannah's ear.

Hannah swallowed, her tongue suddenly thick and her throat dry. "Yeah," she managed, and felt ridiculous standing there gaping like some puck bunny. It had nothing to do with his fame, she realized, and everything to do with a simple visceral reaction to an incredibly sexy guy.

A guy who'd been four years behind her in school, and more of a cocky pain in her neck in those days than someone she'd like to—

"Hey, Hannah."

She stared up at him and felt uncharacteristic heat creep up her neck. "Oh, hey, Cam. I heard you were back in town."

Willow met Hannah's gaze and nodded, a knowing smile touching her lips. "Coffee, Cam?" She stuck out her hand. "I'm Willow, Ethan's partner."

He shook her hand and smiled easily. "I'd love some coffee to go with my breakfast."

"You got it."

Hannah was so relieved by Willow's rescue. It gave her a chance to get her head on straight and stop acting like a silly girl with a crush on the cute boy in chemistry class.

This was her opportunity to talk to Cam. She had to get her act together and be normal.

"Eating on the go?" Cam asked, making polite conversation. The crowd was talking again, but in a low hum, and watching Cam's every move. It would be comical if it weren't so disconcerting.

"I was going to take it back to my office, yeah." She smiled up at him. Lordy, she loved tall men. Always had.

"Oh. I was going to ask if you wanted to eat with me, but that's cool."

Hannah tried not to gawp and recovered as gracefully as she could as opportunity was dropped neatly into her lap. "Oh, well, sure."

He leaned forward. "If I sit alone, I'm going to feel like a spider under glass. Everyone staring and finding me incredibly fascinating and scary."

She snorted. "You? Scary?"

He gave a half shrug, and she couldn't help it, she was charmed. The way the crowd was acting right now, he might be right. He'd take his seat and go to eat, and everyone would stare.

A smile flirted with her lips. "I suppose I could take a few minutes for a bite."

"Go find a seat," Willow instructed. "I'll bring your food out when it's up, Cam."

"Thanks." He sent her a wide smile and then let Hannah lead the way to a small table toward the back of the small dining area.

She made her way to the table, her stomach in strange little knots. Odd. Nervousness was not generally her thing. Then again, this could be the serendipitous opportunity she'd been waiting for, couldn't it? And if that were the case, the success of the benefit relied on how well this meeting went. It had absolutely nothing to do with Cam Collier and his big shoulders and crazy sexy hair.

They were just at the table when Cam spoke up. "So is your office nearby?"

"Actually, it's just a few steps away." She gestured with her hand, forgot she was holding the coffee, and a bit sloshed over the rim and onto her hand.

It was *really* hot.

But she wouldn't let on. Instead, she reached for a chair with her free hand and put the coffee on the table, surreptitiously wiping her wet hand on her coat.

Great start, Hannah.

She put down her bag and shrugged out of her coat, hanging it over the back of the chair. She was really glad she'd worn her favorite sweater dress today. It was a knit column that hugged her figure and was in a soft gray that went extraordinarily well with her fiery hair. When she went to sit down, she caught Cam's gaze. It was warm and approving, and there was a snap of chemistry between them she couldn't—and didn't want to—deny. That they found each other visually appealing was quite nice, really. So what if she was older than him? There came an age when that didn't matter anymore, right?

"You look good, Hannah," he said quietly, his voice a low rumble so no one nearby could hear.

The fizz from a moment ago turned into spark that sizzled along her limbs and settled in her core.

"So do you, Cam." She lifted an eyebrow and gave him a sideways smile. "Really good."

"It's the five a.m. workouts," he replied, taking a sip of his coffee. "Never thought I'd say this, but I miss them."

She tried not to think about him in a gym. To be honest, his physicality was a huge turn on. Not that she was ever going to act on this. He was Rory's best friend, for heaven's sake. And even cancelling out the age difference, there was the sheer fact that Hannah didn't do flings. Didn't do relationships at all, really. Besides, after Christmas,

Cam was headed straight back to Denver to finish out the season.

She wanted him for the benefit. Nothing more.

They'd only been seated for a few minutes when Willow brought out Cam's eggs and turkey sausage. Hannah now wished she'd got something other than a breakfast sandwich. She could just imagine lifting it to take a bite and having cheese stick to her mouth or something drip into her lap. She removed it from the bag and opened the wrapper, gathering the English muffin into her hands and hoping for the best.

She had just taken a nibble when a small voice sounded at her elbow. "'Scuse me, but can I have your autograph?"

The little guy couldn't have been more than seven, cute as anything, with a cowlick, a missing middle tooth, and sparkly blue eyes.

"Sure," Cam answered easily. "I don't have paper. Is a napkin okay?"

The little head bobbed so fast Hannah was surprised he didn't get whiplash.

"Do you play hockey?" Cam asked, while Hannah handed him a pen, a goofy smile on her lips.

"Uh huh. I started last year."

"Cool. You play at the rink here?"

Another enthusiastic nod.

Cam signed the napkin and held it out. "I learned to play hockey here, too. Here you go."

"Thanks!" The kid looked at Cam as if he hung the moon and the stars and then dashed away. Hannah heard him exclaim to his parents, "He signed a napkin! Cool!"

"Does that happen a lot?" she asked.

He laughed. "Yeah. But it's cool. I was that age once."

"It's good to be home, then?"

He regarded her with a strange expression. "Well, I guess. Except for the concussion and all."

Heat crept up her neck. What was wrong with her? What a dumb question. "Of course." She smiled and covered her embarrassment as smoothly as she could. "Not the best circumstances for you at all. But still, your family must be glad to see you. And Rory, too."

He lifted his coffee cup and looked toward the window. "Sure. There's nothing like a Darling Christmas."

There was something in his voice that didn't quite ring true, and it left an awkward hole in the conversation.

Cam eventually filled the gap. "So Oaklee says you run the real estate office here in town."

"Just a few doors away." She was also a silent partner in Willow's yoga studio. Hannah wasn't the kind to shy away from opportunities.

"You always were independent and driven." He speared a piece of egg with his fork. "I'm not surprised you're running your own business rather than working for some corporation somewhere.

You always struck me as someone who would like being their own boss."

She put down her sandwich and picked up her coffee. "Huh. I never thought you would have noticed. I mean, I was graduating high school when you were a freshman. And then you left town."

He met her gaze, and the lopsided grin returned. "Hannah. I was a fourteen-year-old boy whose best friend had a smokin' hot older sister. I noticed."

The blush from earlier came rushing back up her neck and face again. "Oh. Well."

He laughed and cut into a sausage link. "You didn't expect me to be so honest."

"Not really." Hannah was normally so calm and collected, but in Cam's presence, she seemed to lose her self-assurance. Besides, it wasn't as if she could say the same. He'd always been cute, but he'd been her little brother's best friend. At eighteen, she hadn't exactly been interested in boys. She'd wanted to be an adult, go to university and date *men*. Not kids who were just learning to shave.

Eighteen to fourteen was a huge age gap. Thirty-three to twenty-nine was not the same. Especially when the man across the table was confident, successful, and at the top of his game.

His gaze held hers for a long moment, until Hannah found it hard to take a full breath. When she could hardly stand it anymore, she dropped her eyes to her sandwich and picked it up in her hands, uncharacteristically self-conscious.

"Relax," he said, his voice low. "It was just a compliment."

Was it? She wasn't so sure. Maybe if she actually dated, she'd navigate this kind of conversation better. Was he flirting? Or was it simply conversation? She could handle land deals with no problem. Coordinate special events and run a chamber of commerce meeting in her sleep. But flirting, sexual undertones, and subtext? She sucked at it. Probably because, according to her ex, she was a ballbuster, and guys didn't want overbearing women. She'd be fine if she was just less...Hannah.

He hadn't wanted her when she was being herself. And that stung more than it ought to. The nickname Oaklee had called her—the General— actually hurt. She knew people found her intimidating. She tried as hard as she could not to let it get to her, but sometimes, the loneliness crept in. Particularly when her best friends were all in happy relationships, moving through the world in couples, and she was on the outside looking in. According to Liam, the ex, no one would ever want a woman who was so determined to wear the pants.

Hannah was always the third wheel, and she smiled her way through it. Maybe no one would ever want someone like her, like Liam said. But she'd rather be alone than be less of herself.

"So what is keeping you busy these days?" Cam asked, seemingly more at ease than she was. "What's the real estate market like?"

"It's a bit of a buyer's market at the moment," she answered and then lifted her cup and took a sip of her coffee. "You looking to buy?"

He shook his head. "Honestly? This concussion has thrown me more than I expected. I need to get back on the ice, but I'm afraid to be sidelined. There's always that little bit of fear that the next time will be a career ender. Plus, I've got two years left on my contract. Who knows if I'll be traded or find myself a free agent in that time? I've got a condo, but I could be in another city, you know? Looking at a permanent house isn't really in the cards right now."

At least Darling was her home. She didn't have to feel as if her life were...transient. Or in the hands of someone else.

"But you're happy?" she asked, curious.

"Not happy about being scratched from the lineup, that's for sure." The café had gotten busier, and she noticed Cam wincing now and again.

"Is the noise getting to you?"

"I wish I could say no, but I do seem to be more sensitive to light and sound. I only have the odd dizziness or woozy feelings, but I'm not headache free yet."

"I'm sorry. That's got to be frustrating." She wrapped up the third of her sandwich that was left and tucked it in the bag. He'd finished his eggs and had one little sausage link left. She realized she hadn't even broached the topic of the benefit yet, and this was the perfect time.

"So if you happen to be at loose ends while you're home, we have this charity thing going on just before Christmas. A literacy event. This is the second year, and all the proceeds go to local literacy programs. You want to help out?"

"What kind of charity thing?"

Hannah took advantage of the question to press forward. "It's a community day of literacy. There are events all over town. Participants can grab a bookmark and get it stamped at each shop, with a draw at the end. The library has a special reading and a used-book sale, and in the evening, there's a ticketed dinner and silent auction."

He raised his eyebrows. "Sounds ambitious."

"Last year, we raised over ten thousand dollars. Corporate donations took us to just shy of twenty." She was proud of that number, considering it had been their first year, and they'd been trying everything for the first time. Darling wasn't a large town, and twenty thousand had helped a lot of kids learn to read.

She folded her hands on the table and looked him straight in the face, trying to ignore how handsome he was. He had such great hair and perfect teeth. Was it possible for a hockey player to have teeth that great, she wondered? His last contract had been in the millions, double digit millions. Twenty grand must seem like a drop in the bucket to him. But to the organizations nearby, it meant resources for tons of kids.

"Will you help out? You saw that kid this morning. Having a local hero like you would be a huge draw. You could read a story at the library and then maybe speak at the dinner. It would guarantee a sell-out crowd."

"You want me to read a book to some kids?" His voice cooled, and he sat back in his chair a bit.

"Well, yes. I know you're not an author, but I'm sure we could find you a great hockey story to share."

His face flattened ever so slightly into a polite veneer. "Have you been waiting for the right opportunity to ask me about this?"

Hannah blushed a little and gave a small shrug. "Sort of. We just found out yesterday that our headlining author has to have surgery and backed out. We could really use your help."

He sighed, and her heart sank. He was not pleased, she could tell. His gaze had darkened, and his full lips were now a flat line.

"Look, I wish you luck, but I came home to recover and enjoy the holiday. Have some privacy. Not find myself in the middle of some big event."

"It would only be one day," she reasoned, desperate for him to change his mind.

"Sure, but I can't even sit in a café without my head reacting. A library full of screaming kids? I'm sorry, Hannah. The answer is no."

Hannah felt the solution slipping through her fingers and leaned forward. "Look, Cam, I know this looks like we're using you for your celebrity, and you're not wrong. But you're a hometown guy, and it's such a good cause. Please help us." She hated sounding desperate, but finding someone willing to come to their little town just before Christmas with so little notice? They'd had the previous plans in place for months.

"I'm sorry, I can't. I'll give you something for the auction. A signed jersey or something."

"Can't, or won't?"

She could have bitten her tongue. Her earlier jitters had fled in the face of his refusal, because she'd seriously thought he'd say yes. She knew for a fact he'd supported charities in the past. Like the one providing sports equipment to underprivileged kids.

But he wouldn't help out the town that had supported him, and frankly, she was disappointed in him.

Her face must have showed it, because he shook his head a little. "You're looking at me like my grandma used to when I lied about taking cookies out of the Tupperware in her cupboard. I'm sorry, Hannah, but I came home to rest. Doctor's orders. And to enjoy the holiday, too. I want to keep a low profile." He toyed with his napkin. "The sooner I recover, the sooner I'm back on the ice. Maybe you don't understand how many requests I get. I need a break."

It wasn't like reading a stupid storybook would set his recovery back, but Hannah knew she wasn't going to get anywhere with him today. She pushed her chair back and stood. "Well, that's that, I guess. I'd better get back to work."

Cam stood, too, surprising Hannah, who hadn't expected the old-fashioned courtesy. "I'm sorry to disappoint you, Hannah. More sorry than you know."

Was he? Was he really? She felt as if the words were mere lip service, so she offered a weak smile. "Have a good day. I hope you get some rest." She couldn't resist adding the last barb. Suddenly, his good looks didn't seem so attractive anymore. Even if he'd been open to the idea in a small way, they would have had somewhere to go with it. But that had been a definitive shut down.

She dropped her garbage in the trash can on the way by, heading straight for the door before Willow could catch her and quiz her on what had happened at breakfast with Cam. Willow and Laurel had been nagging her about her love life more lately, and she really didn't need the curiosity. She and Cam were not going to be a thing.

It wasn't that she didn't understand wanting to spend a low-key Christmas to recover from his concussion. She wasn't entirely unsympathetic. He just had to see what a great event it was and how many kids could benefit. But it wasn't in her nature to give up on what she really wanted. It was what made her a good Realtor and businesswoman.

She went back into her office, sat in her chair, and rolled up to her desk, reaching for her keyboard.

Maybe if Cam saw the numbers, he'd be more inclined to help. Because the last thing this event needed was Hannah reading to kids. There was nothing exciting or special about that.

Absolutely nothing.

Chapter 3

CAM DECIDED TO GET some fresh air after the encounter with Hannah, so he left The Purple Pig and made his way down Main, trying to inhale slow, deep breaths. His pulse still pattered at his throat, a result of the anxiety he'd felt the moment Hannah had made her request. There was no way he could sit in front of a crowd of kids and read out loud to them. Not an ice cube's chance in hell. He could just see it now. A group of children all starry-eyed at the big hockey star, only to realize how unheroic he was when he started stumbling over the words or reading too slowly.

Hannah had no idea what she was asking, and he wasn't about to tell her. Besides, he hadn't lied. He really was home to recuperate and spend the holiday with his family.

Even he knew that was a technicality. He'd said no because reading was a gigantic struggle for him, and nothing he would ever do in public.

He'd gone exactly a block and a half when he heard his name being called. When he turned, Oaklee was bearing down on him, presumably on her way to work. Damn, this town really was small.

"Good morning," he said, waiting for her to catch up.

Oaklee stopped and stared up at him. "What's wrong with you?"

"What do you mean?"

"You look like a constipated bear. What put you in a bad mood? Or is your head hurting?"

Why had he thought coming home was a good idea?

Oaklee didn't know about his *problem*. No one did, and he wanted to keep it that way.

"I'm just tired, Oaklee. If you haven't had a concussion, you probably don't get it."

"Then why are you out here?"

He started walking again, toward town hall, where she worked. "I wanted some fresh air."

"So you went to the café?" She nodded at his to-go cup and his rapidly cooling coffee.

"What's with the third degree?" he asked, his teeth grinding to the sound of her heeled boots clicking on the sidewalk as she kept up with him. Funny how certain noises seemed to set him on edge. "Yes, I went and had breakfast. With Hannah, actually."

"Oh! Did she ask you about the benefit?"

Cam stopped in the middle of the sidewalk and stared at his little sister as it all became clear. "Damn. Did you put her up to that?"

"It might have been my idea. She was majorly stressed about it yesterday. So you're going to do it, right?"

"No, I'm not. I'll donate something, but I'm not going to replace whatever author you were supposed to have."

Oaklee put her hand on his arm. "Bro. This is not cool."

He loved his sister. He did. So he was as gentle as possible when he answered, "Neither is setting me up to do something I'm not comfortable with, Oaklee. I would hope you'd understand that."

"I understand that you could have given Hannah thirty minutes of your time on a Saturday, and instead, you probably offered a jersey. It's not like you, Cam."

Her eyes were soft with concern rather than censure, and he let out a sigh. "Maybe coming home was a mistake."

She linked her arm through his and they started walking again. "Why would you say that? Mom and Dad are thrilled. And so am I. I don't see enough of my big brother."

He didn't know how to phrase his discontent without sounding spoiled and privileged. "It's just...everywhere I go, people generally want something. And it's not a bad thing. I know I'm blessed. I appreciate my fans, I really do. At the same time, I miss being a regular guy. I kind of thought I'd have that opportunity at home, you know? And I'm home less than twenty-four hours and already someone wants something."

Her lips lifted in a smile. "Waaah, waaah."

Cam chuckled. He knew better than to give his little sister a pity story. One of the things he liked about her was that she didn't take his crap. It still blew him away that she and his best friend were seriously in love.

"I know, it's a tough life I lead."

"Please, just think about it?"

"Oaklee, let it drop, okay? I'll donate, but I'm not doing some story time at the library. Now, aren't you late for work?" he asked, lifting an eyebrow as he glanced down at her.

"Yeah, I guess." Oaklee was pouting now.

"You might be able to get around Mom and Dad with that look, but it's never worked on me. Put your lip away."

She laughed then, and he felt some of the tension dissolve between them. He walked her to the parking lot of town hall and watched as she headed inside. His baby sister was all grown up. Of course, he'd known that already, but it was strange seeing her here with her own place and a job and a relationship... So many things had changed since he left, and yet they'd stayed the same, too.

The walk had done him good, so he headed back to where he'd parked by the café. The air had a crisp bite to it as he shrugged his shoulders and looked at the other storefronts in the building. Next to The Purple Pig was a yoga studio, and next to that, Darling Realty. Hannah's office.

Hannah, with that Gallagher red hair and eyes that seemed to see right into his solar plexus. Not to mention the rockin' bod she had going on. She had legs for miles in those boots today, and that dress... It had hugged every lean curve. She'd been older than him in school, but she'd always been hot. Rory would kill him for saying so, but he'd always had kind of a thing for Hannah. And not just her looks, either. She had zero tolerance for bullshit and had never dated dumbasses. Particular and discriminating, that was Hannah.

He wondered if he met any of her criteria now that he was older and a lot more successful than he'd been back then. If his money made him less of a dumb jock in her eyes.

Oaklee was right about one thing. It was a good cause, and so he went to the Darling Realty door and opened it, stepping out of the cold and into the warmth. He didn't like how he'd left things with Hannah this morning, and during his walk, he'd come up with a way to help her and ease his conscience at the same time.

"Can I help you?" The receptionist looked up and her mouth fell open. "Oh my God. You're Cam Collier."

He smiled his standard smile and nodded. "That's right. Is Hannah in?"

She nodded quickly, her eyes wide. "I'll just go get her. Hang on."

He waited as she scurried away and took the opportunity to look around the reception area. It was very Hannah, dressed up with lovely touches but very clean and efficient looking. A gentle gray covered the walls, with prints featuring Darling landmarks scattered strategically. The reception area chairs were darker gray, and there was not a thing out of place at the receptionist's desk. It was both professional and welcoming, and he liked it a lot.

"Cam?" Hannah entered the area, a frown etching her brows. "What's up?" Her eyes lit up, and she smiled. "Have you reconsidered?"

"About the library? No. But I went for a walk and came up with an idea."

She was disappointed, he could tell. Her shoulders drooped a little when he said no, and her smile dimmed a bit. He didn't like disappointing her, he discovered. But worse than that would be the look on her face when she realized he was exactly the wrong person to be reading in front of a crowd. He did have one thing to offer, though.

"Come on into my office, then." She looked over at the receptionist, who was still staring. "Sheila, if anyone calls, I'm unavailable, okay?"

"The house inspection for Jim Hernandez is due in today. And we're waiting for a counteroffer from the Bajwas."

"I won't be long." She beckoned to Cam. "Come on in, Cam."

He followed her into her office and took a breath as she shut the door behind him.

There were windows on one wall, with slatted blinds that were open enough to let in the morning light but still retain privacy. Her office reflected the reception area, with those restful grays and beautiful prints. But there was more of

Hannah in here, too. Fresh flowers on the credenza. A laptop open on her desk, and what looked like a day planner. And a coffee mug that proudly proclaimed, *Realtor...because Bad Ass isn't an official job title.*

"Nice mug."

"Thanks. Santa put it in my stocking a few years ago."

He tried to imagine her in fuzzy pajamas, opening a Christmas stocking, and he found the image more alluring than he ought to. Hannah was always put together. Thinking of her soft and mussed from sleep did something to him that he wasn't sure he liked. Or maybe he liked it a little too much.

"So," she said, leaning back against her desk. "What's your idea? I was just running some numbers on the benefit, actually. Both expenses and then where the funds go and how many children it helps." She reached behind her for a sheaf of papers and handed it over.

He took them and scanned the sheets, pretending to read them. It wasn't that he couldn't. It was just that he'd have to sit down and really work his way through so things weren't jumbled. He cleared his mind and forced his thoughts back to the matter at hand. "I appreciate you printing this out, but just tell me straight. How much do you need financially to make this a success? I can help there. I'll donate to the auction, and I'll underwrite any expenses you incur."

She stilled. "You want to underwrite the benefit."

Hannah stared at Cam and didn't know what to say. On one hand, the offer was very generous, particularly since all their communication and promotion had to be redone—without Jillian's name and face on it. On the other hand, he was throwing money at the issue rather than giving of himself.

She must have hesitated too long, because he took a step forward and put the papers back on her desk. "I'll make a donation, too, of course."

"A donation," she parroted.

"It's not that I don't think it's a good cause. I do, of course I do!" He put his hands into the back pockets of his jeans. "I just want to be in the background. Out of the spotlight."

She wavered. While having him read at the library and perhaps speak at the dinner would be amazing, she also respected that he wanted some privacy. This morning had been proof enough that he was recognized wherever he went. As cute as the little boy had been, it had interrupted his breakfast. And yet he'd been lovely and gracious. She wasn't sure why he was so hesitant to participate, but she was smart enough to not look a gift horse in the mouth.

"I appreciate the funds, of course," she said quietly, meeting his eyes. "But we won't have much of an event if we don't have someone special lined up."

"I'm sure if you explain about the cancellation, people will understand."

They probably would. But Hannah would still feel as if she'd failed.

She sighed. There was still time. There was a chance she could find someone, right? Someone who was not Cam?

Someone who was not over six feet of sexiness that made her lose her focus the moment he stared into her eyes, imploring her to understand?

She knew what Willow would say about this new fixation on Cam. Willow would say she needed to get laid. And Willow might not be entirely wrong. It had been a very long time. So long she wouldn't own to it if asked.

"Hey," he said softly, coming forward. "I have my reasons, Hannah. Please don't be mad." A lopsided grin flickered on his lips. "If I remember right, an angry Hannah Gallagher is a fearsome thing."

She couldn't help it. She laughed. He looked so innocent and cute right now as he teased her. He'd always been able to do that, she realized. Even when he was a kid. She'd be annoyed at him and Rory, and he'd flash her a grin that melted away her frustration. Not that she'd ever let on. He'd always had charisma. Some of it was cocky, but mostly it was just a natural thing that was hard to resist.

Like right now.

"I know you have your reasons. And to be honest, you shouldn't have to justify anything to me. I'm just disappointed is all."

"I don't like disappointing you."

"If I remember right, you don't like disappointing anyone."

Silence fell between them as he stared at her. Maybe he didn't expect her to see him so clearly, but there were things they had in common. Drive, for one. He couldn't have made it where he was now without it. And a need for approval. She'd watched him look up into the stands for his parents during every peewee game. Heard the interviews where he'd confessed to letting his team down or the fans.

Neither of them liked to fail. It suddenly dawned on her that this trip home must, in some way, feel like a failure. He was away from his job, away from his team, forced to recover. Did it make him feel weak? Heck, she was an amateur athlete, doing half marathons and, last fall, her first half Ironman. And she knew how frustrated she'd gotten when she had to step back from training with an injury. This was his career. He was the team captain. Totally different thing.

"Sorry," she said quietly. "I didn't mean to say that."

"You're not wrong," he answered. "I don't like disappointing you, either. So will you believe me when I say that I've said no for a good reason?"

She nodded. There were things he wasn't saying, but a lot that he was, and she appreciated that.

"Thank you, Cam." She pushed away from the desk and went to stand before him. "For coming to see me and explaining, and for your offer to help. I accept."

She held out her hand for him to shake, and he folded her fingers inside his larger, warm hand. He held on for longer than was proper, while his dark gaze delved into hers.

And then he did the last thing Hannah expected. He tugged on her hand, pulled her closer, and kissed her.

Every rational thought skittered out of her brain at the first contact of his mouth on hers. His lips were soft and yet firm as they moved over her mouth. She let out a little sigh and melted against him. His arm came around her and pulled her against his bomber jacket. It smelled of leather and fresh air and whatever cologne he'd put on that morning—something deliciously fresh and manly that made her want to lick his neck.

He was kissing her, and she was thinking of licking his neck. What kind of madness was this? And yet she was helpless to stop. He was an exceptionally good kisser. Firm when he needed to be, gentle and teasing in between, and always, always in control. She loved that, she realized, as he cupped the side of her face with a wide palm and took the kiss deeper. It was sheer bliss to let him command the kiss and for her to just follow.

When their breath labored and the kiss turned a bit wild, Hannah stepped back, shocked at how quickly they'd gone from a handshake to sucking face in her office. Her office, for Pete's sake! Her chest rose and fell with panting breaths, and every part of her tingled with arousal.

"Wow," Cam said, running a hand through his hair. His breathing was ragged, too, and one quick glance at his jeans told her she wasn't alone in the arousal department.

She had to get a hold of herself. "I can honestly say that is the first time I've ever sealed a bargain in that manner."

"It was definitely...unexpected."

"Unexpected? You kissed me."

"Yeah, but I didn't imagine it would be like that." His dark gaze seared her now. "Damn, Hannah. Just...damn." His eyes twinkled at her. "I've wanted to do that since I was thirteen. If I'd known you could kiss like that, I would have done it much sooner."

She shouldn't be flattered, but she'd heard so much criticism in the past that she drank up the praise like she was parched in the desert and it was life-giving water.

"I'm as surprised as you are," she replied, smoothing her hands down her dress.

"Have dinner with me," he said. He'd regained his composure and channeled the cockiness she remembered so well. "Tonight."

He didn't have to say the words for her to know that he wasn't just asking her to dinner. And despite the chemistry that clearly sparked between them, she was not the type to throw caution to the wind and have a fling.

What was more, he knew it.

"I think I'll pass," she replied, hearing the regret in the words but standing by them anyway. "This isn't a good idea, Cam."

"Are you sure? Because it felt like a very good idea about two minutes ago."

"We both know you're not asking me out to dinner. Or at least, not just dinner. And I'm not prepared for anything more than that."

It hurt just to say the words. Because Hannah got the idea that being with Cam would be something spectacular.

He stepped back a little. "Then I'll just say if you ever change your mind..."

It was tempting. So very tempting. She desperately wanted to say yes. But sex... It was something Hannah took very seriously. There had to be emotions involved, and a genuine caring. Maybe not exactly love, but close to it. It was how she was built. And after years of being criticized, both in the bedroom and out, she didn't let herself be vulnerable like that very often.

"Thank you, Cam."

"You're welcome."

He let himself out, though she heard him stop at the desk and say something to Sheila, who giggled in response. Hannah smiled to herself. He was such a charmer, and he knew it. And yet it wasn't insincere.

And he kissed like the devil. She put her fingers to her lips and sighed. His invitation was more tempting than he knew. But Hannah wasn't sure she could take one more hit to her pride. The thought of being with Cam and him finding her wanting was more than she could bear.

Chapter 4

CAM DIDN'T SEE HANNAH for the rest of the week. He did as he was supposed to and took lots of down time. He monitored his symptoms and was pleased with how they seemed to be disappearing, though he knew he had to be symptom free for several days before he would even be cleared for basic workouts. He ventured into town and did some holiday shopping, and then into Burlington where there was a wider selection. This Christmas was different. Normally, he shipped gifts to the family, but this year he was going to be here. He intended to purchase them all and wrap them himself, too.

He also kept himself glued to the sports channel and what was happening with the league. He missed team meetings and being in the locker room. He got lots of emails, but reading them was onerous.

Replying was just as difficult.

He was sitting on the back deck, having coffee and enjoying the brisk air, when he heard the fence gate open. "Hey, you out here?"

Rory. Cam smiled and called out, "Yeah, on the deck. Come on up and have a seat."

Rory was the best friend Cam had ever had, and he'd missed him a lot when he went away to play major junior. Rory had been charged with watching out for Oaklee. He'd also been game for anything when Cam had been home in the off-season. It was the one friendship from his youth that had sustained. And yet Rory didn't know Cam's secret, either. Normally, it didn't bother Cam as much as it did now. He'd developed ways of hiding his disability. And though he'd never been formally tested, he was pretty sure that his reading and writing issues were because he had dyslexia.

Rory climbed the few steps to the deck and shook his head as he stared at Cam. "Seriously, it's cold as balls out here. Why are you on the deck?"

"I miss the ice." Cam grinned at his friend and took a sip of his coffee. "You want a coffee? I can make you one."

"Naw, I'm good. I had coffee with Oaklee before work today, and another with Ethan when he stopped over to stash the boys' gifts in my garage. If I have a third, I'll be spinning around like the Tasmanian Devil."

"Ethan's boys are getting big."

"Yep. New toboggans for Christmas, and a hockey net for the front yard. Kind of difficult to hide those away from curious boys."

Rory sat in the chair beside Cam and grimaced as the cold surface greeted his butt. "Dude. My grandmother would tell me I'll get hemorrhoids from sitting on something this cold."

"Wuss," Cam replied. "So what brings you over?"

"I don't work until two. And there's something I want to talk to you about."

Cam drank the last of his coffee and gave Rory a skeptical look. "If you're here to plead the case for the literacy benefit—"

"No. Not that Oaklee didn't ask, but I said no way am I getting in the middle of that. That's not it."

Rory's smile had disappeared, and he shifted on his chair. Cam frowned. He hoped this wasn't anything to do with Oaklee. Rory was his best friend, but if he hurt Oaklee, Cam might just have to knock him into next week.

"What's going on?"

"Well, the thing is...you're her brother, and you're my best friend, and I kinda feel like I need to talk to you before I..." His voice trailed away and then he straightened. "Before I ask her to marry me."

Cam wanted to grin from ear to ear, but he figured it would be fun to make Rory sweat a little. "You're asking my permission?"

"Not exactly. But I think I need your blessing."

Cam crossed an ankle over his knee and looked up at the cloudless sky. "Huh. You didn't ask for my blessing before taking her to bed, as I remember."

"Jesus, Cam," Rory blurted out, giving Cam some perverse satisfaction. What was the point of having a best friend if you couldn't give him some shit now and again?

Cam looked over at Rory and chuckled. "Just sayin', bro. Hell, you guys have been together over a year and are living together. Nothing I say would make a difference, nor should it. She loves you. You love her."

The look on Rory's face was so relieved it was comical, so Cam added, "But if you ever hurt her, I'll crush you. Got it?"

"You and what army, invalid?"

Oh, trash talk. Cam's favorite thing. He lifted an eyebrow. "Have you seen my teammates?"

Rory met his raised eyebrow with one of his own. "Have you met my brothers?"

They both laughed, and Cam held out a hand. Rory shook it and there was a moment of something between them, of friendship and respect and affection that had never wavered over the years. "Hey. If you guys get married, that'll make us brothers, too. Congratulations, Rory. I'm happy for you both."

"Thanks. Hopefully, your dad will feel the same."

"God, you really are old-fashioned. And my parents love you. When are you planning to pop the question?"

"Just before Christmas. I don't want to do it Christmas morning. And if I do it before the holiday, she won't expect it."

"You've got it all figured out."

Rory shrugged. "Everything has pretty much fallen into place since Oaklee and I decided to make this into a relationship. Before it was just—"

He stopped talking, and his ruddy cheeks turned even more red. "Uh…"

"Hooking up," Cam said mildly. "Excuse me while I try to erase that picture from my mind."

"Yeah, well, you should try it sometime. Your single status is kind of legendary."

Cam got up from his chair. "I'm going to make another coffee. There's decaf if you don't want to be wired. Mom says that caffeine gives her hot flashes." He grinned. "So does red wine, but she hasn't stopped drinking that."

They went inside, and Cam made more coffee. The house was empty, and he thought about how much cozier it was than his condo. Living alone was good in some ways but lonely in others. Just seeing a dirty plate and knife in the sink from his dad's morning toast was kind of nice.

As the coffee brewed, Rory unfortunately picked up where he'd left off. Cam's single status.

"So you're not dating anyone?"

"Not at the moment." He went to the fridge to get milk, wondering what Rory would say if Cam admitted he was thinking about "hooking up" with Hannah. He wasn't sure Rory would be as magnanimous about it as Cam had been about Oaklee.

"Dude," Rory said, in a tone that made Cam chuckle. "Back in the day we…well, you know. Neither of us had a shortage of dates. But these days we never hear of you dating anyone. Are you okay?"

God, he'd missed Rory. There was nothing but utter concern in Rory's last question, and it was a balm to realize that despite the years and miles between them, their childhood bond was still strong.

"I'm just really private," he assured Rory. "And to be honest, I don't know if I want to try to have a serious relationship when I could move around at any time, you know? And even when I'm in one place, there's so much season travel. It's a lot to ask of a partner."

It wasn't like he hadn't tried it once. He had. With a sweet girl named Alyssa. It was the one and only time he'd truly been in love. But after a few months of new-relationship bliss, a strange vibe had developed in their relationship. Alyssa hated when he was gone on the road with the team all the time, and she got really sideways over girls hanging around the locker room. Cam, for all his flirting, was not the kind of man to mess around with random women, and certainly not when he really cared about someone else.

That had been when he was in Boston. When he got traded to Denver, that was it. Alyssa had broken it off. She'd been finishing school, and they'd both known that trying to keep something going long distance was asking for trouble. If she didn't like him doing away games, how would she handle him living in an entirely different state? The jealousy and arguments had ended up killing their relationship more than any mid-season trade.

"Maybe you just haven't met the right one yet."

"Maybe," he answered.

They took their coffee into the living room and moved on to other subjects, but Cam couldn't get the kiss with Hannah off his mind. He couldn't offer anything long term, and she wasn't into hookups. And that left them exactly nowhere. Whatever attraction they had for each other was going to go unexplored. And that, he realized, was a crying shame.

—— ℓℓℓ ——

Hannah tugged her white knitted hat over her hair and gave a last look in her hall mirror. Two inches of snow had fallen this morning, which made it absolutely perfect for the tree lighting tonight. But it also meant bundling up in hat and mittens for the occasion. With one last adjustment of her jacket, she tucked her phone in her jeans pocket and headed out the door to make the walk to the Green and the huge tree set up near the Kissing Bridge.

It was already dark, and Hannah let out a happy sigh, taking in the lights decorating each house and yard. Inflatable snowmen and Santas waved happily in the breeze, and eaves and shrubs were decorated with glowing bulbs of various colors. There was foot traffic, too, as the lighting was guaranteed to bring out a good crowd. Indeed, by the time she made it to the park, all the nearby parking spots were occupied, and a throng had gathered.

A church group had set up a hot chocolate and cookie station, raising money for their Christmas adopt-a-family. The high school choir was also lining up in rows to lead the caroling. Hannah stood back for a moment and simply watched, her heart full. Darling was home, and while it had its faults, right now, it was the perfect place to be.

She spied her family at a distance. They were to the left of the tree, gathered in a group, with her mom and dad at the center. Ethan and Willow were there with the two boys running around everyone, and Brenna was bundled under blankets in a stroller. Aiden and Lauren were also there with a nearly identical stroller holding a sleeping Maggie, and the twins, Claire and Cait, were handing out cookies. Hannah stayed on the outside, ever conscious that she was the oldest and single. Loved but sometimes not quite fitting in.

And no one to blame for it but herself. She was the one letting her feelings hold her back, and she knew it.

As she watched, Rory and Oaklee joined the Gallagher clan. Her throat tightened as she realized everyone looked so content. Meanwhile, she was lonely. Not that she ever showed it or would ever say such a thing. Not Hannah Gallagher, the General, the power-through woman who made mountains move.

"You're not with the others. How come?"

Cam's smooth baritone voice sent shivers up her spine, and she turned to face him. "Oh. Well, I just got here."

He seemed to accept her answer and smiled. "This is just like I remember it. It's comforting that some things don't change, isn't it?"

Was it? She loved this place and this moment, but would she be doing this every December for the rest of her life? She might like to have a change at some point. Some...adventure. A challenge or two.

"The snow makes everything perfect," she said instead. "When they turn on the lights, it's going to be gorgeous."

"Do you want to join the others?"

She shrugged. "I don't know. Who are you hanging with?"

"Right now, you. Mom and Dad decided to stay home. Mom's got a cold, and Dad's fussing. It's kind of cute."

"I'm sure my family wouldn't mind you joining in. If you want to."

His gaze plumbed hers. "Sure, why not?"

They made their way over to the Gallaghers and were separated by conversation and excited children bobbing about. Oaklee got Cam a hot chocolate; Hannah took a turn holding Brenna and adoring her sweet little face. She loved being an auntie. After Ethan's first wife died, she'd pitched in to help with childcare while Ethan went back to work. Now, she couldn't wait for the baby girls to get big enough so she could take them on outings and spoil them rotten.

Shopping trips and girly nights with Fun Auntie Hannah were going to be a thing.

When Brenna started fussing, she gave the baby back to Willow and stood back, waiting for the tree to be lit. As the mayor grabbed a microphone to make a brief speech, it seemed as though the family units all clustered together. Even the twins stayed beside each other, leaving Hannah and Cam on the fringes. His arm came around her, holding a steaming cup of chocolate. "You didn't get any," he murmured.

"Thanks." She tried not to be affected by the observation and the remedy. It was considerate of him, and she was glad to have him at her shoulder. The eyes of the town were on him, she could tell. And why not? He was their hometown boy, their very own celebrity, attending a long-standing Christmas tradition.

"Seen with me twice," she whispered. "That's how rumors start."

"Meh. They start anyway. At least this way, I have someone to stand with. Everyone else in my life is paired up. It's weird."

She snorted. "Tell me about it."

"Is it still a rumor if it's true?"

"Nice try, Collier. Still not going to *dinner* with you."

He tried not to laugh and started coughing instead, earning him some curious looks. But then the choir started the first carol, and the crowd started to sing along with "Jingle Bells".

One carol followed another. Hannah sang along softly; she had a decent voice and adored holiday music. To her surprise, Cam's deeper voice joined in a few times, too, and she felt an unexpected kinship to him. His body was just behind hers, close enough she could sense the size and warmth of him, close enough she wanted to lean back and discover what it would be like to rest in his embrace. Instead, she stayed still, listening to his slightly off-key singing.

She did not want to like him. She didn't want him to be nice. That was what was going to get her into trouble, wasn't it?

When the caroling was over, and her hot chocolate long gone, he put his hand on the small of her back. "Do you want company on the walk home?"

"As long as you understand it's just a walk home."

His eyes glittered, and that silly smile flirted with his mouth. "Of course."

They said their goodbyes, and everyone scattered. Hannah was sure people noticed them walking off together, but it would never be possible to go anywhere with Cam and be invisible. It was a simple walk home in the snow. Nothing more.

They didn't say anything during the walk, not until they were climbing the hill on her street.

"How's the head?" she asked.

He sighed. "Okay. I had an appointment yesterday in Boston. Every time a symptom returns, I have to set the clock back. But right now, I've been symptom free for five days. I can start light exercise. Go me."

She laughed. "What do you consider light exercise?"

"Well, I'm going to start with my morning run again and hope for the best. I've been going squirrely."

"If you want company, let me know. I run most mornings."

She didn't know what had possessed her to invite herself, but it was out there now. Besides, there was something alluring about the idea of running alongside Cam. She was a physical person but didn't often have a partner to share that with. There was Willow, but she was into yoga rather than triathlons.

Their steps slowed a little. "I might do that," he said. "It's nice having a workout buddy."

They reached her house and paused on the sidewalk. "Thank you for the walk home, Cam."

Their eyes met, and that delicious feeling wound its way through her body again. "Don't," she whispered. "Not in the middle of my street."

"Don't worry," he responded, his voice low and sultry. "After the other day, I know better than to kiss you in public. The tree won't be the only thing lit up."

Her lips twitched despite her struggle to remain firm. "I'm not inviting you in."

"Okay."

She stared at him for a minute, until he shrugged. "Han, when a woman says she's not interested, that's it. I don't push."

Her mouth dropped open at his honesty, and she appreciated him so much more. They both knew it wasn't because she wasn't interested. But she'd set boundaries, and he was honoring them. Damned if that wasn't sexy.

"I don't need to," he added with that silly smile curving his lips. The moment turned light again as she rolled her eyes and let out a skeptical breath.

"Bunnies lined up around the rink, huh?"

"Sure." He winked at her. But then his gaze turned dark and serious again. "But you know they're not there for me."

She frowned, her brows knitting together. "What do you mean?"

"They're there for who they think I am. They're there for the guy they see at center ice and on the sports interviews and the replays on the TV. I know that. Which is why I don't go home with bunnies."

Hannah was impressed, by both his actions and his insight. She'd never thought of it before, but that kind of life sounded rather lonely.

She was tempted to ask him in anyway, for a drink or something, but she wasn't sure if he was allowed alcohol right now. She was also a little afraid he'd misinterpret her intentions, so she kept the thought to herself.

"You're surprised," he said, shoving his hands in his pockets.

"Yes and no. You ate that stuff up when you were a kid, at least if Rory is to be believed. But what teenage boy wouldn't? You've outgrown that kind of thing, I think."

"Thank you," he replied quietly. "I've tried."

Silence fell again, and the snow started up, too, so that big, fat flakes floated down around them.

"Listen," she whispered, closing her eyes and tilting her head to the sky. "You can hear the snow fall."

The delicate shush of the flakes filled the air around them. Hannah opened her eyes and saw that he'd closed his eyes and was listening, too, and her heart did this strange little flip, seeing his long lashes resting on the hollows beneath his eyes, and how the flakes settled on his hair.

Uh oh.

He opened his eyes and caught her staring at him. "Hannah. Let me walk you to your door. Because I'm going to kiss you goodnight, but not here in the middle of the sidewalk."

Now her pulse was really thumping, and her stomach was doing somersaults. She felt about fifteen, when she'd had a crush on Ben Fraser, and he'd reached over on the school bus and held her hand.

She led the way up the walk to her front door, inserted the key with a surprisingly steady hand, and went inside. He followed and shut the door behind him. Yet he stayed there, with his back to the door, not venturing farther.

"If you don't want me to kiss you, say so," he murmured, his soft voice riding along her nerve endings.

She wanted a lot more than a kiss but was afraid to admit it, afraid to take that step. She swallowed, trying to sort out what to say, when he took a step forward, cupped her face in his hands, and planted the sweetest ever kiss on her surprised lips.

It wasn't like the other day in her office. He only lingered a few seconds and then was gone again, leaving her lips tingling and wondering what had just happened. It was simple and rather chaste and utterly wonderful.

"Goodnight, Hannah Banana," he whispered, and before she could say another word, he was out the door and leaving footprints on the snow gathering on her walk.

Chapter 5

HANNAH DIDN'T KNOW WHAT to make of that kiss. She laced up her sneakers and pulled on her hat before heading out the door. Maybe a good run would clear her thoughts.

The temperature hovered at about twenty-five degrees, not too cold, and she started down the hill at a warm-up pace. Twice now, Cam had kissed her. He hadn't pushed either time, hadn't asked for more than she could give. She appreciated that. The problem was, she wanted more. It surprised her to realize it, but it had been over three years since she'd even contemplated a relationship. Liam hadn't wanted to stay with someone who had to "control everything." Hannah knew she was a lot. She was a strong personality and had always been a high achiever. But she was tired of apologizing for it. More than that, she'd often wondered if Liam's remarks had been designed to cut her where she was most vulnerable, because he didn't want to be with a woman stronger than he was.

Maybe that was unfair. Maybe not. But Cam's comment about fans hanging around for the person they thought he was had struck a chord. People had this idea of who Hannah Gallagher was, but they'd be surprised to know she had insecurities and weaknesses same as everyone else. Feelings. Needs and wants.

She went down Main and diverted from her usual route to head toward the suburbs on the north side of town, where the Colliers lived. She wasn't up this way often, but it was a pretty area of town, and older than the newer subdivisions. Tidy houses and neat yards were punctuated with mature trees. Most of her clients were after new builds, but she loved showing these older properties. They weren't as flashy, but they held a permanence and history that the other new houses didn't.

She went through the intersection where the entrance to the neighborhood met the main road and started down the other side. It would curve around town and come back along Fisher Creek, where she could either head back home or cross the bridge to the golf course. She'd only gone maybe forty yards when a voice called out behind her. "Hey, Han! Han, wait up!"

She kept her feet moving as she turned around and saw Cam coming toward her, dressed in sneakers, sweats, a hat with his team's logo on it, and a fleece jacket. He looked so good, and not like he should be on anyone's injured list. He caught up with her easily, and she didn't make a fuss. She just started running again, and he kept pace.

"Fancy meeting you here," she said dryly, and Cam laughed.

"I told you I was going to start running. Is this your normal route?"

She could lie and say yes. Instead, she said, "No, but I felt like something different to clear my mind this morning."

"Oh." A few seconds passed with nothing but the sound of their feet hitting the concrete sidewalk. Then he added, "What do you need to clear it of?"

Hannah glanced up at him and decided that being honest and blunt had served her fairly well throughout her life, so there was no reason to be different now. "You, actually."

"I'm glad to hear it. I couldn't stop thinking of you last night, either."

Well, damn.

They ran in peace for a while longer, to the main part of town and toward the bridge. Their breath came easily, the respiration of two people in good shape who enjoyed the exercise.

Hannah spoke next, as if the conversation had never broken off. "The thing is, I'm not quite sure why you've kissed me. Twice."

"Um, it's kind of obvious, Hannah. Didn't I tell you you're hot? I kissed you because I wanted to. I'm assuming you kissed me back because you wanted to, too."

He wasn't making this any easier.

"I mean, what do you plan to get out of this? Where do you see this going?"

He was prevented from answering for a few moments as someone in a car honked, and he lifted a hand in a wave. They crossed the bridge and turned right, heading toward the golf course.

"So," he started, speaking between breaths. "You want to know what my intentions are. Why start something when I'm only here for a few weeks."

"Well, yes."

"I haven't really thought about it. But you're different from me, so you're looking at all the angles. Wondering how the pieces fit together."

She didn't answer. He was a hundred percent right.

"Look, Hannah, I head back to Denver after the holidays. My career is there. Maybe I'll stay there, maybe I'll get traded. I really don't know what the future holds. That's why I don't do relationships. During the season, I'm in one city after another. If we make the playoffs, I don't finish until June, and I'm back on the ice in September."

"So you keep things casual."

"If that. I mean, I try to keep it so I'm a player on the ice, and only on the ice, know what I mean?"

And she respected him for it. "So this is just..."

"Two kisses. It's two kisses with a girl I knew a long time ago, who, to be honest, turns me on. But if you're wondering if I'm looking for a life partner in all of this, I'm not."

There was a finality to his voice that was unmistakeable. She wondered where that came from, and if the intensely private Cam Collier was hiding a broken heart somewhere.

"And if you don't want me to kiss you anymore, we should probably stop running into each other. Because I like kissing you. A lot."

How she was still running and keeping her breath even was a mystery.

"It hasn't exactly been a hardship," she admitted. "Even if you won't speak at the benefit."

"Ouch. Nice dig, though, to deflect from your feelings about it."

"Hey, I didn't come here for a callout."

He laughed. They'd gone around the golf course and were heading back toward town. Normally, Hannah went over the Kissing Bridge and then along the Green, but she was wondering if that was a good idea today. They would not stop, that's for sure. The legend of the Kissing Bridge—that those who kissed on it would love forever—was just that, a legend. But she wasn't going to tempt fate in any way.

"I'm not looking for anything big, either," she admitted, though that wasn't exactly true. She'd admit to herself and no one else that she was lonely. That she sometimes longed for someone to share the evenings with, the breakfast table... maybe even babies. Just thinking about it made her heart hurt a little. But not Cam. Clearly, he was not a candidate for *that*.

They crossed the bridge and went down the Green, then worked their way back to where Hannah would normally climb the hill on her street and go home to get ready for work.

As they neared the stop sign, Cam kept pace with her and said, "Thanks for the run. It felt good to get out. And for clearing the air."

She looked over, and he was grinning that foolish grin again. Half the time she wanted to wipe it off his face, and the other half she wanted to burst out laughing. He was incorrigible.

"So long as we're clear," she replied, turning the corner and leaving him behind.

He said nothing, just kept on the road heading toward his parents' house. She halted and turned, watching him jog away. His butt was so very firm, his legs strong, and he'd hardly broken a sweat during their run. She'd be a bald-faced liar if she said his physicality wasn't a huge turn on. But it was more than that. It was his easygoing manner. The only time he'd been difficult was when she'd broached the idea of him reading for the benefit, but other than that, he was as chill as anyone she'd ever met.

She wondered how he'd accomplished that, since it was in such contrast to his ambition and drive. Cait and Claire were always saying that Hannah had no chill.

Her breath evened out as she walked up the hill to her house and decided that Cam's temperament was going to be one of life's mysteries she would probably never solve. And that was okay. He'd be gone after New Year's anyway.

―ελε

Cam took a deep breath and prepared himself for a Friday evening at the rink. Connor was playing tonight, and the Gallaghers were big on showing up to cheer him on. Rory and Oaklee were going, and Cam couldn't say no to a kid who was super excited to be playing hockey. So he parked the SUV and made his way inside, looking for the Gallagher cheering section. They weren't hard to find. All he had to do was look for the red hair. The twins were more strawberry blond, Ethan and Aiden kept theirs cropped short, and the strands were more rusty than red. Rory had the lone dark head, like his mother, and Hannah's was a glorious mane of bright auburn, trailing over her shoulders.

Damn. They'd run together a few times this week, but her hair had always been up under her hat. He loved it down. Wanted to sink his hands into it.

Wanted to do a lot of things, actually.

All week, their interactions had been frustratingly platonic. A few runs around town. One stop at her office to give her the sponsorship money for the benefit. Crossing paths at the Ladybug Garden center, when he went to buy a huge poinsettia for his mom and Hannah was buying a wreath from one of Laurel's employees, George, who made them by hand.

He couldn't stop thinking about her. And while the runs had helped him burn off some energy, there was a lot more bundled up inside him, pounding to get out.

Oaklee waved him over, and he nodded at several people as he made his way through the stands. He was used to the stares and had expected them tonight. He'd say hello to people he hadn't seen in a while, probably sign a few autographs, and get nostalgic about how he'd been on that same ice twenty-five years earlier, with his first hockey stick.

He joined the group and smiled widely, feeling instantly at home, as he always did with the Gallaghers. He shook John's hand and gave Moira a hug. They'd served as second parents to him during his childhood. Oaklee patted the bench beside her and Rory, and he sat down, resting his elbows on his knees. Down on the ice, around thirty seven-year-olds skated, wearing helmets and gloves and carrying sticks during the game warm-up. Connor's little brother, Ronan, sat with Grampa John, while Willow had baby Brenna on her lap. Aiden had Mandy in his arms, the baby bundled in a cute sweater and hat, while Laurel sat with yarn and needles, either knitting or crocheting something—Cam wasn't sure. Apparently, the twins had gone on a coffee run, which just left Hannah as the odd person out. She sat on the bench below him, and he reached out and tweaked a hank of her hair.

"Hello, Peeta." She turned around and gave him a bright smile, though her eyes showed she was surprised he'd done such a thing.

"Peeta?" he responded, leaning forward.

"P-I-T-A," she answered. "Like the bread. Stands for pain in the—"

"Right." He smirked. "Got your attention, though."

"If you're flirting, you need to work on your skills. Or maybe you save your mighty skills for the ice."

Beside him, Oaklee snorted.

"Maybe I like pestering you."

Rory joined in. "You sure loved bugging her when we were kids. Remember the time you asked her if she kept spare tampons in her purse?" Rory was already laughing when he added, "I swear, Hannah, I've never seen you blush like that in my life."

Cam did remember. Hannah was being a stuck-up senior while he and Rory were freshmen. She'd acted as if they were pesky little ants, always in her way and doing dumb things. Which, to be fair, they were—the current anecdote was a prime example. But her holier-than-thou attitude had always inspired Cam to be particularly impish. He'd loved getting under her skin.

"You guys were gross pimple-faced brats," she countered.

"Hey." Cam shook a finger at her. "I'll have you know I had excellent skin."

Oaklee responded now. "Oh, sure, Cam. The problem with you and Rory was that you two were very pretty, and you knew it." She rolled her eyes and Hannah laughed.

The kids went off the ice, the ref came out, and then both teams lined up at center ice for the face-off. There was a brief cheer, and then Hannah turned around again, looking up at Cam.

"We reordered all our signage and were able to put a rush on everything, so thanks," she said, her voice lower than it had been a moment ago.

"Glad I could help." He frowned. "Still no luck finding an author?"

She shook her head. "It's the weekend before Christmas. People have plans. No one wants to travel then. We got our first author because her family is nearby, and it worked out that she could go home for Christmas. That kind of magic doesn't happen twice."

Except he was here. And refused to help. He did feel guilty about it, whether she realized it or not. A few times, he'd almost reconsidered but then rejected the idea.

"It's only what, two weeks away?"

"Two weeks from tomorrow, yeah."

He nodded slowly. Then Hannah stood and said, "Scooch over. Trying to talk to you this way is killing my neck."

He shifted a little closer to Oaklee and made room between himself and Ethan. She settled in beside him, bringing the scent of vanilla and something floral with her. He didn't know if it was perfume or perhaps just her hair. Whatever it was, she smelled wonderful.

"Did you get the stuff I had couriered? It should have arrived today."

She shook her head. "It might take an extra day, being the holidays and all."

"I'll double check the tracking. It should be a nice addition to your auction, Hannah."

"Thanks." Once more, the unspoken thing was there between them. He was doing well, feeling good. He was here tonight, supporting Connor. So why was he so set on not participating in a more public way? He heard the questions in her mind without her needing to put voice to them.

For the first time in forever, he wondered if he should just say it. He could trust Hannah, couldn't he? What would happen if he straight up told her why he had said no? He glanced away from the ice and ten hurtling children and took in her profile. Hannah was a good person. Yeah, he and Rory had enjoyed annoying the crap out of her as kids. But he liked her, a lot. And she wasn't some stranger. She was the kind of woman—the kind of friend— who would keep a secret.

He mulled it over while watching the game, clapping and giving a shout of encouragement as Connor's team scored. The twins had come back with coffee, and the scent of the brew filled the air around them. At the end of the first period, a handful of locals ventured over to say hello and ask for autographs. For the first time in three weeks,

Cam actually felt like himself. No lingering threat of a headache or fatigue. He hadn't had dizziness for days. Maybe this concussion wasn't as bad as everyone had thought. He had an appointment next week for another evaluation. Maybe he could even be back practicing on the ice before Christmas. He could always fly back for the holiday so he'd be with his family, as promised.

When the second period started, everyone took their seats in the stands again. Hannah had shifted to his other side and was talking to Oaklee, not about the benefit, but about the last chamber of commerce meeting and something about profit percentages and local retail traffic for the Christmas season, and how it was down slightly over last year. As he eavesdropped, he suddenly realized what it was about Hannah that intimidated him. It wasn't her looks, though she was—and always had been—stunning. It wasn't that she was older than he was. Or that she had a reputation of being a bit of a ballbuster. He could handle all those things. He liked a challenge, after all.

No, it was her brain. Hannah had always been the smartest person he knew. If she'd wanted, she could have gone on to be a CEO of a major corporation, and done it with ease. Clearly, she liked what she did, enjoyed running her own business, loved real estate. Rory said that she was involved in a few other ventures as well, as an investor.

Hannah was everything he wasn't. He struggled to read. He could do math, but even that had been a challenge as he'd had difficulty reading the questions. He'd had a tutor once he left school to play full time, and he'd been pushed through academically because he was a prodigy on ice.

But he couldn't compete with Hannah Gallagher in the brains department.

And it would be painfully obvious if he went ahead and told her his reasons for not speaking at her event.

No matter what he did, he would disappoint her.

He focused on the game, watching the kids, watching Connor in particular. He was a strong skater, fast for his age, and pretty steady. He had good ice awareness, too, but the stick looked awkward in his hands, and he struggled to control the puck. Granted, he was only seven, but Cam thought it might be fun to take him out on an outdoor pond and give him some tips. He'd mention it to Ethan and Willow later.

The other team scored, and the crowd on the other side of the ice stomped their feet and hollered. As the teams lined up for the face-off, Hannah's leg brushed against his. He looked over at her and found her watching him, the gleam in her eyes telegraphing something he hoped he was interpreting correctly.

They'd been doing this dance for well over a week. And maybe he wasn't the mental giant she was, but he could hold his own when it came to the bedroom. His physicality had always been his best asset. This was far more in his comfort zone.

He slid his hand down and grazed a finger over her jean-clad knee. She was wearing tight skinnies that were tucked into those brown boots she liked so much. She gasped slightly at the covert touch, and his lips curved in silent gratification. He grazed the outside of her thigh for long seconds, a tacit reminder this was not an accidental touch. But he didn't look at her. He didn't need to. He could feel the tension in her thigh muscles, and anticipation settled low in his pelvis.

Hannah was in fantastic shape, strong and lean. He imagined her body curled around his and let out a deep breath, pulling his hand away from her leg. If he wasn't careful, he was going to be sitting here with a hard-on for the rest of the game.

They didn't talk after that, and after the game was over, Willow invited everyone back to The Purple Pig for hot chocolate and cookies. Hannah was going, and the invitation was extended to Cam as well. He was going to offer to drive her over, but she joined Laurel and Willow, who were walking with the babies. Instead, Ethan invited him to visit the team in the locker room, and Cam readily agreed. He loved this kind of thing. One of his favourite days of the year was the open team practice on March break, when the local youth got to interact with the players.

Connor was instantly a celebrity as he introduced his Uncle Rory's friend, Cam. Cam chatted to the team, offering tons of praise and a few hints to up their game, and then he and Ethan, who was holding Ronan's hand, collected Connor and his duffel and headed out of the rink.

"You want to drive with me, buddy?" he asked Connor.

"Seriously?"

He chuckled. "Sure. Throw your hockey bag in your dad's truck, though. P-U."

Connor laughed and raced off to Ethan's truck, then he trotted back and hopped up in the seat next to Cam. "Hey, thanks for coming to the locker room. The guys were like so excited!"

"No problem, buddy. You did a good job out there. You're a good skater."

"I am?"

"Sure are. You want to do some stick work sometime? I kinda miss being on the ice."

Connor looked at him with eyes as large as saucers. "Um, duh," he replied. "My dad made us an outdoor rink this year. It's kinda small, though."

"It's big enough. I'll talk to your dad, okay?"

"Okay. Thanks, uh..."

"Just call me Cam, Connor."

Connor grinned so big that Cam could see the two teeth he had missing. Damn, he was a cute kid.

But when they got to The Purple Pig and walked inside, Connor disappeared and Cam's gaze homed in on Hannah, laughing at something Laurel was saying as the two of them carried cookies to the tables that had been pushed together to seat the entire family.

Hannah. The night wasn't over for them. If he had his way, it was just beginning.

Chapter 6

HANNAH HAD NEVER BEEN so aware of a man in her entire life.

Sitting beside Cam at the rink had been an interesting experience. First of all, it was clear as the nose on his face that the building was his home, whether he was on or off the ice. His body language had been more relaxed than she'd seen since his arrival, his smile ready and genuine. It was his comfort zone, and that casual confidence only made him more attractive to her. There was something about a confident man that turned her crank, and while Cam had always had a certain low-key arrogance about him, tonight she realized it was most powerful when he was able to simply be himself.

It was something she envied.

He'd taken the time to sign autographs, again, and then gone into the locker room with Connor's team. It was all Connor could talk about now, and Cam just smiled and laughed along as if it was no big deal. As if he were no big deal.

But to her, he was a big deal. His refusal to appear at the event was still something that puzzled her, because every other thing she was learning about Cam Collier was that he was a really nice guy with, as he put it, a smokin' hot bod, and a career so spectacular that he was one of the few men who didn't find her threatening. If anything, he'd gone on to definitely out-achieve the achiever.

Of course, they wouldn't have a relationship. But it had been months—years—since she'd been involved with a man, and for Pete's sake, it was Christmas. If he was interested, why not? He'd go back to Denver, and they'd chalk it up to that one Christmas they had a fling. Not that anyone had to know.

And if it was out of character for her, so what? She was thirty-three years old. She could do something crazy if she damned well wanted.

It was eight thirty before the cookies were gone and the mugs emptied. Ethan made noises about getting the boys home for bed, and the babies were already asleep in their mothers' arms. Hannah and Oaklee got up and cleared the mess, loading the dishes in commercial dishwasher as Emily, the café manager, finished closing procedures. When Hannah came out of the kitchen again, Cam was moving the tables to their original position and tucking the chairs in properly. Damn, he fit in so well. He always had. Rory snagged a chair, and the two of them shared a laugh. Maybe this was a mistake. Maybe a fling should be with someone with no ties to the family at all. It had so much potential to be awkward.

But someone else wouldn't be Cam. Wouldn't be tall like Cam, wouldn't have the same hair, or the full lips, or the hard, muscled thighs she'd gotten a glimpse of during their runs. No, she wanted him. And the way he'd touched her in the stands tonight told her he wanted her, too.

They all left through the front door, Emily locking behind them, and Cam appeared at her shoulder.

"I'll drive you home," he said, his voice low. It wasn't a suggestion. It was an invitation and an acceptance all in one, and her body responded to the low timbre of his voice by breaking out in goose bumps.

"I guess that would be okay," she answered easily, hoping the rest of the family didn't pick up on their edgy energy.

The interior of his SUV enclosed them in a cocoon of intimacy. He cranked up the heater as the temperature had dropped, and silence filled the space as he pulled away from the curb and headed down Main to the turnoff to her street. Had she ever been this aware of a man before? Had she ever wanted one quite this much? It had all changed tonight, with the nudge of her knee against his, meeting his gaze, and seeing acknowledgment in his eyes.

Her pelvic muscles tightened. Oh, this was going to be so good.

It took maybe two minutes to get from the café to her house. She looked up at it, gleaming in the December darkness. She'd turned on the lights before leaving tonight, and the eaves, front railing, and shrubs twinkled with clear lights. The railing lights illuminated the wreath on the front door, and a warmth filled her heart at the sight. She loved this little house. It wasn't as big and fancy as some, which had surprised her family. Instead, it was cozy and welcoming. Of course, she'd gutted a lot of the interior and made it her own. Maybe she was going through this world solo instead of half of a pair, but this was *home*.

And Cam was going to be inside it. She'd never brought a man here before, and she tried not to read too much into that fact.

He unclipped his seatbelt, the click unusually loud in the darkness. Her breath caught in her chest as he got out and went around the hood to open her door.

She stepped out and looked up at him. For a moment, she wondered if he was going to press her against the door with his hard, strong body and kiss her. The hungry look in his eyes certainly telegraphed that he wanted to. But instead, he held out his hand, and she took it, hoping he couldn't tell how much she was shaking. This wasn't like her. She was the kind of woman who doled out great advice but rarely took it herself. Who teased her friends about getting laid but went home alone. Who advised those she loved to relax, but scheduled her own life to the hour.

Nothing about this thing with Cam was scheduled. Not even a little bit.

He waited while she unlocked the door, and they stepped inside.

She'd turned the outside lights on but not inside. The house was dark, lit only slightly by the tangential glow from the mini-bulbs on the porch and in the evergreens. She took off her coat. He took off his, too, and hung them both on the carved hooks in the foyer. She unzipped her boots and toed them off; he removed his shoes and left them on the mat. Neither of them had said a single word since leaving The Purple Pig. And before she could think of what she could possibly say now, his arms came around her, his hands gripped her butt, and he lifted her up until her legs instinctively wrapped around him.

Then he kissed her.

It wasn't wild and uncontrolled. It was a full-on, deliberate meltdown of her senses as his mouth possessed hers. He took four strong steps, and she found her back pressed against the support wall between the kitchen and hall. Cam pinned her there with his body, and she held on, gasping as his mouth slid away from hers and instead raced down her neck. If she could have tilted her head back, she would have, but it was pressed against the unrelenting wall as he slid his tongue into the hollow of her throat, sending shivers of delight rippling through her body.

"Cam," she finally said, the sound strangled with desire.

He still didn't say anything, and for some reason, she found it incredibly arousing. Instead, he tilted his hips, keeping her in place while his fingers got busy with the buttons on her shirt.

The soft brushed cotton slipped open, and he reached behind her and flicked open the clasp of her bra. Her breasts weren't overly large. On a generous day, she'd call them a C cup, but the sound of approval from Cam's throat made her feel as if they were the most amazing things in the world. She was a tangle of shirt and bra, with a bra cup riding up toward her neck, but she didn't give a damn as he fastened his mouth on one very ready nipple.

She cried out, and her hips jerked against him. He was in total control, and she was rapidly becoming a boneless, desperate mush. "Too many clothes." Her voice was strident in the silence. "Let me down, Cam."

He didn't acquiesce for a few moments as he feasted on the other breast, his hot mouth undoing her bit by bit. But she pressed against him again, and he braced his hands on her bottom and let her body slide down the wall.

Once she was free, she found the strength to meet him equally. She pulled off her shirt and bra and left them on the floor, then reached for his sweater and pulled it over his head so that his torso was delightfully naked. Oh, glory. Muscles curved and dipped everywhere, shoulders and arms and pecs and a delicious six pack before everything dipped low into the waistband of his jeans. His eyes were dark fire as he met her gaze and then reached for the button of her jeans. She reached for his at the same time, and somehow they stumbled out of them in the hallway, until she was only wearing bikini panties and he was in boxer briefs that hugged his ass and thighs like a dream. It hugged something else, too, and once again her muscles tightened in anticipation.

He reached for his jeans, pulled something out of the pocket, and then reached for her. They were in the hallway now, and she knew she should lead him to her bedroom, but he caught her in his arms and managed to slide his hand inside her panties. She cried out again, overwhelmed by the sensations racing through her, but not so overwhelmed she couldn't meet him halfway. Her hand molded to the ridge in his briefs, and he groaned as he kissed her, the sound vibrating from her mouth throughout her whole body.

She pushed down his briefs and took him in her hand, her grip firm and purposeful. In response, he got her panties down to her knees, and for a few frantic moments, they pleasured each other with their hands.

"Cam...I can't stand up any longer. You've got to take me to bed, Cam."

He pushed her panties the rest of the way down, and his underwear, too, and once against picked her up so she was straddling him. "Which door?"

"The last one on the left."

He was walking, and she was sucking on his neck, and within two seconds, he was in her bedroom and kicking the door shut with his foot. Then, instead of putting her down, he pinned her against the door. "Hang on," he ordered, and she tightened her legs around him. She heard a tear and felt his hands move, then realized he'd put on a condom.

She wished he'd hurry.

They never made it to the bed. He adjusted her, then slid inside her, right against the door to her bedroom. It was elemental, beautifully physical, and she gave herself over to the sensation of him filling her again...and again...and again. At one point, he reached down between them, and she called out with pleasure as spasms rocked her body. Moments later, he thrust so hard she wondered if they'd break the door.

And then he stilled, his breaths coming fast, her body limp, her brain empty.

Only then did he carry her to the bed and let her down gently on the comforter before collapsing beside her.

Cam needed a minute to catch his breath and feel his body again.

He hadn't expected her to be so primal, so responsive to his every touch. Maybe he should have anticipated her response. After all, Hannah never did anything halfway. And he hadn't been wrong. Her body was a pure delight, all small curves and tight muscle and breasts that were the perfect size, round and firm and yet soft, too.

They'd driven him crazy from the moment he'd unsnapped her bra.

For God's sake, they'd left a trail of clothing from her foyer to the bedroom. He'd expected there to be some urgency. He hadn't expected it would be incendiary.

"Hey, Han? Bathroom?"

A low chuckle sounded beside him. "First door is the closet. Second is the en suite."

He got up from the bed and went to take care of the condom. When he returned, she was still sprawled on the bed, naked as the day she was born, and holy hell, she was beautiful. His eyes had adjusted to the dark, and he could see her burnished hair spread out on her pillow, the hollows of her hips, the tips of her breasts. He'd brought one condom. One. It was the only regret he had of the evening.

And now he was standing naked at the foot of her bed.

She started to laugh, a soft chuckle that made him smile in response. "What?"

"You look good naked."

"So do you, Hannah Banana."

She raised up on her elbows. "Come here," she said, "and catch your breath."

He went back to the bed and lay down beside her, turned onto his side so he was facing her profile. How could it be that he wanted her again so soon? Why had he thought one condom would be enough?

Hannah was demanding. He should have known better.

"Sorry it was so rushed," he said, bracing his elbow and resting his head on his hand. It hadn't even been fifteen minutes since he'd parked at the curb.

"It was perfect." She sighed, leaning her head back. She was still braced on her elbows, so the movement made her breasts jut forward.

He couldn't dispute it. He hadn't been with a woman for a long time, but this…this was one for the books.

Maybe because for the first time, he hadn't been with someone who saw him as Cam the Superstar. He was Cam, the pain-in-the-ass friend of her little brother. And if he'd rocked her world, she'd destroyed his—in the best possible way.

"Do you have to go right away?" she asked, finally dropping down from her elbows and shifting to her side beside him.

He laughed. "I'm a big boy. I don't have a curfew."

"Except people will see your SUV. And you're staying with your parents."

"Well, well. You're worried about what people will think."

She met his gaze in the dim light. Somewhere down the street, there was a dusk-to-dawn lamp, and it gave enough light to show her features in black and white. He reached out and grazed her hip with his fingers, then the hollow of her waist.

"Actually," she said, "I don't care. People can mind their own business. Or talk. I just keep doing my thing."

"Which is something I've always liked about you."

"Thanks."

They were quiet for a few moments. Then Cam felt the need to come clean about what he figured were expectations.

"I've been symptom free for several days now. I'm going to see if I can practice with the team after my next follow-up appointment."

"You must be happy about that."

"I am. But even if I practice, I don't think I'll be in the lineup until after New Year's. I still plan to spend Christmas with my family." He took a breath and held it for a moment. "And with you." There was a hesitant moment after he said the words, where he nearly added, "if that's okay."

She touched his hand where it rested on her hip. "Listen, we both know what this is and isn't. Your life is there. Mine is here. Right now, we're insanely attracted to each other. That's all this is, Cam. You don't have to worry about me getting over attached."

He should feel relief, but instead, unease settled through him. Was he really so forgettable?

Then he gave himself a mental shake. That wasn't what she was saying at all. She was just being realistic about their situation, saving him from having to say it, that was all.

She reached out and touched him, soft, fluttery touches that he revelled in. "You feel so good," she whispered. "You have a six pack. I can feel the ridges with my fingertips. Is it wrong that your body turns me on so much?"

"If it is, I'm equally guilty," he confessed. His hand slid from her hip to the soft spot on her inner thigh. "Hannah, I only brought one condom."

"Well, shit."

He laughed out loud then. He liked her so damned much. She was smart, funny, hot. There actually wasn't anything about Hannah he didn't like.

"Don't worry," he murmured, sliding closer, slipping his hand between her thighs. "I have a few ideas."

"More than one way to score, Collier?"

"Mmm." He leaned forward and nuzzled at her breasts.

Her hands slid into his hair. "It doesn't always take a slap shot, right? I mean, you could come up on the wing and catch a rebound—"

"We could swap hockey jokes all night," he replied, kissing his way toward her navel as her breath released on a hiss. "But my mouth is gonna be a little bit busy."

And it was.

Chapter 7

HE ENDED UP STAYING the night.

Hannah woke at seven, a full hour later than normal, and stretched, her muscles flexing and releasing beneath the soft sheets. Cam was beside her, his hair flat on one side, and his long lashes resting on the crests of his cheeks. At some point, he'd gone to the hallway and retrieved his shorts. Hannah had been too lazy. She was still completely naked.

Cam Collier. Go figure.

Her cheeks heated as she remembered last night. Maybe they'd only had one condom, but they'd been inventive. A few times, actually. Hannah was used to being in control, but she'd been in total surrender mode with Cam. Surrender not only to him, but to her desires, surprising not only him, but herself as well. The word wanton came to mind. And Cam... He'd been amazing. Everything.

She let out a slow, quiet breath. Okay, so they were sexually compatible. That's all this was. Letting loose, blowing off steam, enjoying each other.

Except she looked at his slumbering face and felt a tenderness wash over her.

It was just because she'd known him so long. He was her little brother's best friend, after all. Heck, she could still remember when Cam's voice had started to change.

She slipped out of bed and went to the bathroom, turning on the shower before grabbing a fresh towel from the shelf. She made it quick, then bundled her hair in the towel and grabbed a second to wrap around her body. Her clothes were all in the bedroom, so taking a deep breath, she stepped outside the steamy bathroom and into the cooler air of her room.

Cam was sitting up in bed, his eyes closed, tension lines around his eyes and his lips.

She hurried to the edge of the bed and perched on the mattress. "What is it?" she asked.

"Headache," he murmured. He opened his eyes and she saw pain there. "Shit."

She kept her voice low as her heart sank. He'd been feeling so good. "Do you feel sick to your stomach?"

"A little woozy, yeah."

"What can you take for pain?"

"What have you got?"

"Acetaminophen and naproxen."

"Naproxen. Acetaminophen doesn't do jack."

She grabbed her robe from the back of the door and wrapped it around herself, dropping the towel. Then she went to the kitchen for the medication, water, and an ice pack. When she returned, she watched as he took the pills and then put the ice pack on the back of his neck. "Here. Keep this here for a few minutes and see if it helps." As he held it, she went to the bathroom and got a ginger tablet. "Take this, too," she said, handing it over. "It'll help settle your stomach." She sat on the edge of the bed again. "Any double vision, blurred vision, that kind of thing?"

He shook his head a little. "No. Just the sick headache."

"I'm sorry, Cam. I know this means you have to restart the clock on being symptom free."

He nodded.

A smile flirted with the corners of her mouth. "I guess we overdid it last night."

He took the ice pack from the back of his neck and looked at her. "Totally worth it," he answered, and her insides curled with both memory and anticipation.

It was Saturday, so Hannah didn't have to go into the office. Truthfully, she had been planning to work on the silent-auction items today, as well as firm up other details with participating businesses. She and Oaklee were meeting later to discuss dinner-ticket sales, which had slowed since the announcement of the loss of their headliner.

But right now, there was nowhere she needed to be.

"Lie down and close your eyes while the meds kick in. I'll go make some breakfast."

"I should probably go. My car—"

"Your car's been out front all night. Another few hours won't matter, and honestly...who cares?" Darling was small. People were going to talk anyway. Hannah tried not to listen to it. Or at the very least, not repeat it. "I'm thirty-three, Cam. I'm a big girl who can live her own life."

He chuckled. "Lucky you."

Her smiled slid off her face. "Oh wait. I never thought that maybe you would like to keep this off the radar. I know you like to keep your private life private."

Cam shrugged and met her gaze. "I don't care about the public, to be honest. Not right now. It's more... I don't want to get sucker punched by Rory for hooking up with his sister. Or, you know, look your mom in the eye and see...you know."

Aw, that was sweet. He didn't want to disappoint her family. She liked that about him. In fact, she was discovering there wasn't a whole lot she didn't like.

"Then it's up to you. If you need me to, I can drive your rental to your folks' place if you think you shouldn't be driving. Or you're welcome to stay. I'm not about to kick you out after a night of debauchery." She wiggled her eyebrows, and he laughed again.

"I'll stay for a while. You mentioned food. It's always a good incentive."

"Now I see you were only after my cooking."

He reached out and slid his hand up the outside of her thigh, underneath the robe. "Not just your cooking. But I'm not sure another round would be good for my head."

She bit down on her lip and got up from the edge of the bed. "Right. Then breakfast it is."

Hannah hurried to the kitchen and once there, tightened the belt on her robe.

She'd make him eggs and avocado toast, and then by that time, she might have figured out where she wanted this to go next.

Cam knew he should put on his clothes and head home. Or go hang out somewhere. Be anywhere but playing house with Hannah Gallagher, but he was sitting in her sunny kitchen for two reasons. One, she'd just fed him an amazing breakfast and poured him a second cup of coffee. And two, his head was still in a fragile state. The pain was mostly gone, thanks to medicine and an extra thirty minutes of quiet in bed while she cooked. But now he had a headache hangover, like it could rebound at any moment.

He was going to take his time. Besides, being with Hannah wasn't exactly a hardship. Her house was lovely, cozy, and welcoming, with splashes of panache that were very her. The sofa he was sitting on was plush and comfortable, but both the throw rug in the middle of the floor and the art above the fireplace mantle were abstract, with splashes of rusty orange in with tan and sage green. The rust color reminded him of her hair, and he sat back and sipped the rich coffee while remembering how her hair had grazed his thighs last night...

The thought was erased from his brain as she entered the room carrying her laptop and a binder in her hands and with glasses perched on her nose. Damned if she didn't look adorable and fiercely smart all wrapped up in one package.

"Whatcha got there?" he asked, angling himself a little and tucking one leg beneath him.

"Stuff about the benefit. I'm going to inventory our silent-auction items today, and later, Oaklee is going to come over, and we're going to go over our ticket sales for the dinner." She frowned. "Last year at this time, we were within ten seats of being sold out."

"And this year you're not?"

She shook her head. "And the price hasn't gone up. The golf club is doing it for the same as last year. The only thing I can think of is that we've cancelled our speaker and are just doing the auction."

"Maybe what you need is something to really bring them in to bid."

She reached into her binder for a sheaf of papers and handed them over. "Well, if you have any suggestions...this is what we have."

He took the papers and scanned them. If he slowed down and really focused, he would be able to make sense of them. A few words he recognized stood out, like the Foxborough Inn, and something yoga. "See?" she asked. "We've got some great things lined up already."

"I, uh, see," he agreed.

"What do you think of this one?" She leaned over and pointed to an item. Any other time, Cam would be able to suss it out by taking his time, but right now, he was flustered and couldn't focus. "Um, Han, things are a little blurred," he lied. Something heavy settled in the pit of his stomach. He was using his freaking injury to cover his disability. What a coward he was. Why couldn't he just tell her?

Because last night, she'd looked at him like he was a freaking god, and he wasn't sure he could bear falling from that pedestal. Everyone seemed to think he was this invincible wonder kid. Instead, he was a fraud. And now, Hannah was looking at him with worry wrinkling her brow and clouding her eyes.

"You didn't say that earlier. Do you need to call a doctor or something?"

He felt even more of a heel for making her worry. "No, I'm sure it's fine. I just need to take it easy. It's just the fine print stuff kind of blurring together, that's all."

Hannah took the sheets back. "Let me drive you home, though. You shouldn't be behind the wheel if your vision is compromised." She leaned forward and peered into his eyes. "And if things get worse, you should call your doctor."

They wouldn't get worse. His vision was fine, and his headache was nearly gone. But he couldn't tell her that. He'd let her think he was sick before admitting a weakness, wouldn't he?

Coward. You could make this thing a success for her if you'd just own up.

Instead, he put his hand on her knee. "What you need isn't something that everyone can bid on, but a draw that only attendees can enter." He grinned. "Like two tickets to a Stanley Cup final game, along with travel and hotel for two nights."

She stared at him.

He shrugged. "I can make that happen. Oaklee can promote the hell out of it on social media and radio."

Her eyes filled with tears. "You'd do that?"

"It's only money, Hannah. What else am I going to do with it?"

It was the right thing to offer. Hannah ran with the idea and within an hour had sent it to Oaklee so she could start designing a graphic.

He was happy to help. He really was. But there was a part of him, inside, that wished he could put that happy expression on her face without having to buy its way there.

Chapter 8

HANNAH GOT BUSIER AS the day of the benefit drew closer. Two house sales closed, and she saw her clients through getting their keys and stepping foot in their new homes. Showings dropped off a bit in the lead up to the holiday, as most people were in Christmas mode and rushing around to do their shopping and decorating. But Hannah hadn't yet put up her tree, nor had she wrapped the presents she'd bought for family. And the day-long event was taking a significant amount of her time. Christmas was a busy time for Oaklee, too, as the town held several events and promotions, and as social media manager, Oaklee was scheduled to the hilt. Hannah didn't feel she could add anything more to Oaklee's plate.

But she still made time for her morning run, though the last few days she'd been running solo. Right now, she was back to her original route, her feet slapping the sidewalk in a steady rhythm as her breath made puffs of air around her face. Her early runs were the one thing that always seemed to keep her sane. Whether it was the endorphins or the deep breathing or what, exercise kept Hannah from being overwhelmed.

She missed running with Cam, though. She hadn't talked to him since she'd driven him home, and she suspected he was skipping the runs due to his recurring symptoms.

She'd wanted to call him or text him, but maybe the one night was all he was after, and truthfully, she wasn't sure more was a good idea. She was in danger of liking him too much. For the first time in a long time, she felt as if she could be herself with someone. Cam had no reason to feel threatened by her "big personality," as her brother, Ethan, put it. The morning after he'd stayed the night, they'd talked a long time about why she loved real estate, why she found business so invigorating, and she'd even let him in on the secret that she was a silent partner in a few ventures around town, Willow's yoga studio included. He'd shared with her, too, about what it was like to be a professional athlete, the pressure, the competitiveness, the fame. They were a pair of overachievers who didn't have to compete with each other. It was just too bad they lived on opposite sides of the country. Maybe they might have explored this thing between them a little further. See where it led.

When she got home, there was a text on her phone from him, asking her to meet him for lunch at the Sugarbush Diner. She knew she should say no. What was the point in prolonging something that had a definite shelf life? And yet she found herself typing back yes for twelve thirty. She wanted to see him. To know how he was doing, and if he was feeling better.

Besides, the diner had the best Cobb salad in Vermont. She'd been indulging in a little too much comfort food lately. She could use fewer starchy carbs and more protein right now.

Hannah walked in at twelve twenty, a few minutes early, and to her surprise he was already in a booth, his menu closed in front of him and a large glass of ice water at his elbow. She slid into the booth and smiled. "Hey. It's good to see you."

His face lit up, and it did silly things to her insides. "You, too," he said. Then he laughed. "This place hasn't changed a bit. Neither the menu nor the Christmas decorations."

There was an artificial tree toward the back, and all sorts of garish tinsel decorating the booths and beams. Each table had a small artificial poinsettia in the middle. "It's delightfully cheesy," Hannah agreed. "And it wouldn't be Christmas at the Sugarbush without all of it."

A waitress came over and took Hannah's order for water, and then Hannah asked for the salad, and Cam ordered a club sandwich with salad instead of fries. "Trying to behave yourself?" she asked, handing over the plastic menus.

He nodded to the waitress and then shrugged in Hannah's direction. "I'm not training, and Mom is determined to make home-cooked meals every day. It's not going to be good if I get too soft while I'm home."

"You're going to miss out on the maple crème pie then," she replied, putting on a sad face. "It's something." Then she held his gaze. "How are you feeling?"

"I saw the doctor. I'm fine. Just a setback, but that morning was the exception. I've been fine since."

"So..."

"So you broke me, Hannah Banana."

There was a gleam in his eye that made her blush. "Shut up," she murmured, wishing the waitress would come back with her water.

"No, seriously. The doc said I probably overdid it. Set me back a little." He leaned forward. "But just so you know, it was totally worth it."

"Cam." Her voice was a low warning. The waitress came back with her water and a refill for Cam, along with a shy smile for the celebrity. Hannah rolled her eyes.

Cam took a sip, and so did Hannah, and then he leaned forward again. "So I bet you've spent the last few days itemizing all the reasons why us not seeing each other again is a good thing."

Busted. "Oh, you think you're so smart."

"I've known you a long time. The thing is, when we really want something, we can always come up with reasons to logically justify our behavior. So for example, I might say that we both know this is a short-term thing, so why not enjoy it?"

She swallowed against a growing lump in her throat and reached down to fiddle with her napkin. Yeah, she'd used that argument before. Including the night they'd gone back to her place.

"Or maybe that this is good because we know each other and there won't be any expectations for more than either of us can give."

"Cam—"

"Because we kind of trust each other."

"Really, keep your voice down—"

"And we *really* like being together."

She gave up. She stopped fingering the paper napkin and let out a sigh. "You overdid it, remember? A repeat is not a good idea."

"*Au contraire.*" She laughed at the expression despite herself. Cam ran his finger along the edge of his glass. "I believe what the doctor said was to pace myself."

The lump was nearly impossible to swallow around now. How could he be sitting there discussing this as casually as they might discuss the weather forecast? "Pace yourself."

"You know. Slow down. Not be in such a hurry. Take my time."

The heat from her cheeks spread throughout her body. "You're seducing me in broad daylight," she whispered, hoping no one could hear them. At least the chatter from the other patrons and the Christmas music playing on the speakers caused some auditory interference.

"Is it working?"

It so was, and she didn't want to admit it. She looked up at him and brushed her hair back off her shoulder. "What would be the point of us being together? I mean, clearly there's chemistry.

I'm not denying that. But you're heading back to Denver. I'm going to be here. And I really don't do relationships." She lifted her chin. "I'm too busy."

He studied her for a long moment. Long enough that she thought he might see through that last statement for what it was defense mechanism. She loved to work. Was there anything wrong with that? And working meant she didn't have time to think about the dearth of sex or intimacy in her life since Liam walked out.

Much, anyway.

"I don't, either. But I like being with you, Hannah. Sometimes it's good to feel, I don't know, alive. Like there's more to life than a puck on the ice and..."

He halted, sat back as the waitress brought their food. He thanked her and then picked up his fork, but he only pushed a piece of cucumber around with it.

"And what?" she asked.

He shrugged. "My body isn't going to let me do this forever. Eventually, there has to be something else. It's kind of scary, because since I was a kid, there has never *been* anything other than hockey. I have no idea what's next. And with this injury... I haven't been able to avoid thinking about it."

She thought about that. Then thought about her high school years, university, getting her Realtor's license, setting up her own business, her entrepreneurial streak.

"Cam, know what? We suck at a life/work balance."

He grinned and finally stabbed the cucumber. "That's kind of what I'm saying, Han. We've got a couple of weeks here where maybe we can be a little better at that. With each other."

"Our families will talk."

He rolled his eyes. "Whatever. We're adults, aren't we?"

"And so will the town."

"Probably. Probably about how Cam Collier is a lucky bastard. You, Ms. Gallagher, are notorious for having high standards. I'm flattered that I've made the cut."

They were actually talking about having a short-term but not-sneaking-around kind of relationship. What she really liked was how Cam seemed to see the very things she'd been criticized for by partners of the past as attributes and qualities.

"You want to go on a date, then?"

He nodded. "I do. A real date."

She got that tingly feeling again, and not because she was thinking of him kissing her or touching her, but that he was asking to spend actual time with her. Enjoying her company.

"What's your idea of a perfect date?" she asked, trying to settle her nerves. She drizzled dressing on her salad and forced herself to start eating.

"I'm a low-key kind of guy. A movie? Maybe ice cream, or a few drinks after." He grinned. "Chicken wings or nachos. A walk in the park. Something that makes you laugh."

Damn, he was good at throwing in those afterthoughts that hit her right in the feels. And she liked all those things, too. She also liked intimate dinners, the theater, and wouldn't be totally averse to a grand gesture or two. But it wasn't necessary. For all her peculiarities and perceived high standards, Hannah could be incredibly low-maintenance.

"What's yours?" he asked. "So I have a somewhere to start."

"You're going to plan a date?"

He frowned. "Well, yeah. But I only want a starting point. It might be fun to throw in a surprise or two."

He'd certainly surprised her last Friday night. If all his surprises were that good, she wasn't going to complain.

"Good wine, cozy fires, anything that makes me feel...special. Like the person I'm with thinks I'm..." Her voice stumbled a bit. "Worth the effort."

He'd been holding a triangle of sandwich, but he put it down and wiped his fingers, focusing all his attention on her. "Damn, Hannah. Any guy who doesn't think you're worth the effort is a fool. All right. Tell you what. Tomorrow night, I'm taking you on a date. I'll pick you up at seven." He frowned for a moment, then his face cleared. "Wear those boots that you like so much, and dress warmly."

Oh Lordy. What was he planning?

"Cam, you don't have to—

"Yes, I do." He picked up his sandwich again. "I might not be here for more than a few weeks, but I can damned well make sure you are treated the way you deserve." He bit into the sandwich, chewed, swallowed, and dabbed his mouth. "The way you've always deserved," he stated, reaching for his water. He took a sip, put the glass down, and pointed at her. "None of those clowns in school ever appreciated you. Including me."

She snorted, trying not to be touched and failing, but covering it with a laugh. "Dude, you were thirteen."

He grinned then, dazzling her with his smile. "Yeah, but I was an *old* thirteen," he replied.

It was so silly she couldn't help but laugh, then she dug into her salad again. It had been a long time since she'd been wooed. If she could only have it for a short time, she was going to enjoy it. And she'd deal with missing him when he was gone.

Because she was going to miss him. Funny how after all this time, everything had changed. They'd been in each other's orbits since they were kids, but in just a few weeks, they'd become so much closer. Not because of his long-standing friendship with Rory, but despite it.

They finished their lunch, and Cam walked her back to her office. They stopped at the door, and the scent of evergreen from the lush wreath filled

Hannah's nostrils. She'd pulled on gloves and wrapped her scarf around her neck, and Cam's nose was red from the cold. But she was warm all over, just from being with him.

"Tomorrow. Seven, and I'll pick you up at your house."

"Seven," she parroted, and made the mistake of dropping her gaze to his lips.

Her eyes darted up again to meet his, realizing there were little flecks of green and gold in the dark depths. The tip of his tongue snuck out and ran along his lower lip, and her breath caught. She should go in. They were in the middle of busy Main Street. And yet she hesitated, long enough that he leaned forward a few inches and placed a soft, quick-but-lingering kiss on her lips.

"Tomorrow," he reminded her, and then turned away.

Her lips tingled, and she watched the pockets of his jeans as he walked away.

Cam Collier, hockey superstar, Darling's golden son, had spent the night in her bed and had just kissed her in the middle of the day on a busy street.

Christmas was a magical time indeed.

Chapter 9

CAM COULDN'T REMEMBER THE last time he'd been this nervous about a date.

He had everything he needed in the back of the SUV. He'd made phone calls today and set it all up the way he wanted. It was not necessarily elaborate or glamorous, but he'd listened to what Hannah had said yesterday, and he'd realized that her perfect date wasn't something crazy and expensive. Rather, she wanted—no, needed— someone to put thought and effort into it. So he'd enlisted the help of Willow for the food and Rory for information about who he needed to call for permissions. Right after Rory had delivered a speech about not hurting his sister that had ended with the words, "Don't be a douchebag."

Cam parked in front of her house and took a deep breath. Tonight wasn't just about a date. Tonight, he was going to tell her the real reason why he wouldn't speak at her event. It was something he'd never come right out and told anyone before. He'd never trusted anyone with it, not even Rory. But it was time. He couldn't run from it forever. Especially when thinking about the future and what he might do after retirement.

She came out of the house dressed warmly and wearing those sexy brown boots that stopped just shy of her kneecaps. The hem of her coat rested below her butt, and she had on mittens and a knit cap that sat sideways, like a beret. She was adorable, framed by the Christmas lights on her front porch. His heart gave a solid thump as she came down the steps and he hopped out to open her door.

"Hi," she said, a little breathless. She smelled delicious, like sugar cookies, and he wanted to taste her skin. Instead, he dropped a kiss on her cheek and reached for the door handle.

"You look great," he said, trying not to choke on his own spit, feeling like he was sixteen and borrowing his father's car to take out a girl.

"So do you," she replied, hopping up into the seat. "I like your ass in those jeans."

Heat rushed up his cheeks, though he had no idea why. She'd been up close and personal with his ass already, but tonight was different. It was... deliberate, and every word held new weight.

He jogged around the hood of the car, got in, and adjusted the heater. "Warm enough?"

"Perfect." She smiled by the light of the dashboard, and his heart thumped again.

Hannah. His brain jolted back by a week to the night they'd spent in her bed. There'd been less thinking then, and more acting on a need, a desire that had been awakened. It had blown his mind, but there was more now. There were feelings involved, tender ones. Cam wasn't sure what to do with that. He'd never been the tender-feelings type.

He drove them through town and then out to the golf course, where a metal gate was across the road. The grounds were closed this time of year, but Cam put the SUV in park and got out, retrieving a key from his coat. The lock snicked open, and he pushed the gate out of the way, then got back in the SUV to drive through it.

"You have the key to the golf course."

"Being me has its advantages. I don't use my celebrity often, but tonight it came in handy."

Once they were through, he got out again and locked the gate. No one would disturb them.

He parked at the far end of the lot by the dark clubhouse. "Ready?"

She nodded. "I guess. What have you got up your sleeve?"

A quick smile, and he jumped out of the truck, then popped open the tailgate as she slammed her door and came around the bumper.

"Good heavens. What have you got in here?"

"Firewood, food, drinks, blankets to keep warm..."

Her eyes were huge. "Cam."

He was wearing gloves, but that didn't stop him from placing one along her cheek and looking into her eyes. "You said cozy fires and wine. You kind of left out stars, but they did come out for you tonight."

She looked up, sighed, and looked back at him. "You're crazy."

For you, he thought, but didn't say it. The thought alone was scary enough. "Come on. I'll get the fire started first and come back for the rest."

There was a fire pit just below the clubhouse, sometimes used in the summer time for special events. It wasn't your typical wheel-rim-in-the-ground kind of pit. Instead, it was stone and mortar, a lovely addition to the grounds, circled with stone-and-wood benches. Hannah sat on a bench while he arranged the wood and some little bits of kindling, then worked for a few moments making sure it lit and would stay lit. Little crackles snapped as the kindling caught, and he blew out a breath of relief. Once the blaze was established, he added a few logs to keep it going. Then he trotted back to the SUV and grabbed the picnic basket and blankets.

When he returned, Hannah was sitting on the bench, leaning forward toward the flames with her hands held out to the heat. He put down the basket, then unfolded one of the soft blankets and tucked it around her lap. "Okay?" he asked.

"This is so nice. I didn't think you'd take me this literally."

"I haven't done something like this for a long time, either." He sat on the bench beside her and reached for the picnic basket. "I'll confess, though, your friend Willow packed the basket. I figured she'd know your favorites."

"Oh Lord. Willow makes the best stuff. What's in there? I missed dinner."

He chuckled and opened the top. He frowned. "A dish of something brown, and a container of what looks like chips. And dessert for later."

"Mmm." Hannah grinned and peeked into the basket. "Willow's homemade hummus and pita chips. My fave."

He took those out first, and Hannah swiped a chip through the dip and held it to his lips. "Try it. She does a remarkable job."

He tasted it and liked it, so they munched on those a while as the fire crackled. He told Hannah about driving to Burlington to shop, and she shared how she hadn't found time to put up her tree yet. He poured warm mulled wine into a cup for her, and cider for himself, because he was driving. The spices teased his nostrils as he lifted the cup to his lips. The cider was perfect, delightfully appley and with mulled spices that made it sublime. He couldn't remember when he'd last had spiced cider or sat around a fire with a blanket. His life had been missing these simple pleasures for a long time.

"Oh, this is delicious." Hannah cupped her hands around her drink and tipped her face up to the sky. "Look at the stars, Cam. It's such a beautiful night."

The fire snapped and crackled, and Cam could hear the traffic from the highway faintly, the sound traveling on the clear air. "Good choice?" he asked.

She nodded, looking over at him. "It's the perfect date."

"Not perfect yet. Hang on."

He reached into the basket and took out a pair of two-pronged forks. He twisted one and it extended to reach about three feet in length. He grinned and handed it to her. "Marshmallow forks. Dessert is s'mores."

Her laughter rang down over the first tee and into the valley. "S'mores. You really did think of everything."

Cam took out the bag of marshmallows, two bars of chocolate, and a package of graham crackers. While Hannah put a marshmallow on her stick, Cam got out two graham crackers and opened one of the chocolate bars, snapping it in half and placing it on the cracker.

Hannah toasted her marshmallow perfectly, and when she moved her stick over, Cam used the top cracker to sandwich the melty treat and pull it off the fork. He handed the finished s'more over to Hannah and took his fork, setting about toasting his own marshmallow.

Lips got sticky, and crumbs dropped onto the blankets, but neither of them seemed to care. Hannah finished her first one and took a healthy gulp of mulled wine before picking up her fork and stabbing another marshmallow. They had two each, then packed the detritus in the basket, which Cam put to the side after topping up their drinks.

"I've now eaten and had enough wine that the edges are getting a little fuzzy," Hannah said, putting her feet up on the bench and pulling the blanket around her.

"So you're cozy?"

"Very."

Cam got up and added wood to the fire, sending up a spray of sparks and renewed snapping as the birch bark caught and flickered. When he sat down again, he sat in a corner of the bench away from her and patted the empty space beside him. "Come on over here and curl up. We can watch the fire for a while."

She did, snuggling up next to him with her feet on the bench, and pulling the blanket over them both. Her head rested in the hollow of his shoulder, and he closed his eyes for a moment, enjoying the sensation. He'd missed this more than he liked to admit. Not wanting to have a serious relationship and also not fooling around with puck bunnies had left him leading a rather monastic existence. He put his arm around her and let out a long breath. He should confess his real reason for not doing the benefit. He wanted her to understand he wasn't just blowing it off or trying to buy his way in without putting in effort.

And he wanted to trust that she wouldn't judge him for it, or look at him differently.

"Hey, Han?"

"Mmmm hmmm?" Her reply was lazy and lovely, and it stirred things inside him he didn't know existed. His heart stuttered, afraid to be vulnerable, and yet somehow longing to connect with her on a deeper level. His throat tightened. What a time to realize he actually believed in love...and missed its presence in his life.

"I need to tell you something."

She twisted a little so she was looking up in his face. "Uh oh. This sounds serious."

"Not too serious," he replied, his heart thundering now. "It's just...there's a reason why I said no to the benefit. A reason I've never actually said out loud before."

She twisted farther and sat up a bit so she could look into his face better. "But you want to tell me?"

"I don't want you to think that I... Well, I don't know what you think. I gave you money, but I didn't give you my time, and I think that's what you really wanted."

Her eyes were bright. "I won't lie. I've wondered why you were so quick to say no and were equally quick to open your wallet."

Cam took a deep breath. It was now or never. "You wanted me to read a book at story time. And give a speech. But those things... Han, you couldn't have asked for two harder things. The truth is..." He swallowed against the lump of fear. "The truth is, I can't read very well."

She smiled. "I didn't realize you were a perfectionist. No one said you had to do a perfect job, Cam."

Oh God, she didn't get it. He tried again. "No, I mean...I've never been officially tested, but I think I'm dyslexic or something. The letters don't make sense all the time. It's like they move around or overlap. Or things like P and B and stuff get mixed up. I mean, I can do it. It's just hard, and I'm super slow. Same thing when it comes to my writing skills."

The smile had slipped from her face. "Cam. I had no idea. I'm sorry. I wouldn't have asked otherwise."

"It's not something I talk about."

She sat all the way up and faced him. "But...you got through school and everything."

"I got through because I was a hockey prodigy. I had a tutor. I scraped through most of my classes, and I'm pretty sure I got marked way up so I could keep playing. When you asked me to read to kids..." His voice caught, and he felt a hundred kinds of stupid. "Any of those kids would probably read better than me, you know? Some hero."

Her bright eyes had softened and looked into his. "You're not dumb, Cam. Having a learning disability doesn't mean you're stupid."

"Let's just say it doesn't feel that way."

"Fair enough."

He was glad she didn't try to dismiss his feelings. "Anyway, I wanted you to understand. I'm not trying to be selfish or unhelpful. If it was anything but reading..."

"It's okay. It really is. One of the librarians is going to do the story hour. What would be really great is if you'd go to the benefit dinner. Maybe even...with me."

He'd made it into the world of professional sports. He had a World Cup gold medal and had held the Stanley Cup. He'd been the NHL MVP twice. He should have confidence up the wazoo. Instead, he was sitting on a park bench in front of a fire feeling as uncertain as he ever had in his life.

"You want to go with me?"

"Of course I do." She put her hand on his arm. "Why wouldn't I?"

Because she was Hannah Freaking Gallagher, honor roll student and overachiever, the ungettable girl. And he was Cam Collier, dumb jock. But he didn't say that. Instead, he leaned forward and kissed her, a long, lingering kiss that warmed him from the inside out.

"You're so amazing," he murmured, pulling her into his arms and kissing her again.

They kissed for a long time, holding on to each other, letting the slow burn of desire keep them warm as the fire burned down. Eventually, they pulled back from the kiss, and he held her close as they looked at the stars poking through the inky blackness.

"Wow," she said quietly. "Good date, Collier. Top notch."

He chuckled. "It wasn't anything elaborate."

"It was just what I needed. And thank you for telling me the truth." She angled her head so she could look at him yet again. "You know you could get tested. Get some help."

"And have the world know I'm an idiot who can't read?"

"Again, you're not an idiot." She spun around and looked him dead in the eye. "If that little boy from The Purple Pig came up to you and said he had a learning disability, would you call him an idiot who can't read?"

He was horrified. "Of course not!"

"Well then, why would you talk to yourself that way?"

She was right, but it was impossible to change twenty-odd years of thinking like turning off a switch. "I know. I know. Except I don't, you know?"

Hannah nodded. "Sure I do. Let me just leave you with this. You could be a real inspiration to people with learning disabilities if you ever wanted to." He was about to protest when she lifted a hand. "I'm not pressuring you. It's just food for thought if you're ever ready."

He nodded, but the thought terrified him. "Right now, I just want to recover from this concussion and get back to my life."

The statement sobered them both. It had been a nearly perfect evening, but there wouldn't be many of these before he had to go back to his life. He tried to imagine being in a relationship with Hannah and being across the country while she was here. It seemed impossible. But imagining her leaving Darling behind to take a chance on him was even more impossible. Her business was here. Her family and stakes in other businesses... She was so entrenched in this community, how could he ever ask her to leave?

And he couldn't retire. He was only twenty-nine. He wasn't ready to give up hockey, and what if they tried it and it didn't work?

But the thought of leaving her behind after Christmas made his heart hurt. It wasn't the same as it had been with Alyssa. He'd loved her, but Hannah... There was already history with her. Their lives were already intertwined in a strange and wonderful way. He wasn't saying he was in love with her, but he cared about her so much.

"You're thinking so hard that smoke is going to start coming out of your ears," Hannah said softly, picking up his hand in hers. "Don't try to figure everything out. And this is coming from someone who plans everything. I don't want to analyze us out of what we might be able to have for a few short weeks. I want to be with you, Cam. I know what this is. But it feels good and right and dammit, we deserve it, don't we?"

He squeezed her fingers. "Someone once told you you didn't deserve it, huh? Who is he? I'll tune him up."

She laughed lightly. Their knees were pressed together, and he loved every single spot where their bodies connected. "You can't beat up everyone. But his name was Liam. He didn't like having a strong woman for a partner. I made him look bad."

Cam snorted. "His stupid loss, then. Because you're incredible. Any guy would be so lucky to have you. You are smart, savvy, dedicated, kind, beautiful... He should have been proud of you, not threatened."

He wasn't expecting tears to fill her eyes, but they glowed in the firelight and shone on her lashes. "Hey, don't cry."

"All the things he used to deride me for, you are proud of. It's so different and great."

"Maybe because we're more alike than we knew, Han. We see what we want, and we go after it. Not by stepping on others, but by working hard and demanding a lot of ourselves." He kissed the tip of her nose. "I like you a lot, but damn, I respect you even more. And that's something new for me."

She nodded quickly, and one tear splashed down off her lashes. "Have you wished that this didn't have to be just Christmas?" she asked and then bit down on her lip, as if unsure if she should have asked the question.

"Yeah, I have. But your life is here, and mine is there. Let's just do that live-in-the-moment thing again."

In response, she shifted and straddled his lap, then kissed him until his brain blanked of all other thoughts than just her. And when the fire burned down, they packed up their gear, threw a bucket of snow on the dying embers, and left the golf course.

Chapter 10

FOR THE SECOND TIME, Hannah woke with Cam in the bed beside her. This time he was awake, his dark eyes watching her, and she smiled as she stretched.

"Well, hello."

"Good morning."

She couldn't remember a time when she'd been this happy in...forever. "How's your head? Better job pacing yourself?"

They'd taken their time last night, and it had been... Well, transcendent sounded cheesy, but it was pretty accurate. She'd been thoroughly loved, and she'd given as good as she got.

"I feel like a million bucks," he confirmed, and reached over beneath the blankets and pulled her closer. "Slept like the dead, too. You're good for me, Hannah Banana."

"Ditto." She ran her hand through his hair, loving the softness, even though one spot stuck up stubbornly. "By the way, thank you for not going in for *the flow* hair that so many players have. Or the gross beards, either."

He laughed. "You don't like facial hair?"

"A little is okay. I just can't see how a full beard can be comfortable when you're getting all sweaty and wearing a helmet."

"I don't like it, either. Besides, I gotta keep the baby face for the ladies."

In response, she ran her hand over his rough jaw. He had stubble there now from overnight, but she didn't mind. A little was sexy.

"What do you want to do today? I have an open house with a client tomorrow, but I'm free as a bird all day." She wasn't going to worry about the benefit next weekend. Everything was in place. Surely she deserved one day off?

"Let's put up your Christmas tree. I'll help."

"Really?" She sat up, clutching the covers to her chest. "You want to put up my tree?"

"Sure, why not?"

Hannah loved Christmas. All the siblings had always gathered to put up the tree at their parents' place. But over the past few years, her brothers had started traditions with their own families. Rory and Oaklee were celebrating their first Christmas in their house. Laurel and Aiden had started their family, and Willow and Ethan had three kids at their house. Priorities changed. Sure, Cait and Claire were still home, but Hannah's mom and dad had put up their tree on Monday night and not said anything to anyone about it. The changes had chipped away at her Christmas spirit. But today, she could get a tree with Cam and put it up and do all the fun things in her own house.

"Oh my God, I'm so excited." She jumped out of bed, not caring that she was naked. "Let's grab coffee at The Purple Pig and then get a tree at the garden center and—"

"Wow. I had no idea this was so thrilling for you."

"Putting up a tree alone is a sad affair. But you're here. Let's do it."

They had a quick shower since Hannah could still smell the smoke from their campfire in her hair. Today, she didn't care about looking perfect, so she rolled her damp hair in a low bun and plopped a cute hat on her head to keep it warm. Jeans, ankle boots, and an old jacket rounded out the ensemble. If there was any pitch on the tree, she didn't want to get it on her good coat.

They stopped at the Pig and said hello to Emily, then took their coffee and headed to the Ladybug Garden Center. The manager, George, was doing a brisk business with trees, but it didn't take long for Hannah to pick the one she wanted. Then she went inside in search of Laurel, who would definitely be working on a busy Saturday before Christmas. Laurel was stacking cookies and squares on a rack inside the shop, a fresh delivery from a local bakery. During the holidays, the garden center did a booming business with decorations and seasonal treats.

"Hello!" Laurel brushed off her hands and moved forward to give Hannah a hug. "It feels like I haven't seen you in forever."

"Everyone's been busy. Including you. This place is hoppin.'"

"Trees and wreaths and poinsettias, for sure. And the bakery started sending shortbread and all kinds of cookies and squares. I swear, no one has to do any Christmas baking at all. They even sent—" she held up a container. "—little jars of buckeyes."

"Sold." Hannah loved the chocolate and peanut butter treats. "We just came for a tree. Mine's not up yet."

"We?"

Hannah met Laurel's gaze. "Me and...Cam."

Laurel's eyes twinkled in response. "Oh, honey. Yee haw."

Hannah burst out laughing. "Stop that! Someone will hear you."

"Oh, whatever. But seriously, you can't even give me juicy deets, because there's too many people, and it's crazy in here." She peered closer into Hannah's face. "There are juicy deets, right?"

Hannah didn't answer, but she felt the heat of a blush rush into her cheeks.

"Ho damn," Laurel said on a low breath. "When's our next girls' night?"

"I am not going to kiss and tell," Hannah said firmly. "That's not my style."

"Well, clearly not with Oaklee. She doesn't need to know that about her brother. Gross. But, Hannah, whatever is going on looks good on you. So yeah, enjoy it."

"I intend to. Now, I was hoping to grab a few things before I go. Including these." She held up the container. "I'm gonna go. We're all set for next weekend?"

"Sure thing. Centerpieces will be ready and delivered Saturday morning, and you already have my silent auction contribution. Aiden and I bought our tickets to the dinner, too. Your mom and dad offered to keep all the kids so all of us can go."

Hannah's heart warmed. That was one thing about the Gallaghers. When something was going on, they had each other's backs. "So everyone will be there?"

She nodded. "All your siblings, anyway. Your folks are going to go to the afternoon events."

An unexpected calm descended over Hannah. For weeks, she'd been stressed about this event, but the truth was, her family was solidly behind her. The town was, too. It was all going to be fine. She felt more love and support in this moment than she'd felt in many years.

Maybe, just maybe, it was okay for Hannah to be Hannah.

Cam ventured into the small store, then smiled at Hannah as he caught her with Laurel. "Hey, the tree's all ready to go. You had a blanket in your truck, so I put it on the roof rack and put the tree on top so you don't scratch any of the paint."

"Hey, Cam."

"Laurel. You're doing big business today."

"It's Christmas. The season of joy and happiness." She smiled brightly at him, and a blush crept up his cheeks.

"Oh God," he muttered.

"Sorry. Or maybe more...sorry not sorry. It's kind of cute seeing you blush."

"Please don't bring this up with Aiden or Ethan or Rory. I'm not ready for the third degree from protective brothers."

"Aw, come on. I mean, just because one's a firefighter, the other's a cop, and the third is a vet, who is around all sorts of lethal medications...why worry?"

He chuckled. "Ha, ha."

One of the cashiers waved at Laurel, so she gave a parting grin. "I gotta go. You two have a brilliant day."

Hannah held the container of buckeyes in her hand and looked at Cam. "Pick something from the rack, and we'll have it with coffee this afternoon."

"Oooh, I get to pick a treat?" He rubbed his hands together, and she laughed.

He chose something she didn't expect: a Christmas Stollen, heavy and dense with marzipan and coated with powdered sugar. It was one of her favourites, too, and not overly sweet, beyond the marzipan, of course. She added it to the buckeyes and a roll of wired ribbon from the wreath section and went to the cash register. Before long, they were on their way back to her house, smelling of spruce needles and holiday spirit.

Cam unloaded the tree while Hannah went to her basement to retrieve her tree stand and decorations at the bottom of the stairs. She'd already moved the furniture aside so she could put the tree in the corner by the fireplace, and by the time Cam wrestled the thing through the door, she had the stand ready and waiting.

With a flurry and fluff of branches, the trunk settled into the stand. Hannah held the tree steady while Cam knelt down and tightened the wingnuts to hold it perfectly straight. When he was done, he got up, stood back, and gave a whistle. "Good choice on the tree. It's perfect."

She thought so, too. Even more because he was here with her. It felt like a very couple-ish thing to do. She wasn't going to analyze it too deeply, either. She was going to enjoy the day.

"Hang on," she said, and disappeared to the kitchen. She came back with her phone and started a holiday playlist, which she put through a portable speaker on the fireplace mantle. "Gotta have some carols while we're decorating."

The playlist was a Christmas Classics one, so right after Burl Ives, Perry Como came on. After turning on the gas fireplace, she gave Cam the tree skirt to put underneath and started unpacking the decorations.

"Lights first," she said, taking out several bundles. They were rolled around flat pieces of cardboard to keep them from tangling, and she tested each set and made sure it was working before handing them to Cam, who could reach the tall branches and around the back better than she could. As she opened a pack of replacement bulbs, she stole a look at him. It seemed impossible that he was here, in her living room, helping her put up a Christmas tree. Tree decorating was an intimate thing, when she thought about it. It was usually an activity for families or couples, or at the very least, people who were very special to each other. Was Cam special to her? Maybe he shouldn't be, but he was. He fiddled with a branch, and a lump formed in Hannah's throat. He was a good man. And she was beginning to care about him—a lot. Not just because they knew each other, but in other, deeper ways.

But she could not fall for him. She couldn't. He was leaving soon. This was a short-term thing she would look back on with fond memories and nostalgia. Right?

"Got the next set ready?"

Cam's voice pulled her out of her thoughts, and she immediately pasted on a smile. "Oh, sorry! I got distracted."

"Really."

If he knew the direction of her thoughts, he'd be out the door faster than she could say "penalty box." She brightened her smile and said, "Yeah. I was looking at your ass."

His eyebrows lifted, and he left the tree to come over to where she was sitting with the bundle of lights in her lap. Her heart hammered as he neared, but he merely reached down and took the lights from her hands.

Her breath escaped with relief.

Except Cam put the lights down on the coffee table and came back, braced his hands on the arms of the chair, and leaned in to kiss her.

It was no chaste peck. Even though he kept his hands to himself, his mouth did lots of talking all on its own. It wooed and persuaded, tasted and devoured, until Hannah was ready to forget all about the tree and start losing clothes.

Then he stepped back, retrieved the lights, and went to put them on the tree.

"I, uh...what was that for?"

"For staring at my ass."

"If I do it again, do I get double the punishment?"

He laughed and roped the lights around the middle of the tree. "Sweetheart, the kiss wasn't the punishment. Walking away was."

Damn him. Hannah smiled to herself and reached for another set of lights.

After the lights, they put garland on in swoops, and then Hannah's ornaments, which were all in red, green, and gold. The final touch was the star for the top. Hannah's tree lights were all white, and the star was gold and trimmed with white LED lights and glittering crystals. She'd paid a lot of money for it and kept it in the original box when not in use. She handed it to Cam, and he situated it on the top of the tree, and then they stepped back and admired their handiwork.

"I like it," she said softly.

"Me, too," he said. He stood behind her and wrapped his arms around her middle, and the bottom of his chin rested against her temple. It was an intimate moment, admiring their tree.

"Are you glad you came home?"

"More every day."

"Cam..."

He turned her to face him and cupped her jaws in his hands, his thumbs resting on her cheeks. "I know the future is... Well, not this. But I'm not sorry, Hannah. I'll never be sorry. Being with you has been so good."

Tears stung the backs of her eyes. "For me, too."

"I've been lonely a long time," he admitted.

She had, too. Longer than she cared to admit. Maybe too long, because she was probably being foolish right now. She should send him on his way before someone got hurt. But she couldn't. She physically could not form the words. And that, more than anything, scared her to death.

Chapter 11

CAM KISSED HER LIPS gently, his heart pounding with both anticipation and trepidation. He was walking a very fine line right now. There was something about Hannah that just got to him. Maybe it was the way she laughed, or how she was so very capable but hid a vulnerability he understood more than she could imagine. She hadn't been staring at his ass earlier, either. He'd seen the look on her face as her hands stilled over the lights, and he'd known.

This fling might be too much for her. For both of them. Especially since it didn't feel like a fling at all.

Not to him, anyway.

She responded, melting against him as he sank his fingers into her hair. He loved her hair, the wild, thick, red mass of it cascading over his hands as she moaned into his mouth. She was so responsive, something he hadn't imagined when he'd first encountered her that day at The Purple Pig. How had he ever thought she was uptight? She was pliant and willing in his arms right now.

"Hannah," he whispered roughly.

"Cameron," she replied, and that was it. The husky way she said his full name—no one ever called him by that—reached in and did something to him that couldn't be undone.

The light had dimmed in the late afternoon, and now the light was provided by the glow of the tree and the flicker of the fireplace. It danced on her face, darkening her eyes and highlighting the hollow of her throat as she tipped her head back. He kissed the base of her throat and licked up her neck, feeling her shiver with pleasure.

He wanted to give her that; undiluted, magnificent pleasure. Slowly, he pulled her sweater over her head, then cupped her breast in his hand, loving the feel of the hard tip as it pressed against his palm. She pulled at his hoodie, and he made short work of pulling it off and dropping it on the floor. Next to go was her bra, and then he picked her up and lay her down on the plush sofa, her body sinking into the cushions beneath him. Her hands were above her head, and he made the most of the invitation as he tasted her breasts before kissing her again.

And still they didn't rush. They savored each touch and taste until the need for satisfaction grew too strong. Cole got up and removed his jeans, then leaned over and removed Hannah's until she was stretched out naked on the sofa.

The light from the fireplace cast shadows that licked her golden skin and shone against her burnished hair. Cole had enough presence of mind to reach for a condom in his jeans pocket, and then he was inside her, feeling her arch against him, hearing her breath as she gasped and moved in rhythm with him. He upped his pace, resting most of his weight on one elbow while he used his opposite thumb to flick her nipple. She cried out, and he adjusted, bracing himself on his hands so that he could lick them the way she needed.

"Oh God. Cam. Cam."

She said his name. She hadn't done that before, and an overwhelming emotion washed over him. Her legs wrapped around his waist, her strong thighs cinching him close, and he pushed harder, her cries urging him on. When she finally came apart around him, he was certain he had never felt this sort of victory ever in his life—and that was saying something. Her hips pulsed against him, and her voice was a hoarse sob as the climax pounded through her, and with it went his last bit of control.

He looked down at her as he came, her dazed eyes staring up at him, and he knew he was in serious, serious trouble.

He'd gone and fallen in love with Hannah Gallagher.

There was no way he could tell her how he felt.

Cam held on to his feelings tightly over the next few days. After decorating the tree, they made dinner together, then curled up in front of the fire and talked for hours before going to bed. On Sunday, they went to her parents' house for

Sunday dinner, where he was completely included, and no one—not even Rory—said a thing about him being there with Hannah. It was almost as if they'd all been forewarned...which he figured they had been. It didn't matter. He enjoyed roast beef and all the fixings, lots of laughs, and Moira's top-notch apple pie. He'd spent a lot of time in the Gallagher house as a boy. It had felt good to be at home there again.

Monday, Hannah was back at work, but he had an appointment in Montpelier anyway. That night he cooked for her—fresh pasta in a Bolognese sauce and salad. Tuesday, he helped her go through her lists for the auction. And Wednesday, he decreed she needed a few hours off and to grab her skates.

He hadn't been on the ice since his injury, but as they sat on a bench on the bank of Fisher Creek, he shoved his feet in his skates, and it felt a lot like home. Blades were as natural to him as a favourite pair of sneakers. They shoved guards over the blades as they made their way to the frozen creek, and then they took off the guards and left them on the bank.

He pushed off, felt the ice beneath his feet, and nearly cried. God, he'd missed this. It had only been a few weeks, but he'd missed it like crazy.

Hannah wasn't quite as sure on hers, but she pushed away from the bank and with shortened strides, made it to where he was waiting for her.

"I'm feeling a bit outmatched," she said, her breath forming clouds. The lights along the walking path cast a soft light on the creek. Farther down, toward the garden center, the creek was wider, and he could hear children laughing. Hannah's nose was pink from the cold, her blue eyes bright and shining beneath a soft knitted cap. How had he not seen how extraordinary she was?

It was going to kill him to leave her. Yet what choice did he have?

"Come on," he said softly, and held out his gloved hand.

She was wearing mittens that matched her hat, and she folded her smaller hand into his. Together, they skated up the creek, Cam slowing to match her speed, which smoothed out as she went along.

They skated along, past the memorial, under the Kissing Bridge, and up toward the traffic bridge that connected one side of town to the other. Hannah's strides were stronger now, and he let go of her hand and skated off, enjoying the freedom, indulging in some footwork, laughing from the sheer joy of it. He wasn't ready to give this up. Not yet. All he was missing was a stick in his hand and a puck on the blade.

Hannah goofed around a bit, too, going around him in circles, doing little half-jumps. She grabbed his hand, performing a twirl that took her right into his arms.

"Hmm," he said, looking down at her lips. "Look at you."

"I'm so rusty," she said on a laugh. "But I'm never going to be like you on skates, so I might as well embrace my mediocrity and enjoy myself."

He pulled her close. "You, my Hannah Banana, will never be mediocre. Never let anyone tell you otherwise, and never hide it."

"Cam..."

"Right." He pushed her away, spun her around, and put his hands on her hips. "You leading the train, Ms. Gallagher?"

She burst out laughing. "There are two of us. That means I'm the engine and you're the caboose."

"Someone's gotta be."

She started to skate, and he matched his strides to hers, working together to make their way down the ice. She surprised him by doing a half turn and skating backward so they were face-to-face. He captured one of her hands, leaving his other on her hip, and grinned.

"What are you doing?" she asked, still skating with strong, even strides.

"Dancing. Hush, and let me lead."

He was no figure skater, but he was nimble enough that he led her through a couple of turns so that he was the one skating backward, taking her with him. As they reached the Kissing Bridge again, he slowed and pulled her in so their bodies were pressed together and she was no longer skating, just sliding forward from his momentum. He clasped her hand tightly, put his wide palm along the hollow of her back, and slowed until they were making tiny circular steps on the ice.

She sighed and rested her head against his shoulder.

"Hannah..."

He stopped moving altogether and kissed her, right there on the ice under the Kissing Bridge, hidden from view. He wanted to make love to her right now, not because of burning need or desire, but because he longed to feel that connection with her again. It both scared and thrilled him. Was this how love felt? Was this love as a grown up? It certainly made all his other feelings pale in comparison.

He loved her. He wasn't sure how to tell her, but he wanted to. Wasn't sure if it was even fair to say the words and then walk away, but it felt wrong somehow not to.

"Hannah, I..."

"What is it?"

The words tangled in his throat. It wasn't the right time. Maybe it would never be the right time. Instead, he leaned forward and kissed her forehead. "I'm glad I came home for Christmas," he said softly, then closed his eyes. Going back to Denver was going to be harder than he ever imagined.

Hannah let out a slow breath and let Cam fold her into his arms. What had he been going to say? He'd been different since Saturday, though she couldn't quite pinpoint how or why. There'd been a naturalness to them being together that hadn't happened before. Even at dinner the other night with her family, he'd struck a fine balance of hanging with the family and yet being...coupley. A look across the table, coming up behind her in the kitchen and putting a hand on her waist, even bringing her a second cup of tea while they watched hockey highlights.

She cared about him a lot. Another time, another place, maybe it would go somewhere. But she was rather glad he'd said he was happy he'd come home and not made any sort of declaration.

She didn't want him to love her. She just wanted to enjoy this time, be able to hold it close in the months ahead when she got lonely again. As she certainly would. Cam once made the comment that she was "ungettable." She supposed that translated to high-maintenance. Was she? She didn't think so.

She clung to his jacket and enjoyed the hug. She wasn't ungettable. What she was, was afraid. Afraid of changing herself, afraid of no one loving her as she was. She stayed in Darling because despite being an achiever, she was not a risk-taker. She could be a big fish in a little pond here. She didn't know how to be a little fish. And it made her admire Cam a little more, knowing that over the years he'd had to work to become a big fish, against a lot of odds and without his family close by. He was so much braver than she was.

Being a big fish meant she was lonely. But at least she wasn't lonely in the middle of the unknown.

Damn Cam for coming to town and making her face that vulnerability.

And damn him for making her feel so alive she was reminded of what she was missing because of the choices she'd made.

Chapter 12

HE WAS HEADED BACK to Denver right after Christmas.

The go-ahead came from the doctor in Montpelier in a follow-up appointment on Friday, and Cam now sat on the back deck, huddled in his winter jacket, frowning at his mixed feelings.

This was what he wanted. To go back, get into training again, return to the ice and the team. And yet the thought of leaving Hannah behind left a hollow feeling in his gut. Saying goodbye was going to be awful. Not just the situation and the actual saying of it, but the walking away and going through his days knowing she was so far away. The end of what they'd only just begun.

The sun was just beginning to creep through the trees, and Cam took a big breath. Today was the benefit, and he was going to help Hannah and Oaklee as much as he could. Oaklee was going to be handling the activities in town during the day, while Hannah was manning banquet HQ at the golf club. He'd given her the details of the trip he was offering in the auction, and she'd done up some sort of display for it. She'd asked if he could meet her at the clubhouse at ten to help her make sure everything was on schedule and perfect.

The sliding door opened and his mom came out, bundled in a fleece jacket of his dad's and carrying two cups of coffee. "You're out here early."

"Just doing some thinking."

"About Hannah Gallagher?"

He nodded. "Yeah. And other things."

"You got in a little over your head, huh."

He laughed and accepted the steaming coffee. "Yeah, I guess I did."

She sat down on a cold chair and sighed. "Well, you're almost thirty years old. I couldn't expect you to stay in your childhood bed forever. You've been gone a lot of nights."

"She's...really special."

"Of course she is. Beautiful and smart and successful. I don't know what the guys around here have been staying away for."

"Because they're idiots," he grumbled, and sipped his coffee. "She's got her own insecurities. She's not a ballbuster. Even if some people think she is."

"Maybe she just needed someone strong enough to go toe to toe with her," his mother said wisely. "And you are that, my stubborn son. So maybe this concussion turned out to be a bit of a blessing."

He frowned and didn't say anything for several long moments. Finally, he looked over at her. "But what now? Mom, I'm going back on the twenty-seventh. I got the all clear to at least practice. I have to go. I have a responsibility to be there. I *want* to be there."

Her face was sad as she looked over at him. "And Hannah's life is here."

"Her family. Her business. Her friends. How can I ask her to leave that behind? We've been together what, three weeks?" He made a scoffing sound and shook his head. "It's crazy."

"Does she love you as much as you love her?"

Her simple question rattled him. His gaze darted up and held hers, as fear and elation rushed together through his system. "I never said I loved her."

"You don't have to. It's all over your face and in the way you talk about her. Besides, you've known Hannah for years. It's not like you just met."

It wasn't, and she was right. It was more like taking an old relationship and shifting it, molding it like clay into something new and beautiful.

"It's not an easy thing to say. And what would be the point?"

She patted his hand. "The world would be a lot better place if people would just say 'I love you' more often instead of holding it inside. Loving someone is a gift. You should tell her."

He was quiet a little longer, and she leaned closer so she could peer into his face. "What is it? What are you afraid of?"

He swallowed against a lump in his throat. "What if I say it, and she doesn't feel the same? What if..." His voice trailed away. "Aw, hell, Mom. I don't even know what I want this to look like, but I'm pretty sure she's not going to go for it. It's a lot to ask of a person. I don't even know what the next five years of my life are going to look like. How do I drag her into that?"

"Why would you have to drag anyone? Life is always one choice after another. It would suck if you didn't at least give her the chance to say yes to something great. Maybe she's feeling the same way and doesn't know how to tell you, too. I hate to tell you this, Cam, but with matters of the heart, it comes down to making yourself vulnerable and taking chances."

He wasn't a stranger to taking chances. Heck, his whole career was based on it. But it was different when his heart was involved. He'd been through this before, and it had hurt, a lot. It would be exponentially worse with Hannah. He was older, wiser, and a lot more scared.

And yet he knew, deep down, his mom was right. The only way this was going to work was if he laid it all out there. As if she sensed he was working through the puzzle of his thoughts, his mom stood and patted his shoulder before going back inside.

Hannah had said enough about her past for him to know that people expected a lot of her. Words wouldn't be enough for her; he needed to show her how important she was to him. And he knew there was one way he could do it, if he was brave enough.

But first, he needed to grab some breakfast and prepare to convert the clubhouse into a winter fairy tale. Then he'd sort it all out.

Hannah was feeling all sorts of jitters, but they were the good kind. Last year had been the inaugural year of the benefit, and this year she'd made a few changes to simplify the setup, and it wasn't all new. Besides, she had a good feeling. Nothing was going to go wrong today. Oaklee was popping into each sponsoring business to make sure their donation boxes and raffles were running smoothly, then checking in at the library to help with the story hour and used book sale. Hannah had already been into The Purple Pig and got a hot chocolate and a cookie. A dollar from each sale today was going to support the cause. Even Papa Luigi's pizza was putting on a special deal over the lunch hour for a slice and a soda, and an extra dollar paid for a ticket in a draw for a New Year's Eve pizza feast. Rory had said he was buying a ton of tickets so they could have the food for their New Year's party all figured out.

She had a clipboard and a handful of volunteers, all busily setting up banquet tables and chairs. She'd rented the linens, and they were pressed and waiting to be placed on tables. There was a podium at the front for announcements by the emcee, a local radio personality who had donated his time.

Boxes lined the back, full of silent-auction donations ready to be displayed. And she had six hours to do it all. Then she could rush back home and change out of her jeans and sweater and into the killer cocktail dress she'd bought for tonight. It wasn't a black-tie event, but it was semi-formal, and she wanted to knock Cam's eyeballs out.

Speaking of, the man himself strode through the door, carrying a tray with coffee and a paper bag nestled between the cups. "Wow. Ready to give this room a makeover?"

She laughed. "You have no idea." She swept out her hand. "I have some volunteers to help with the room setup, and you, mister..." She smiled up at him. "I've got twinkly light kinds of things for you to do."

"Coffee first?"

"God, yes."

He handed her a cup and then leaned down and kissed her lightly. "I'm not really into PDAs, but I wanted to do that," he murmured, pulling back. A quick glance showed a few of the ladies staring, and he smiled shyly. "Oops."

"Oh, it's not like this town hasn't been talking anyway." She grinned at him over top of her cup. "Besides, you're my date tonight."

"That's right. I washed my special sweatpants for the occasion."

"Ha, ha."

He'd also brought breakfast sandwiches, which she was thankful for, because she'd had sugar for breakfast between the hot chocolate and the cookie. They took ten minutes to eat, and then she showed him where the decorations were and what she wanted to do with them. "The white trees have LED lights on them. The idea is to do a group of three on either side of the podium and make it a little magical. There should be extension cords in the boxes. And someone from the garden center should be here anytime with centerpieces and extra poinsettias."

"Great. All under control."

"I'm going to put the linens on the display tables and start setting up auction items. Sound okay?"

"Of course."

She left him then, but she stole glances at him as he moved around setting up the trees, plugging them in and rearranging them again. She had several donations for the auction, and she put his in the very center as the big draw—the trip to the Stanley Cup final. The Foxborough Inn had donated a weekend stay-and-dine getaway, Willow had offered up ten yoga classes, and even Rory had put together a healthy pet-care package filled with treats, toys, and a certificate for a pet checkup and vaccinations. The donations went on and on, and Hannah's heart warmed as she put one after another on the tables, along with the description and bidding sheet for each.

There was even a beautiful crocheted baby blanket by Amelia Evans, who had been Hannah's mother's school teacher, and who must now be at least eighty. The work was precise and perfect, done in a pale yellow, like liquid sunshine. Hannah ran her fingers over the delicate yarn and felt a wistful tug at her heart. What would she ever do with a blanket like this? She probably wouldn't ever have kids. The clock had begun to tick softly a few years ago.

"Wow, that's pretty." Cam's voice sounded at her ear, and she jumped a little, pulling her hand away.

"Yeah. Did you know Amelia taught my mom? And yet here she is, still finding the time to donate something for this charity."

"As a teacher, she probably appreciates the cause," he said. "So what do you think?"

She turned around and smiled, enchanted. "Oh, Cam. Who knew you'd have an artistic eye?"

He'd placed the trees perfectly and plugged them in so the lights glowed at the front of the room. Then he'd somehow taken the rest of the little lights and twined them with the greenery that hung around the door to the banquet room, making it sparkle. "I wish I had more to do something around perimeter of the room, you know?"

"No, this is perfect. Laurel's centerpieces are going to look after extra sparkle, don't you worry. The lighting is going to be perfect."

She'd just said the words when Aiden stuck his head in the door. "Shrubbery!"

Hannah rolled her eyes and then burst out laughing as Aiden and Cam went through a Monty Python bit about shrubberies. Before long, the two of them were lugging in the centerpieces and poinsettias. Hannah rushed to get a tablecloth, and when the last of the delivery was inside, she grabbed Cam's arm and pulled him over.

"Okay, so look at this. Laurel came up with the design, and George put them together." George had, until the last year or so, been a homeless veteran on Darling's streets. Now he was Laurel's manager and lived with his girlfriend, Lindsay, right here in town.

Precisely in the middle of the table, she put a two-inch thick circle of wood. On top of that went a small wreath that George had made, and in the middle was a glass candle holder and a thick, white candle inside. "Each table will have one of these. There are fifteen tables. Add these with the rest of the lights, and the ones I have to intersperse on the auction tables, and it'll be magical in here."

The volunteers were nearly done setting up the chairs at each table, and then the caterers arrived. Hannah disappeared to direct them to the clubhouse kitchen, and when she looked out again, Cam was snapping a tablecloth and letting it fall onto the table, then adjusting it with a critical eye. One of the volunteers said something to him, and he laughed, answered, and worked together with them to make sure everything was just right.

How lucky was she, anyway? This had to be some sort of Christmas miracle. And it would be over as soon as the season was over, but for right now, it was pretty amazing.

He was amazing. Way more than she'd realized the day he'd said he wouldn't read at the library. He'd succeeded despite what she suspected was a significant learning disability. He'd risen to the top in competitive sport, in a way thousands of young players only dreamed.

Cam Collier was a special, special man.

"Ms. Gallagher?" One of the catering staff needed her attention, so she dragged her gaze away and turned to help.

She could think about their relationship later. Right now, she had to keep the day running on schedule. She didn't have time to worry about anything else.

Chapter 13

CAM BUTTONED THE SUIT jacket and smoothed the lapels. He was no stranger to tailored suits. They were regular game-day attire, and he made sure they fit him well. He'd paired the dark gray suit with brown shoes and a shirt in the lightest shade of blue. He knotted the tie and tightened it, then ran his hands through his hair and shrugged.

He wasn't sure he was ready for tonight, but there came a time in a man's life that he couldn't run anymore. That something became important enough to stand for. Or someone, rather. That was Hannah for him. He wanted to try to make this work. Surely they could come to some kind of compromise? He could come back to Darling over the summer. Maybe she could travel to Denver now and again during the season.

Anything but saying goodbye.

And he knew that to convince a woman like Hannah, he needed to not just say the words, but show her how much she meant to him.

Just thinking about it made his stomach twist with anxiety. He'd almost rather get knocked in the head again, but he would do this. For her. For them. And to be a better person than he'd been in the past.

The parking lot at the golf club was already filling up when he arrived. Hannah had insisted on meeting him there, since she would be going a bit early to ensure everything was perfect and to be on hand when people started arriving. He stepped inside the banquet room, and soft, jazzy Christmas music met his ears. A bar was set up in the corner —that was an addition since he'd left at two—and a tuxedoed bartender was mixing drinks and pouring wine.

He didn't see Hannah yet, but he knew she had to be here. Instead, he zeroed in on Rory and Oaklee. His sister looked stunning in a red cocktail dress, and Rory was practically beaming.

"Well, you two clean up nice." He leaned over and kissed Oaklee's cheek. "How did the afternoon go?"

"Perfectly! The weather was amazing, so we had great crowds on Main, and I think there were maybe fifty kids at story hour. It looks like the individual efforts paid off, too. The used table was doing a booming business, and Papa Luigis could barely keep up with pizza orders. Hannah's thrilled."

"Speaking of, have you seen her?"

Oaklee shrugged. "Yes, but she disappeared a few minutes ago. I'll go see if I can find her."

Oaklee kissed Rory's cheek and slipped away. Rory's smile slipped a little, and he met Cam's gaze.

"Tonight's the night, man. After the benefit, because we're all dressed up. I've got champagne in the fridge, and I'm gonna pop the question."

Cam grinned widely. "Look at you, scared shitless. Way to go, man. It's not every day that a guy gains a brother who is also his best friend."

Rory laughed a little. "Yeah, well, I know you've been hanging around my sister. Should I grill you about your intentions?"

This time, it was Cam's grin that faded. "Ask me after tonight," he said quietly."

Rory's jaw dropped. "Oh my God. You're not proposing..."

"No, of course not!" Cam's heart nearly stopped. "It's all too new. But... Well, Hannah and I just need to talk, you know?"

"You're smitten."

Cam raised an eyebrow. "Very."

"My sister is a handful."

"And a half."

Rory laughed then, a genuine, happy laugh. "Don't hurt her. But damn, bro...I can't think of anyone better to handle her shenanigans."

"God, I need a beer. I can't believe you said shenanigans."

They were just about to head to the bar when Hannah and Oaklee came through the door.

Cam's heart stuttered.

Oaklee was beautiful, but Hannah... She was incandescent. Her gold-sequined dress sparkled and glittered in the flickering light, modest in its cut, but stunning in its fit. Her hair was down, the whole fiery length of it curled about her shoulders.

"You are in so much trouble, dude," Rory said, clapping him on the shoulder.

"Shit," Cam answered.

Rory disappeared, and Cam met Hannah's gaze across the room. She gave him a slow smile and a wink, and he knew he was in way over his head. He ignored the stares and hellos aimed his way as he crossed the room, never breaking eye contact. And when he finally reached her, she put her hand on his arm and kissed his cheek while he caught his breath.

"You... Wow, Hannah. Just...wow."

"You like it?"

"I could say something like how it makes me want to get you out of it, but that's not true. I want to enjoy the whole evening, knowing the most gorgeous woman in the room is my date." He reached down and took her fingers in his. "When a candle burns this brightly, you want to stay close to it, you know?"

"Cam..."

"Let's enjoy the evening. Everything is in place, and according to Oaklee, today has been a booming success. Your hard work is over, Han."

And his was just beginning. He fought back the nerves that threatened to derail him.

They circulated together. Cam signed a few autographs, caught up with old teammates from his childhood days, and shook hands with the mayor and his wife. Hannah sipped on a glass of white wine while he indulged in a single beer. He had to drive later, and he also wanted his wits about him. Catering staff circulated with appetizers, and the mood was warm and festive as the dinner hour neared.

The emcee tapped on the mic and announced that dinner would begin in five minutes.

Hannah and Cam were seated at the front, along with the rest of the Gallaghers: Rory and Oaklee, Aiden and Laurel, and Ethan and Willow. Cait and Claire were at another table with their friends, but as Cam looked around, he was reminded of how wonderful this town was, as well as the Gallagher clan. He hadn't spent enough time with family over the years, but maybe now that would change.

The emcee opened the event with a welcome, and then invited Hannah to the podium. Cam smiled at her as she rose from her chair and made her way to the microphone.

"Good evening, everyone. Doesn't this place look beautiful? I'd like to thank all the volunteers who came out today to help with our setup and decorating, and also to so many who took part in our many activities throughout Darling today. I'm thrilled to announce that our preliminary numbers exceed that of last year, and we have a total of eleven thousand, two hundred and sixty-six dollars, all of which will go to our various literacy charities. Thank you so much for all your support!"

A round of loud applause followed, and as it died down, Hannah added, "If you haven't placed your bids on the auction items at the back, you can do so until eight p.m. Thank you again, and enjoy this wonderful dinner."

She made her way back down to her seat, and Cam noticed she didn't even look ruffled. Public speaking scared the hell out of him, but Hannah spoke with ease and authenticity. "You're amazing," he whispered, leaning over toward her as she sat.

"All this flattery is going to go to my head." She sent him a wry smile and reached for her water goblet.

"I hope so. You should realize how wonderful you are. And that people admire you for it."

Her blue gaze met his. "Cam."

"I mean it, Hannah. Screw anyone threatened by you. They're afraid of being eclipsed by the sun, but if they were smart, they'd bask in the glow."

To his surprise, her eyes glimmered with unshed tears. "Thank you," she whispered. "I needed to hear that."

He didn't say anything more, because he wanted to keep things easy for at least a little while longer. Instead, he reached over and squeezed her hand. Then they were served their entrée, and the banquet room echoed with the sounds of happy voices, cutlery, and soft music.

When their plates were removed and the candy-cane cheesecake was served, the emcee stepped up to the microphone again. Hannah's brow puckered, and she braced her feet as if to push back her chair, but Cam steadied her with a hand on her knee.

"Good evening again." The emcee's voice cut smoothly through the chatter, which immediately died down. "At this time, I'd like to invite Darling's favorite son, Cam Collier, to the podium."

He felt Hannah's gaze on his face, but he ignored it. He couldn't look at her, or he wouldn't get through this. Instead, he stood, put his napkin on his chair, and went to the small stage.

The light was on him. He was no stranger to that. And no stranger to seeing a group of people before him, either. He wasn't a public speaker, but he wasn't shy. No, it was the subject matter that had him freaked out.

But he could do it. For Hannah.

"Good evening." He ran his hand through his hair and chuckled nervously. "Okay, so I'm going to be honest. I'm really nervous about being up here.

"Many of you have known me since I was a kid strapping on my first skates. I have a million great memories of growing up in this town. I played hockey at the rink, ate burgers and fries at the Sugarbush, and had my first legal drink at Suds." A few laughs came from the crowd and he grinned. "I went to school here, at least I did until I was sixteen, and my family is still here—my mom and dad, my sister Oaklee. And my 'other' family, too

—the Gallaghers. If there are any stories about me as a kid, Rory's name is probably in there, too."

More laughter sounded in the room. But this was not the time to reminisce about boyish antics.

"But there is something you don't know about me," he said, and then cleared his throat. "It's something I've only ever told one person in my life. I've done a very good job of hiding it, and if anyone ever suspected, they kept it to themselves or pretended it didn't exist. The truth is...I am not a good reader."

He let out a breath, then continued. "When I say I'm not a good reader, I don't mean that I'm a bit slow or I don't like it. I mean I have trouble with transposing and confusing letters, so I often miss the meaning of what I'm trying to read, or I give up because it takes me so long. I use the term 'not a good reader' because I have never been tested or evaluated. There are two reasons for that. One, I was afraid someone would find out, and I wouldn't be able to play hockey anymore. And two, I'm fairly certain now that some people did know, or at least suspect, and they pushed me through my schooling because I was good at putting a puck in a net."

He met Hannah's gaze. Her eyes were wide and her lower lip was quivering, and his throat tightened.

"Now I've made a career of doing just that. And I stayed quiet because I was ashamed and felt... stupid."

He smiled at Hannah. "But you know, it took a good knock to the head to bring me home. And when I got here, Hannah was determined I would help out with this benefit. I disappointed her when I refused to read at the library today. I was still ashamed of my secret, you see. In my head, I was that ten-year-old boy again, terrified of being called on to read in class, afraid that I'd start, and the kids would laugh at me. I have a great life. But I still have insecurities.

"I wish someone would have intervened with me earlier. Teachers told my parents that I struggled and my mom read with me every night. I went to extra help, but it wasn't enough. I wish that there had been a program for me, or specialized tutoring, but those resources weren't available in Darling twenty years ago. That's where this benefit comes in. Thanks to the generosity of all of you, and the people who attended today's events, several charities will be the beneficiaries of much-needed funds."

He looked to Hannah again and felt a wave of love wash over him. She had given him such a great gift, and she didn't even know it. He swallowed around the lump in his throat. "Here's the thing. It's never too late. Never too late to be evaluated or to learn. I'm happy to announce that I'm going to be partnering with two local programs to provide resources and tutoring as early intervention, and also to assist adult non-readers.

People like me, who maybe slipped through the cracks and are ready to try again."

A round of applause echoed through the room, and he waited a few moments before he wrapped up.

"Thank you to Hannah Gallagher, the force behind today's events, for all her hard work. I have always been a bit in awe of Hannah's ambition and energy. Now I know it's all fuelled by the biggest heart I've ever known. Thank you, and enjoy the rest of your evening."

More applause echoed as he stepped down from the mic. Oaklee was crying, wiping under her eyes with a finger, and Hannah looked absolutely stunned. He got to his seat, but before retaking it, he leaned over and gave her a small kiss on the lips. He didn't care who knew right now that he'd fallen for her. He'd been waiting a long time to find someone he truly cared about enough to give his heart to. She needed to know he was willing to show the world how he felt about her. He got the feeling not many men had been.

When he finally sat down, he felt about fifty pounds lighter. Now there was just one more thing to do tonight. Tell Hannah the truth about his feelings.

Chapter 14

HANNAH SAT THROUGH DESSERT trying to look unaffected while inside her feelings were anything but. She had not expected that, not tonight. Not ever. Cam had explained everything the night of their date by the fire, and she'd accepted it without any qualms. No, she had not expected the grand gesture tonight. Partnering with charities was lovely for him to do, but he had made a personal sacrifice very publicly, and she knew, deep down, that he'd done it for her.

No one had ever done something like that for her before. Not ever. And now it was out there, a big something, and she had no idea what to do with it.

She played with her cheesecake, dipping the tines of the fork into the fluffy confection over and over. He'd looked into her eyes while speaking, and she'd felt something strange and wonderful and terrifying. It had been sneaking up on her for a while. She had gone and fallen in love with Cam. And love was something she hadn't done for a very long time.

People kept stopping by their table to say hello and to shake Cam's hand. Hannah made sure to smile winningly. After all, she was his date and the coordinator of the event, and it was on her to shine. She laughed and chatted as she always did, as she'd always done no matter the situation. Hannah Gallagher, who always had her shit together. Except right now, something was off. Inside, she was falling apart, and she should be ecstatic. At this moment, she had everything.

The winning auction bids were announced, and the guests began filtering out shortly after nine. Ethan and Willow and Aiden and Laurel disappeared, since their parents were babysitting the kids overnight, and the couples had a rare and treasured night alone. She looked over at Rory, who was positively radiant with his love for Oaklee. It was so beautiful it made her chest hurt. Cam was hugging Oaklee, and he kissed her cheek before she joined Rory to head home. When Cam came back to her side, his eyes were misty.

"Jeez, Collier, you getting all sappy tonight?" She tried a joke to lighten the tightening in her chest. Cam shrugged. "I'm sentimental. Rory's proposing tonight."

Her mouth dropped open. "He is?"

Cam nodded. "I've known it was coming for a while. He came to ask me—and my dad—for permission. It was sweet, actually. I know a lot of Rory's secrets, but I also love him like a brother. I'm happy for them."

"Me, too," Hannah said, but her voice sounded strangled. Cam looked at her strangely.

"You okay, there?"

"I'm fine. Just tired. It was a big day."

"Then let me take you home."

He held her hand and then opened the door for her as she got into the SUV. *I love him.* The words echoed in her head over and over, but she kept trying to push them away. She couldn't love Cam. He had just said he was leaving right after Christmas to go back to Denver. Leaving to go back to his life where he was rich and famous and too...everything for Darling, Vermont.

Too everything for her.

The drive through Darling had a surreal quality. Hannah's insides were in turmoil, but the town was postcard perfect with the recent snow on the ground and the beautiful lights and decorations. It was the Saturday before Christmas. Maybe people inside had gone shopping today and were up wrapping presents. Maybe they were having hot chocolate and watching holiday movies by the light of the tree.

Maybe they were getting engaged. Making love. Holding on for dear life.

Hannah let out a slow breath as Cam pulled up in front of her house. "Can I come in?" he asked softly.

"I'm pretty tired," she answered, avoiding looking in his eyes.

"There's something else going on with you. You haven't looked at me or said a word the whole way home. And I want us to talk about it, Han. We don't have much time left."

That was the problem, wasn't it? Not much time. But a whole Christmas sleigh full of feelings.

"Hannah? Will you look at me?"

She did, her insides quivering. What he'd done tonight was brave and generous and so unexpected. Why had he done it? She was afraid to hear that answer. Afraid and longing to at the same time.

His eyes were dark in the dim light of the vehicle, his lips unsmiling. "I love you, Hannah."

Oh God. He'd said them. The words. The three words she craved and needed and also didn't want to hear from him.

"You don't. It's only been a few weeks."

His eyes were wide and earnest as he held her captive with his gaze. "What does time have to do with anything? I've known you most of my life, if that's the case. But I've never felt this way about anyone before. What I did tonight... I was ready to do it because of you. You have never made me feel stupid or foolish. Instead, you make me feel... like I can do anything."

She could barely breathe. A bit of it was elation, and the remainder was panic. Why was being loved by Cam so frightening? Maybe it wasn't the loving exactly, but what it would mean for them. It was everything tied to it. She shook her head and bit down on her lip.

"You're leaving in a matter of days. We live across the country from each other. This wasn't our agreement."

But his gaze never wavered. When she remained silent, he let out a breath and said, "I didn't want to do this here in my car. But I will if I have to. If that's what it takes. I know it wasn't our agreement, but I want to try to make this work, Han. I've got to go back. We both know that. But I can fly in, or you could fly to see me...and in the off-season, we can figure something out. I know it's not perfect, but don't we owe it to ourselves to try? This doesn't happen every day." He reached for her hand. "It's never happened to me. Not like this." He squeezed her fingers. "Is there even a chance that you love me too?"

"You don't love me." She met his gaze and thought back over the last few weeks. "We've had fun, Cam. And the sex...it's been amazing. But..."

He pulled his hand away and put it on the steering wheel. "No buts. I was there, Hannah. I was there when you came apart in my arms and said my name. I was watching your face every moment. I get that you're scared. I just don't know why. Why don't you trust me?"

It wasn't him she didn't trust...not really. She knew he meant everything he said. But she'd seen the pictures and TV appearances where sports stars took their glamorous wives and girlfriends. She would never fit in there. Darling was where she belonged. Big fish, small pond. What if she gave up everything to be with him, only to have it crash and burn? She'd have nothing. And how could she come back home with her tail between her legs? How could she fail, and so publicly?

And she couldn't say any of this to him, because she was too afraid. Not just of failure, but of a broken heart. The last time, she'd bounced back. She wasn't sure she would after Cam. He was too... everything. Everyone thought she was so confident. Instead, she was a huge coward. It was her dirty little secret.

"My life is here," she said quietly. "My business. My family. Everything that is important to me."

Hurt flashed across his face, touching his eyes and making his full lips drop open in surprise.

"So you haven't fallen in love with me, too," he murmured. "Okay then. Okay."

"Cam, I—"

"No, you're right. This wasn't what we agreed to. And I didn't mean to fall for you, Hannah Banana. It complicates everything. But I was willing to give it a try. It doesn't work unless we're both willing to do that."

"You're invited to Christmas Eve at Ethan's," she reminded him. "I don't want you to stay away because of me. And there's New Year's Eve at Rory's..."

"I don't know about Ethan's. I'm going to have to skip New Year's. I'm hoping to be back in the lineup." He looked like he wanted to say more, but reconsidered and sat back in his seat.

Silence fell. Here she was, in a killer dress, all in a plan to finish the evening with him stripping it off her. She'd envisioned getting him out of his suit and into her bed. Now they were just... awkward and sad.

He looked over at her and gave it one last shot. "Hannah, whatever you're afraid of...can't we try to work on it together? I'm afraid, too. The last serious girlfriend I had was crazy about dating a pro athlete and not so happy with the travel schedule and the idea I could change cities and uproot our lives. I have my own hang-ups. It says a lot that I want to try again with you."

She wanted to say yes. But a few weeks together was different than a relationship. Once the newness wore off, would Cam still love the woman she was, deep down? Or would it be like before, where her initiative became ambition, and her organizational abilities became control-freak issues?

When it came right down to it, she didn't trust him enough to believe he'd feel the same after the bloom was off the rose. And she loved him enough to know that to try—and fail—would break her heart irrevocably.

Better to rip the Band-Aid off now, and do it quickly.

"I love that you want to, Cam. I really do. And this has been so amazing. Let's just leave it that way, okay? Our own little Christmas fling that we can look back on with good memories."

"Look back on with good memories?" He shook his head, his voice filled with disbelief. "Sorry,

Han. I'll be leaving Darling with a bit of a broken heart. I think I'd rather just forget."

If she was hoping to end this on warm and nostalgic terms, those words disabused her of that idea. She sat back, startled by the coolness in his words. She didn't want this to end with harsh words and regrets, but it looked like it was going to. Because they hadn't had a fling at all. Hearts had been involved, and they both knew it.

She gathered up her clutch purse and put her hand on the door handle. "Goodnight, Cam. And I'm sorry."

"Me, too," he replied, his voice tight.

***

It was five a.m. on a Sunday morning, and Cam breathed deeply the cold air that had the distinctive ice smell of a hockey rink. Ice time for local teams started at seven, so he'd come out early, needing to feel blades on ice and a stick in his hand. He didn't care that he hadn't been cleared. He was fine. No one else around, no possible contact. He spent the first ten minutes skating, running drills all by himself with only the sound of his skates cutting in the ice for company.

A bucket sat at the edge of the blue line, pucks lined up and waiting. Cam stopped, adjusted the stick in his hands, and made contact with the first one, the weight of the puck and the snap of the stick so familiar that it was like an extension of his own appendages. He made his way down the line, missing the net a few times, correcting and firing puck after puck. Focusing on nothing but the black rubber disks in front of him. When he'd shot the last one, he went to the net, rounded them up, and lined them up again.

Last night, when he'd looked down from the podium, he'd been so sure of her. So certain she shared his feelings. This morning, he was hurt and angry and needing the comfort of the one thing in his life he could count on.

Except in the back of his mind were all the thoughts that had crowded him when he'd first arrived home. What if he sustained another concussion? What if his career ended? Hockey was in his blood and would always be a part of his life in some way. He knew that. But this... He slapped the blade of his stick on the ice, the sound echoing through the arena. How could he be married to this, knowing that even if he stayed healthy, in another ten years he'd be nearing the end of his career?

Maybe the lesson was that nothing was certain. Maybe that's what he'd take back to Denver with him.

The physical exertion felt good, so he kept it up until he looked over and saw Ethan standing at the bench, watching him with a sober expression. Hannah's brother. He wasn't sure he was up to talking to a Gallagher today.

Ethan lifted a hand. "Good morning."

"Hey." Politeness dictated he at least be civil, so he skated over to the boards. "You're here early."

"Eight a.m. ice time with Connor. I was just heading to Mom and Dad's to pick up the boys and I saw your vehicle in the lot. You're feeling better?"

Cam knew Ethan meant the injury, so he nodded. "Yeah. I had one setback when I was home, but I've been symptom free for a bit. Thought I'd lace up this morning before the ice gets busy. Feels good."

"You don't look like it feels good. You look like you're ready to clock someone." Ethan grinned and took a step backward, out of reach.

"Hannah dumped me last night." Cam hadn't expected to say the words, but they came out of his mouth anyway. He gripped the stick tighter. "I didn't see it coming."

Ethan's face flattened in surprise. "She dumped you? What the hell?"

"Just what I asked myself. I didn't sleep much, but this morning, I thought this might help clear my head."

"And has it?"

"Not really. I read her all wrong, Ethan. Anyway, maybe it's good you know. I don't want things to be weird with the family. I promised Connor I'd practice with him, and I will in the next day or two. But I'm gonna skip Christmas Eve, and I'm heading back to Denver right after the holiday."

Ethan's eyes held disappointment. "I'm sorry, Cam. We have all been rooting for the two of you. Hannah is great and deserves to be happy. She also needs to be jolted out of her comfort zone."

"I don't know what to say to that one."

Ethan laughed. "Believe me, I do not want the gory details. But she lit up every time you were together. You did, too. Darling and her business here and the big family...it's low risk for her. She never has to fail here. You represent something crazy, and you don't come with guarantees. Even if she does care for you like you do for her, that would probably stop her up."

Cam leaned against the boards. He hadn't thought about that before. Was Hannah just really afraid to take a chance? Did she maybe love him too?

"How do you know all this?" he asked Ethan.

Ethan smiled. "Bro. I've known Hannah all of her life. We're the oldest two. To be honest, I think we both felt the weight of expectations. By the time we were in school, there were six of us. Mom and Dad were always busy. Hannah and I had to step up a lot, and she got used to meeting expectations. I think she's always been worried about what would happen if she didn't."

"You didn't feel that way?"

"Hannah was the only girl until the twins came along. I had my brothers to distract me. And I still felt that sometimes. Until my wife died. Then I let go of expectations... Well, I didn't at first. But I did once I fell in love with Willow."

His face softened as he said his wife's name. It was sweet and sent a bittersweet jolt to Cam's heart. Did he look like that when he spoke about Hannah?

Lord, he was a lovesick puppy, wasn't he?

Ethan gave him a nod. "Maybe you shouldn't give up yet. Hannah's stubborn, but if anyone can change her mind, it's you."

But Cam had his own issues. He didn't want to have to beg and convince someone to be with him. He'd done that before with Alyssa, and it had flopped. No, Hannah needed to be all in, meet-in-the-middle, ready to try if this was going to work.

"Listen, thanks for the advice. I appreciate it. Not sure it'll change anything, but it helped my state of mind."

"No problem. Hey, none of us would mind having you officially be part of the family. And now I should go. I gotta get the boys and make sure we're back."

Ethan waved goodbye, and Cam set to work cleaning up his pucks, changing out of his skates, and stowing his stuff in his SUV.

Then he went home for a shower and breakfast. And a long day ahead of him that didn't include Hannah.

It was a bitter pill to swallow.

Chapter 15

HANNAH WIPED HER FACE with another tissue and cursed out loud as she dropped it in the wastebasket. She didn't cry over guys. She just didn't. She hadn't since Liam had said so many things that had cut her to the quick the day he'd broken up with her.

Back then, she'd cried because Liam had turned all the things she liked about herself into faults. Now, she was crying because Cam loved her for those things, and she couldn't bring herself to trust him. To trust that it would last. Or worse, he loved Darling Hannah. But would he love Denver Hannah? Would his friends like her, or would they wonder what in the world he was thinking?

She kicked the garbage can, spilling soiled tissues over the bathroom floor. For a confident, strong woman, she had huge self-esteem problems.

Her dirty little secret.

She'd sent Cam away and was now sitting alone in her little house in her little town, only a few days away from Christmas and hating every moment.

A cup of coffee restored her a little, along with a bowl of berries she picked at while sitting at her kitchen table. She didn't want to stay here alone and didn't want to go anywhere, either. Not looking like this. Her eyes were red and swollen, and her hair was a rat's nest pushed up in a messy bun and held with an elastic. She dressed in yoga pants and a sweatshirt of Cam's that was much too big for her. It still smelled like him, and she wrapped her arms around herself to intensify the scent. She was going to miss him so much. His smile and laugh, his stupidly thick eyelashes... everything.

Her cell rang, and she saw Rory's number. A lump formed in her throat. Did he already know about the breakup and was calling to read her the riot act? It was no secret everyone loved Cam. He could do no wrong. Even her own family would take his side. Not that there were sides to take. It was just... Oh, why had she thought a fling would be a good idea?

The ringing stopped, but a few moments later, it started again. Worry settled in the pit of her stomach. What if something was wrong with their folks or one of the kids? She took a breath and answered.

"Hey, Han," Rory said in reply. He sounded far too cheerful for there to be anything wrong.

"What's up? It's barely nine on a Sunday morning."

"Oh, you know. Just having coffee. Making some eggs. Picking a date for a wedding."

The line went silent as what he'd just said sank in, and then tears burned her eyes again. "Oh,

Rory. You proposed last night?" She'd forgotten Cam had mentioned it, she was so wrapped up in her own broken heart.

"I did. And she said yes."

"Well, of course she did." Hannah didn't have to force happiness into her voice. Oaklee and Rory were so clearly made for each other. "Congratulations, little brother."

"Yeah, well, you're next," he said joyfully. Hannah's chest tightened as she fought to keep her voice light.

"Oh, there's no rush there. Have you told Mom and Dad?"

"Yeah, we told them just now. But you're the first of the sibs. You're my big sis, you know? And Oaklee loves you."

Aw, heck, now she was definitely misty. "I love her, too. I'm thrilled for you both."

"Good, because we're already talking about having Cam as best man and you standing up with Oaklee. Awesome, right?"

It was such a blow to her already tender feelings that she felt sick to her stomach. "Aw, there's lots of time to plan. You need to celebrate now." She wasn't going to ruin his perfect day with her drama.

"All right. Love you, Han."

She could finish the call without sobbing. She could.

"Love you, too, Rory."

She ended the call, but then the sobs came. Big, gulping, gasping ones that made her head ache. She wasn't sure if she was more hurt that she and Cam had broken up, or upset at herself for ruining everything because she was a coward.

Her hand hovered near her phone. She could call him, tell him she'd been wrong. But it wouldn't take away her fears or make everything okay. So she withdrew her hand and laid her head on the table. After a while, the weeping ceased, and she got up and drank a glass of water and took something for the headache. Then she got under the blanket on the sofa and stared at the Christmas tree they'd decorated together until her lids grew heavy and she fell asleep.

———eee———

Monday she was back at her desk, clearing away backlogged items on her to-do list now that the literacy benefit was over. Oaklee was handling the final tallies, and in the new year, they'd look at dispersing the funds to the selected charities. It had taken a lot of Hannah's work hours, so she was happy to throw herself back into her job.

And if she used work as a distraction, so what? She hadn't heard a peep from Cam. Christmas Eve was right around the corner. She would go on as usual. Efficient, energetic, driven Hannah Gallagher, who was a whiz at biz but sucked at relationships.

Every time her phone rang, she wondered if it was him. Or if it would be one of her family asking her what the heck was wrong with her brain. But nothing. Either Cam had kept quiet, or they were all buzzing around talking about it behind her back. She wasn't really sure which she preferred. Generally, she was a deal-with-it-straight-on kind of woman. But now...

She missed him. The reason why she kept staring at the phone or out her office window was because she wanted to hear his voice. Get a glimpse of him.

The day ended, she packed up her tote bag, and walked home in the dark. Her house was dark, too, and she flicked on lights to take away some of the emptiness. Maybe she was like Oaklee and needed a dog. Or a couple of cats. She could become a crazy cat lady.

Dinner was something easy to throw together: roasted squash, with marinara and goat cheese. She supposed she could wrap presents, turn on the TV and watch one of the zillion holiday specials that were on. She still had the present she'd bought for Cam sitting in her closet. She'd had a jersey from the Darling peewee team—where he'd first started playing—made up with his name and number. It was custom, so she couldn't take it back. And he still hadn't called or texted, so giving it to him was out of the question. He clearly wanted nothing to do with her.

The doorbell rang and she jumped, the blanket she'd put over her legs as she drank her after-dinner tea sliding off her lap. She wanted it to be him, though she had no idea what to say if it really was him on her front step.

She opened the door and instead found Laurel staring back at her. Her sister-in-law, and one of her dearest friends. Laurel held up a bottle of wine. "I figured you might need this after the last few days."

Hannah's lip wobbled. "So you heard?"

"Yeah, I heard. Cam told Ethan yesterday morning. Ethan told the rest of us. When no one heard from you all day today, I figured I'd better check on you."

"I'm fine."

"Oh, girlfriend." Laurel stepped inside and handed over the wine. "You are so not fine."

"Well, I will be." Hannah lifted her chin, trying to stay strong while she was incredibly touched that Laurel was being a true friend.

Laurel hung up her coat, took the wine from Hannah's hands again, and shook her head. "It's cute that you think that. Come on, Han. It's Cam freaking Collier we're talking about here. Hot, rich, nice guy, and he loves you. How can you possibly be fine?"

The doorbell rang again, and Hannah's heart leapt. She opened it to find Willow standing there, holding another bottle of wine and a paper bag in her opposite fist.

"What is this, an intervention?"

Willow grinned. "If it needs to be. It's cold as balls out here. Let me in."

Hannah stepped aside. She wasn't going to win this one, and she knew it. And she probably deserved it. She'd done her fair share of nosing in when Laurel and Willow had been dating her brothers.

Laurel took over opening the wine, and Willow took a container of homemade truffles out of the paper bag. "Dark chocolate. Excellent for pairing with that red. And by the look of your eyes, wine and chocolate are very, very necessary. What the hell are you doing, walking away from a man like that?"

Laurel handed Hannah a glass and looked over at Willow. "Hey. We're not here to judge. Hannah has her reasons."

"Just like you had yours," Hannah said to Willow, gesturing with the glass in her hand. "Don't forget, you walked away from Ethan, too."

"Because I was stupid. We're here to keep you from making the same mistake."

Hannah laughed. "I love you guys."

"We love you, too. Let's go sit down, and you can spill your guts. Then we'll figure out what's next."

Hannah's heart warmed. Even though she'd been afraid to see anyone, having her two closest friends come to the rescue made the crushing pain in her chest ease just a bit. They went into the living room, where Hannah's tree was lit and casting a gorgeous glow over the room.

"Oh, now, that's a dandy," Laurel said. "George pick that out for you?"

"George and...and Cam."

Willow sank down into a chair and took a sip of wine. "Okay, babes. What happened? Because two nights ago, he was looking at you like you hung the moon and stars. And you were making googly eyes at him, too."

Hannah sipped the wine—it was very good, and she savoured the taste on her tongue for a moment. "I got cold feet, you guys. That's it in a nutshell. I'm terrified. So it was just better to end it now, before things got out of hand."

Laurel burst out laughing and reached for a truffle. "Out of hand? Sweet pea, it's been out of hand since the first night he stayed over. Lordy, you two can't be in the same room without giving off sparks. That kind of thing can be scary. Really intense, really fast."

Willow nodded. "It was that way with Ethan. Scared me to death."

"If you guys are going to talk about having sex with my brothers, I'm going to need more wine and a set of earplugs." But Hannah grinned, her heart a little lighter.

"Then let's talk about you and Cam. What's got you so scared?"

Hannah took a long drink. Then another. The answer was simple yet so difficult to say.

"Honestly? Change. I'm afraid of all the changes it would mean to my life, and I'm really not sure I'd fit into his life at all. He doesn't have a...a normal life like the rest of us."

"So you're just going to give up without giving it a shot? How do you know you won't fit in if you don't try? I have a hard time believing that Cam is any different back in Colorado than he is here. He's a good guy with a good heart. He works hard. He isn't a jerk or a snob. He never behaves in a way that gets him in the news, either. It's not like he'd go back there and pull a Mr. Hyde."

Hannah tried a truffle, focusing on the dark, rich flavours. She brushed her fingers on her jeans and let out a long sigh. "Look, you guys. I know it's me. But I guess it's just...this is Christmas, and Darling, and maybe we got caught up in something that won't last. How can I uproot my life for that?"

Willow's gaze widened. "Did he ask you that? To move to Denver?"

"No, he just said he wanted to talk and work something out. Not say goodbye. He told me he..." She swallowed around the lump that had come and gone a million times since Saturday night. "He told me he loved me."

Laurel and Willow practically swooned before her eyes. "And you said no?"

"What if it all goes wrong? What if I get my heart broken?"

Her question hung in the air for a few moments. Then Laurel came and sat beside her and took her hand. "People survive broken hearts all the time. Sometimes we have a life all planned out for ourselves and something throws a monkey wrench into it. But it doesn't mean we stop trying."

"But what if I've built a life I love?"

Willow studied her glass and then looked up, her eyes soft with understanding. "Hey, I get it. Ethan stepped into my life and disrupted all the peace and tranquility I'd built for myself. I had made my world a safe space, and he forced me out of it into something risky and unpredictable. And I'm not sorry, of course I'm not. But I understand the fear, Hannah. I do."

Hannah reached over and took Willow's hand. "I know you do."

Laurel nodded. "And after my divorce, I was really not looking for a romance. Particularly not with Aiden. But there he was. I'd had my perfect life and lost it. I wasn't so into giving someone that much influence again."

"But it changed for you both. It doesn't mean it would for me."

"Ah," Willow said wisely. "That's where I think you're wrong. The truth of the matter is, our lives would look very different if we hadn't ended up being loved by—and loving—two fine men. It wouldn't be like this for me with anyone else. How about you, Laurel?"

Laurel shook her head. "Aiden's it. He tells me the truth when it's hard, and he loves me all the time. No one else gets me like him. And I can totally be myself and know that it's okay."

Willow looked at Hannah. "Ever felt that way about anyone, Han?"

They were so right. Why would this be the same as before if everything else was different? She was different. Cam was, too. He understood her when others didn't. Got her insecurities and loved her because of them. "I've never loved anyone like this before. It scares me to death."

"That's how you know it's real," Laurel announced, and reached for the other wine bottle. When she'd topped up the glasses, she held hers out for a toast. "To love. It's crazy and scary and wonderful. And totally worth it."

Willow held out her glass, a smile playing on her lips. Finally, Hannah held out hers, too, and closed her eyes and she touched her rim to theirs. "To love. God help me."

They finished off the bottle, and by the time they got to the end, they'd come up with a pseudo plan that Hannah would re-evaluate when they were all sober. But before the two women put on their coats to leave, they made Hannah promise to go through with the plan.

Rory—the only Gallagher man who wasn't on diaper duty—came and picked them up and drove them home, and Hannah ate the last truffle before heading to bed. She had a big day tomorrow, and only a short window of time to get what she needed.

Chapter 16

THE LAST THING CAM wanted to do today was go to the park and pose for family pictures on the Kissing Bridge. Oaklee was adamant, though, because he was so rarely home, and they were hardly ever all together. He could think of other ways to spend Christmas Eve. Watching movies and having a few beers with his dad. Doing some light conditioning, a skate at the rink maybe. Definitely not something in public. And hopefully not with Hannah there. She had broken it off, and she hadn't texted him or called, not once. He was more than hurt by it. He missed her. It said a lot that she could walk away so easily.

"Cam, come on! The photographer is going to be there right at two."

"Fine." He rolled his eyes and left his old room behind. He wasn't sure when he'd be home again after this trip. For Oaklee and Rory's wedding, certainly. But an extended visit... It would probably be a long time. To his surprise, he felt a bit homesick already about it.

Oaklee went in her car, while he went with their parents. Oaklee would be leaving afterward to go to Ethan's for Christmas Eve with the Gallaghers. His folks were going out to a neighbours', as they did every year. He'd be sitting home alone.

After they got parked, they walked the short distance to the bridge. Oaklee was already there with Rory, and the photographer appeared to be making some adjustments before starting the shoot. Cam stood back and enjoyed a bittersweet moment. His sister and best friend looked so happy together. Oaklee was radiant, and Rory couldn't stop smiling. Rory had brought their dog along, too. The caramel-coloured ball of fluff pranced around their feet until Rory gave a command and offered a treat. They were already a family, weren't they? He had a vision of his sister as a mom and got so sentimental he had to turn away. He'd be an uncle someday.

But it was bittersweet, because he didn't want to be standing here alone. God, he'd come home, and all he'd wanted was peace and quiet and to get back to Denver as soon as possible. He still wanted that, but he wanted so much more. He wanted Hannah, and her love, and the privilege of loving her in return. Funny how the first victory felt hollow without the second.

The dog was behaving so nicely that they decided to snap the engagement pics first. Rory and Oaklee had made their relationship official on the bridge in a very public fashion; it only seemed fitting that their pictures be there as well. Oaklee's hair was down, and she wore a red coat and scarf, looking festive and bright as Rory put his arms around her. The pup sat at their feet. Then there were shots with them kneeling by the dog, and a kiss with the leash dropped by their feet. Cam would have thought it hokey if it weren't so genuinely sweet and celebratory.

Then it was time for the family. Oaklee, Cam, and their parents posed at the arc of the bridge, and once again, Cam's latent sentimental streak made an appearance. His family was pretty amazing when all was said and done, and he appreciated them more than they could know.

He was going to miss them when he returned to the team.

"Cam, we'd like for you to change your shirt," Oaklee said, putting her hand on his arm.

"What?" His mood took a shift into annoyed. "What's wrong with my sweater?"

"It's missing something."

That was not Oaklee's voice. It was Hannah's, and it made his heart stop. He turned around to find her standing there, holding out a box, but what was more, she was wearing his team jersey.

She looked adorable. He couldn't stop staring at her, as if afraid she would go away if he so much as blinked. "Han," he said softly, and she smiled a little.

"It's your Christmas gift."

"You want me to open it here?"

She nodded. "Yes, please." She held out the box with hands clad in thin gloves the same shade of blue as was in the jersey. He didn't understand why she was wearing it, but one thing at a time.

Everyone had moved off, giving them a smidge of privacy. He took the box and placed it on the end of the concrete wall of the bridge, then undid the wide bow and ribbon holding it together. When he lifted the lid, a smile lit his face.

"My peewee jersey!"

"Only a few sizes larger. So you can wear it now."

"Right now?"

"It's big enough to fit over gear. I think it'll fit over your sweater."

He lifted it up. It was a home game jersey, white with red and black, with his name and number on it. The same number he'd had since he was eight.

"This is cool." He pulled it over his head and down over his sweater. It felt a little awkward, but he didn't care. "I love it, Hannah. But why here? Why now?" He looked her in the eyes. "After what happened, why give me a present at all?"

She came forward and took his hands. "Because I was afraid, and I let that colour my decision. I lied to you, Cam, and that was the worst mistake of my life. I hope it's not too late. You should know that I love you, too. I fought it the whole time, but at the benefit, when you got up to speak...I realized exactly the kind of man you are, and I couldn't fight it anymore. Then when you said you loved me..." She stopped, bit down on her lip.

"You bolted," he finished for her.

She nodded.

"Why are you wearing my jersey?" he asked. He wanted to hope but wasn't sure he should. He needed her to say the words, but more than that, he needed her to mean them.

"Because I don't want to be afraid to take chances and miss out on something incredible. I've spent my whole life being the responsible one, the one who always lives up to expectations, the one people can rely on. And that worked for me. It validated me when people said I was bossy or too loud or too smart. Sliding into that role gave me a measure of safety, so I wouldn't have to risk being somewhere else and having those attributes...thrown in my face."

He was starting to put the pieces together. "You mentioned your ex before, but it's more than that, isn't it? It's me?"

"Not you. No one has ever accepted me as you have. But more... What happens if I go to Denver with you? Meet your teammates and their wives and girlfriends, the puck bunnies outside the dressing room? What are they going to think of me? I'm an achiever, Cam, and I can organize things. I don't know how to be...your girlfriend."

He wanted to say, "Is that all?", but he knew that this was so important to her it had nearly driven them apart.

"Hannah. The only thing you have to do to be my girlfriend is love me. Everything else we'll figure out. And some of those people might surprise you. We all have our hang-ups." He lifted his hand and touched her cheek. "I wanted to come to you and beg you to reconsider. But I was so afraid you'd decide it wasn't worth it—I wasn't worth it—and walk away anyway. We can figure it out. All I need from you is a promise that you'll be there with me."

She nodded, her eyes shining. "I want to. I love you, Cam. It took me by surprise and blew me away, but I fell for you hard. I'm not ready to say goodbye to Darling, but I'm more than willing to travel back and forth for a little bit and then make bigger plans."

"I was thinking I could come back and do a hockey school in the off-season. Spend some more time in Darling with my family. And yours."

"And I could maybe split time between Denver and here."

"See? We're doing it already."

She looked up at him and smiled, her eyes shining. "I'm sorry. I'm sorry for what I said after the benefit, and sorry we wasted time. I was foolish and afraid. For all my business smarts, I am not a risk taker in my personal life. But I know better than anyone that the higher risks yield the best returns."

"Mmm. I love it when you talk like that."

She burst out laughing. Then she lifted her chin and said, "Now will you kiss me please? I'm dying over here, wanting one. Wanting you."

He didn't need any prodding. He stepped the few inches closer and pulled her into his arms, claiming her winter-kissed lips. Suddenly, everything in the world was right again. She gripped the fabric of his jersey and pulled him closer until they heard whistles and clapping from the end of the bridge.

"Oh, geez," she said, putting her forehead against his chest.

"Might as well get used to it," he said. "You kissed me on the Kissing Bridge, and you know what that means."

"That our love is gonna last forever? You don't really believe in that stuff, do you?"

He cupped her face in his hands. "Look at your family and tell me it doesn't work." He grinned. "Now. We have Christmas Eve at Ethan's to get through. We're going to eat food and play with kids and you're gonna hold babies, and then, after they've had a goodnight story from their Uncle Cam, I'm going to take you home and make this one Christmas to remember. You still have that gold dress, right?"

Her cheeks were pink with cold, but her blush deepened as she nodded. "I might have."

"Good. And when it fits your schedule, I'm going to fly you to Denver so you can see my apartment and meet my houseplants and some of the guys that are my other family."

"I love you, Cam."

"I love you, too, Hannah Banana. I'm glad you changed your mind."

She laughed and took his hand. "You're lucky. Because once I set my mind to something..."

He squeezed back and wondered if he'd ever thought he could be this happy. "You get the job done. I know." He planted a kiss on her temple. "In fact, I'm counting on it."

———eee———

February

Claire Gallagher sat with the rest of her family on a Saturday night, watching the hockey game. Cam was playing, and everyone was gathered in John and Moira's living room, having a few drinks, eating popcorn, and cursing out the ref. Everyone except Hannah. She was in Denver for a few weeks, and things were hot and heavy with her and Cam. Claire looked around and found her twin, Cait, looking at her phone. Something had been off with her lately, though Claire couldn't put her finger on what.

"Look, you guys! Hannah's on TV!"

There was a break as the goal net had come off the post, and the camera panned around and settled on Hannah. Hannah was dressed in a team jersey and had her hair up. She looked...happy. And beautiful. But it did mean that Claire and Cait were the only ones left who were single. Rory and Oaklee had a wedding date for the summer, and it wouldn't surprise her if either Willow or Laurel got pregnant again.

The camera moved away after a few moments, and the game recommenced. Aiden went to get another beer and put his hand on her shoulder. "You okay, squirt?"

"I'm fine. Hannah looks good."

"Well, she decided to stop letting fear drive her decisions. And now she's happy, so good for her."

Claire felt Cait's gaze on the two of them. "Do you think they'll get married?"

"Yeah. Hannah's gonna want some babies soon, and since they can't keep their hands off each other..."

"Aiden!" Moira's voice came across the living room. "Eeew."

"Sorry, Ma." But he grinned and winked at Claire. "You want another?"

"Naw, I'm good. I'm going to go to bed soon anyway."

But before she did, she looked around the room, her heart filled with love for her family and a little bit of longing at being left out. Her gaze touched Cait's, and they shared a thought, as they often did as twins. *Sucks not having a partner*.

But Claire hadn't given up hope. And she wanted a happy ending for her sister, too.

Everyone deserved their own happy ever after.

The End

About the Author

While bestselling author Donna Alward was busy studying Austen, Eliot and Shakespeare, she was also losing herself in the breathtaking stories created by romance novelists like LaVyrle Spencer and Judith McNaught. Several years after completing her degree she decided to write a romance of her own and it was true love! Five years and ten manuscripts later she sold her first book and launched a new career. While her heartwarming stories of love, hope, and homecoming have been translated into several languages, hit bestseller lists and won awards, her very favorite thing is when she hears from happy readers!

Donna lives on Canada's east coast. When she's not writing she enjoys reading (of course!), knitting, gardening, cooking...and is a Masterpiece Theater addict. You can visit her on the web at www.DonnaAlward.com and join her mailing list at http://www.DonnaAlward.com/newsletter .

Milton Keynes UK
Ingram Content Group UK Ltd.
UKHW041444071023
430131UK00001B/6